MURDER
UNDER A
GREEN SEA

MURDER
UNDER A
GREEN SEA

=== PHILLIP HUNTER ===

Mirror Books

This book first published by Mirror Books in 2019

Mirror Books is part of Reach plc
10 Lower Thames Street
London EC3R 6EN
England

www.mirrorbooks.co.uk

ISBN 978-1-912624-16-4

Chapter One

Martha was wearing her best shoes when she stepped over her husband. She strolled over to the window, opened the curtains with a grand gesture and blinked as the bright, white morning hit her. When she felt able, she opened her eyes enough to see, to her left, the sun's reflected light bursting back from the Thames, silhouetting a barge hauling its heavy load of tar-black coal. Then she looked directly down at Grosvenor Road and, from that perspective, tried to gauge what kind of day it would be.

She opened the window and smelled soot and smoke lingering on the cold air. She heard the clack-clacking of a horse pulling a milk cart. She watched the milkman, a small figure, far down, far off, hunched over the reins, dragging on a cigarette as his horse plodded its way back to the depot. The horse seemed as tired as the man, its head down, its limbs heavy and slow.

There was light traffic on the road below, a handful of people milling about on the pavement or strolling along. Nobody was doing much of anything urgent, which, she felt, was how it should be. There were too many people these days taking things far too importantly and getting very urgent about them all.

She watched the movement four floors beneath her: a few cars stuttering along; a bus pulling to a stop in front of the chemist's; one or two cabs searching for trade; a lorry carrying barrels of something, two nannies in neat uniforms chatting to each other as they pushed prams. It was all exactly as a Saturday should be.

She continued to watch this casualness casually for a minute or two, thinking that it made her feel secure, for some reason, all this life, this motion; people doing their daily things, unaware of her observing them. It was as if the world wasn't really complicated at all. And certainly not urgent.

After that, she looked at Max. He was lying face down on the Persian rug. He wasn't moving, as far as she could tell. He certainly didn't seem to be breathing. Apparently, there was no life in him at all. Still, that was nothing new. She wondered vaguely whether you could drown in a deep rug. Or would it be suffocation?

She decided she'd better go over and see whether the old man was, in fact, dead. She kicked his Oxford brogue with her powder-blue leather shoe. His foot moved and fell back to where it had been.

She placed her feet in front of his eyes. She had very nice legs, she knew, and the heels on these shoes made her calves more firm, more shapely. Martha felt it necessary, every now and then, to remind her husband how lucky he was to have a wife with such lovely legs.

Meanwhile, Max was not dead – a fact he was very much regretting.

Of course, he could be dead, if he wanted to be. The trouble was that being dead would require that he first stand up, and that was something he didn't think possible at that moment, or ever again.

Martha opening the curtains didn't help. Previously, his head had been thumping. Now that the bright morning light was trying to burn him to a crisp, it was thumping and splitting.

He heard Martha approach.

"Are you dead?" she asked his face.

"Yes."

"Hmm."

"I'm not well."

"Well, you *do* look pale."

"I feel pale."

Martha sighed and glanced at her watch. "Get up, darling. Flora will be here in a couple of hours."

"I'm too pale to see Flora."

"That just seems rude, Max. Anyway, what time did you get in last night? Why didn't you come to bed?"

"I didn't want to wake you."

Martha knelt and put a cool hand on Max's hot cheek. Slowly, and with great care, Max opened his eyes. "You have beautiful legs," he said.

"I know, darling," she said, as if he'd told her that the ceiling was above them. It was self-evident.

She stroked his jaw.

"I've got a lump on my head."

"It's not on your head. It *is* your head."

"It hurts. My lump."

"Why were you drinking?" Martha said softly.

"I was celebrating."

"Celebrating what?"

He made an attempt to stand. Somehow, he succeeded. Martha rose gracefully, too gracefully, in fact, given the height of her heels, as if she were proving to Max how lamentable his effort had been.

"Celebrating what?" she said again.

"I can't remember. I was too drunk to take much note."

Martha took a step back and looked her husband up and down. "Will you need any help crawling to the bedroom?"

"Uh, yes."

She put her arm around his waist and he rested his arm along her shoulder and together, in a much-practised manner, they proceeded out of the sitting room and into the hallway.

"Hitler," Max said.

"What, darling?"

"Hitler. That little Fascisti bastard. That's why I was drinking."

"You were celebrating Hitler?"

"No. Not celebrating. He's rearmed the Rhineland."

"Has he?" Martha said, straightening the vase on the sideboard they were passing. "My God. What will he think of next?"

"And Mussolini's invaded Abyssinia."

"Oh."

"You do know where Abyssinia is, don't you?"

"Certainly I do. My cousin Lewis went there when he was in Kenya. He lost a lot of money in that tea company, as I remember. In Kenya, I mean, not Abyssinia."

Max stopped walking and took his arm from Martha's shoulders. He turned to face her. "Do you care?" he said.

Now she looked at him. "Darling, if I could fly out and save Abyssinia, I would. But I can't. And neither can you. Come on, let's get you to bed."

She put her arm through his, but he brushed it off. "I'll be all right, as soon as you stop moving the floor around."

"You aren't going to be sick, are you?"

"I don't know."

"Well, try not to be. I'm meeting my mother for lunch in Piccadilly, and Flora's not in till ten today."

"I'll do my best to save it all for Flora."

"If you would."

Max started again to move along the hallway, stopping now and then to wince in pain.

"Oh, poor baby. I'll get a wet cloth and some aspirin. And drink lots of water."

"Thanks."

They finally managed to make it to the bedroom, where Martha helped Max out of his jacket, which she hung up in the wardrobe. "Who were you with?"

Max sat on the edge of the bed and Martha stood behind him, gently rubbing his shoulders. "With?"

"Last night."

"Oh. Uh, a man I knew once. From the regiment. Man called Daniel Burton."

Two small vertical lines appeared between Martha's brows. She looked like a child who was attempting to decipher some mystery of life. "You know," she said, "you've never mentioned meeting anyone from the regiment before."

Max didn't have anything to say to that. He put a hand through his hair, slicking it back.

Martha watched him for a moment, then put her hands on the back of his shoulders and kissed him on the neck. Max didn't respond, and his body seemed to Martha to be rigid, tense. She removed her hands. "But you still haven't explained why you were drinking," she said. "And, besides, Hitler rearmed the Rhineland a couple of weeks ago. Start of March, wasn't it?"

"You remembered."

"Of course. You wrote a piece about it for the paper."

"Yeah. Buggers spiked it."

With that, Max fell backwards and lay still on the bed, waiting for death.

Chapter Two

When he awoke, Max felt at least reasonable. He'd drunk as much water as he could, and had taken some aspirins and seltzer. But it was the hair of the dog that did it, a large Scotch from the bottle in the bottom drawer of his tallboy. And sleep.

He probably would've slept for another day or so if it hadn't been for that racket in the kitchen. That would be Flora. Martha did everything silently and elegantly. Flora... well, Flora didn't.

He crept into the bathroom, shed his crumpled smoke-soaked clothes and had a quick cold bath. By the time he'd dressed in fresh clothes, Max felt ready to take on the world. Or, perhaps, get drunk again.

He headed towards the noise of clanging and bashing and muttering.

Flora was a willowy girl, too much limb for elegance, too much opinion for decorum, and far too much lip for anything, really, except working in solitude or with an understanding employer. She'd been inherited by the Daltons when their previous maid – Flora's mother – had been forced to hand in her notice so that she could spend more time with her father, Flora's grandfather, who, as a result of senility, or possibly alcohol, had been sliding downhill for some time to the point where he'd been arrested for an offence referred to only as 'public lewdness'.

Or, as Flora put it, "He went out in his briefs and flashed himself to some ladies."

Flora's mother had explained to Max and Martha simply that the old man was 'unable to look after himself proper.' Max had given Flora's mother a donation 'for the general wellbeing of her father'.

When he entered the kitchen, Flora was on her hands and knees, her rear end poking up while her head and shoulders were stuffed into the oven. She cursed and mumbled, and Max heard at least one mention of bleedin' duck fat. At least, that's what he thought he'd heard.

Max cleared his throat, sending Flora's skull bashing into the roof of the oven. She cursed and clambered out, rubbing the back of her head.

"Hello, sir," she said, climbing to her feet and straightening her pinafore.

"Flora, please don't call me sir," Max said for the hundredth time. "Call me Max."

Flora sniffed. "Sorry, sir. Mrs Dalton said you was feeling a bit delicate, so I thought I'd better leave you."

"Mm," Max said, knowing that Flora would never have used a word like 'delicate' unless Martha had emphasised it, which was a dig at Max, one of her sarcastic asides. He went over to the sink and gulped some tap water from a white tin mug.

"Shall you be wanting a breakfast, sir?" Flora said.

"Ugh," Max said.

"Eggs is good for hangovers, Eric says."

"Eggs is?"

"Oh, yeah. I could do 'em scrambled on toast." Flora smiled. Her face was flushed and there were beads of sweat on her forehead, sticking down wisps of dark blonde hair.

Max didn't particularly want eggs, or anything else for that matter, but Flora seemed eager to help, and he didn't want to disappoint her. "Eggs'll be fine," he said.

He took a seat at the small table and watched as Flora dropped one of the eggs on the floor and a piece of bread into the sink. Still, she managed to make a decent meal and Max ate it with surprising relish while Flora quietly abandoned the oven and set about ruining the rest of the kitchen.

"Overdid it a bit last night, eh?" she said as she scrubbed the life out of the ceramic sink, throwing the odd handful of scouring powder in for good measure.

"Yes."

"Well, I hope you had a nice time."

"I don't really remember," Max said around his eggs. "It had something to do with Hitler and Abyssinia."

"Abbey who?"

"It's a country. Mussolini invaded it a few months ago."

Flora shivered and scrubbed the sink harder than ever. "Mussolini. I don't like him," she said. "Them uniforms give me the frights. Him and Hitler and Stalin. Never trust a bloke in uniform, my dad says."

9

"I agree," Max said, finishing his meal, laying the knife and fork on the plate and patting himself down, trying to locate his cigarettes.

"It's like the whole place is getting ready for a war," Flora was saying, getting into her stride now. "I mean, what's a bloke in uniform for if it ain't for a fight?"

She stood up and arched her back to straighten it then ran the back of her hand over her sweating brow. "I reckon the only people doing well are them making uniforms."

Max was silent for a moment, jaw tight. "Too many bloody uniforms and nobody gives a damn what those uniforms mean," he said, darkness in his voice. "We're sleepwalking towards another damned Armageddon."

His eyes blazed for a moment. He became aware that Flora was quiet and still, her arms held tightly by her side, the scrubbing brush still in her grip. She was breathing heavily, her mouth open. And her eyes were wide, staring at Max.

"Give me a fag, Flora," he said.

She reached into the too-large pocket at the front of her pinafore and removed the packet of cigarettes and a box of matches, which she handed to Max.

"Thanks. If Martha notices the smell, I'll own up, so you might as well light one yourself."

Flora smiled and chucked the scrubbing brush into the sink. "Thank you, sir."

He passed the cigarettes back and Flora lit one up and leaned back against the kitchen worktop, eyeing the dirty frying pan that she was now going to have to clean. Scrambled eggs were a bugger to get off. Almost as bad as bleedin' burned duck fat. She sucked the smoke down deeply and let it out slowly. Max had a go at that and burst a lung. He could feel the smoke grate the membranes inside.

"God," he said, eyes watering.

"Me Dad," Flora said, by way of explanation.

"He's a docker, isn't he?"

"He's a foreman," Flora said. "Has blokes under him."

They were quiet for a while. Max seemed momentarily to drift away and Flora seemed to be waiting for him to return. "I'm sorry I got angry just now," Max said finally.

"Don't bother me, sir," Flora said, though Max knew that was a lie.

She'd been with a man a year or so earlier, and he'd been rough. Sometimes, Flora had come to work with a black eye or a dried cut on her lip. Neither Max nor Martha ever made mention of it, but they offered to put Flora up in the study should she ever find herself in need, as they put it. She was scared of the violence that emanated from men, and Max felt ashamed. "I just become…" He sighed, not knowing exactly what he became.

"It's them bleedin' uniforms, sir," Flora said. "Pardon my French."

"Yes. And the men wearing uniforms are crushing those who aren't."

He glanced at Flora. "You know what they're doing? In Europe? They're dividing people up and stomping on the ones they don't like. Stalin's doing it and Mussolini. Hitler's doing it. He's the worst of them, making the Jews and Gypsies scapegoats for everything. Taking away their citizenship."

Flora looked down at her hands.

"Didn't you hear about that?" Max said.

"What's that?"

"The German citizenship laws."

"Uh…"

"In Germany."

"I don't really know about all that sort of stuff, sir. Eric does. He's very well read up, reads books and broadsheets."

Eric was the young man who worked as an assistant to Mr Stone, the butcher. Eric and Flora had been going together for a few months and she now rarely entered into conversation without mentioning his name, often in relation to whatever subject was at hand. Eric, it seemed, was a paragon of knowledge, as well as a skilled butcher. And a decent man to boot.

Martha had suspicions that Flora's constant praise of Eric was because she was secretly in love with Max. The more Flora praised Eric, the more Martha felt convinced. It was as if Flora subconsciously felt the need to convince everyone that she wasn't really in love with Max at all, and that Eric was clearly the one for her. And Martha, being herself very fond of Flora, went out of her way to ignore her suspicions.

It was, in its way, one of the politest love rivalries in history.

The two male counterparts in this affair, being men, were completely oblivious of all the subtleties. Indeed, they were each perfectly happy to admire the other's qualities to the point where Flora became confused as to who she was supposed to be marrying.

For Eric's part, he was smitten but had suspicions that he wasn't good enough for Flora. Every time she entered Mr Stone's shop, Eric would seek to win her affection by slipping her the odd sausage or beef offcut.

On occasion, he would give Flora – in lieu of his own – a pig's heart, wrapping it in newspaper and placing it in her basket with a wink. For Eric, this act was of great importance, and took on symbolic significance. It was his telltale heart. Eric never stole this offering, though, since he would always admit his action to Mr Stone and ask to have the amount docked from his wages, which, having himself once been in love, Mr Stone would mostly fail to do.

"How can they make them non-citizens?" Flora was saying. "What's gonna happen to 'em?"

"That's a very good question," Max said quietly. "Anyway, that's why I got cut last night, because we're all going to hell in a handbasket."

Flora gave that some thought while she smoked. "My sister's a machinist at a tie makers down Brick Lane, and her boss is a Jewish fella. Mr Rothman. Me dad invited him over for tea once, and he brought my mum flowers. Flowers, and he didn't even know her. Can't imagine Hitler and that lot bringing flowers."

"I couldn't have put it better myself."

"It's a pity someone don't shoot him."

"People like him are twisted," Max said. "The straighter you shoot, the more you miss."

"Bleedin' uniforms," Flora said, glancing at Max with a slightly nervous smile.

"Yes," Max said, smiling back.

He mashed his cigarette on his empty plate and waved away the smoke. Flora spat on the palm of her hand and doused the cigarette tip there. She dropped the stub into her pinafore pocket.

"By the way," Max said, "has Martha mentioned the dinner this evening?"

"She told me on the way out."

"Will you be able to work?"

"Oh, yes, sir. Thanks very much."

"You don't mind? I mean, you weren't going to see Eric or anything?"

Flora shrugged. "Nah," she said. "Eric's busy tonight. I saw him yesterday and he told me he was sorry he couldn't see me tomorrow as he had to go meet his pals. Then he tells me if I come by the shop Monday, he'd give me a bleedin' pig's heart."

By this, Max assumed that Flora wasn't keen on Eric's pals. And she wasn't fussed about pigs' hearts either.

"May I ask who's coming tonight, sir?"

"Um, I forget."

"Will Mr Lindsey be coming?"

"Lindsey? He'll probably turn up. He can smell free booze from Wimbledon. Why?"

Flora blushed. "Well, sir, last time he was a bit, um, a bit forward, sir."

"Was he? Well, if he's ever forward again, you have my permission to knock his bloody head off."

Flora blushed more and decided that was a good time to tackle the frying pan, eggs and all. "Yes, sir," she said over her shoulder, a wide smile lighting up her glowing face.

That was another thing Max liked about Flora, her smile. You can tell a lot about a person by the way they smile, or don't. With Flora, it was a wide smile that made her eyes sparkle. It was open, honest.

There was a knock at the door, and Flora, who was still desperately trying to remove all evidence that the frying pan had ever been within a hundred miles of an egg, dropped the offending item into the sink with such urgency that it threw out half the water. She scuttered off to answer the door.

That'll be Martha, no doubt, Max thought. Probably forgotten her money or something. God, I hope she hasn't brought her mother back.

Chapter Three

There was the clinking of teaspoons on cups, and a low hum of voices, although Martha couldn't see many people talking. She glanced around the small café, letting her eyes wander from one table to the next. The people were mostly young or middle-aged, in couples or small groups. The men seemed mostly solemn, and the women mostly quiet. It looked like a painting by Degas or Manet, everyone waiting for the artist to tell them he'd finished now and they were free to move.

There was one young couple that caught Martha's attention. They weren't quite as well dressed as many here – the woman in a cotton blouse and tweed skirt, the man in a plain dark grey suit – and they weren't solemn at all. They chatted excitedly about something, the woman gesticulating with her hands whenever she spoke, the man ready to smile or agree, his eyes wide.

This couple made Martha sigh for reasons she couldn't explain and, perhaps, wouldn't want to.

Martha's mother, Mrs Webster, looked up from her diary, saw Martha's expression and frowned tightly. "Have some tea, dear," she said. "It'll get cold."

Mrs Webster was a firm sort of woman, tall and erect, with an unwavering gaze that gave to many people the impression of a sergeant major in the British army. Even seated, she gave that impression, which is hard to do. She wore a French-made woollen skirt and jacket, which was tightly buttoned with a diamond leaf brooch on the right shoulder. On her feet were low leather shoes and on her head was a solid, practical hat firmly pinned to her firm hair.

"There's something wrong," Martha said.

Her mother sipped her tea and put the cup down precisely on the saucer, as if she were demonstrating for her daughter, and everyone else in the place, the *right* way to drink tea. "Hmm?" she said.

"With Max. There's something wrong. I think he's lost something, and I don't know what it is, and I feel I should know."

"What are you talking about, dear? Lost what? Are you speaking materially? Has he lost a sock?"

"No," said Martha, knowing she'd made a terrible mistake.

Her mother knew precisely what Martha had meant. And Martha knew that she knew, which meant that Martha was about to receive a lecture of some sort. "Ah," she said. "Then you mean it in a metaphysical way. Things are far too metaphysical these days, if you ask me. Everybody wants to examine the Universe and their place in it. Why they can't all accept things and get on with it is beyond me. Your husband would be better off looking for his sock, in my opinion."

Martha felt her face redden. "Mother," she said, "please. It has nothing to do with metaphysics, as you call it. He's sad, and I don't know why, and I can't reach him."

Mrs Webster considered this for a moment. She wasn't insensitive, after all. "Max needs a career," she said finally. "Men need to work and do their duty. That's how they fill those voids. I'm sure Max just has a void that needs filling. He needs to do his duty."

"He fought for his country. How much more duty should he do?"

"His duty to *you*, Martha. To his wife."

"Anyway, he has a career."

"Writing isn't a career. It's a hobby. I mean, if he sold any of his books or wrote something important, it would be different."

"He does sell books. His last one on the Peninsular War has sold almost a thousand copies. And the *Telegraph* called it masterful."

"But he doesn't sell *lots* of books. He's not *famous*."

"So you'd prefer that he wrote romance novels or something."

"Yes," Mrs Webster said, firmly. "If they sold."

"It's something to do with what's going on in Europe. Hitler and Mussolini and all that sort. It's as if he thinks he should be out there fighting them." Martha sighed and said, "Oh, I don't know."

She was quiet for a moment. It had been a mistake to speak to her mother – it usually was – but there was nobody else she could talk to. She drank some of her tea, which was getting cold. She deliberately put the cup down on the tablecloth to annoy her mother.

She found herself looking again at the young couple over by the window. The man was now explaining something to the woman, using his hands to shape the explanation in the air. The woman watched his hands move, but her gaze kept returning to his eyes, then her eyes would become soft and Martha's, mirroring the woman's, would soften too, and something inside would hurt.

Martha moved her view to the window and the world beyond, cabs and buses, people strolling along in the bright crisp spring air, shadows opposite like blocks of angles, all bright or black in the sunshine even though there was a chill to the wind, an ice on the air that Martha imagined came from the Russian steppes. It was a feint, only pretending to be spring out there while the winter lingered out of sight.

Her mother said something, and brought Martha back to the heaviness of reality. "What did you say?"

"I said, he only married you for your money."

Oh. So her mother was still on that subject, was she? "He married me because he loved me. And I loved him."

"Loved?"

"Love. Loves. Please don't twist my meaning. Besides, what's wrong with marrying for money? You did."

"That's different. Women are permitted to marry money. What else do we have? You young people think that we've won something because we have the vote, but that was just a sort of conjurer's trick. They gave us the vote and while we all watched it and were in awe, we missed the other part of the trick, the part in which everything else stays the same. After all, we have a vote, but for *whom* do we get to vote? Men."

Mercifully, the waitress appeared and placed three plates on the table. Martha had gone for the baked sea bass with Béarnaise sauce. Mrs Webster was on another of her dieting fads. This one had something to do with mushrooms. Consequently, she was having mushrooms with everything and couldn't understand why she wasn't losing weight. In fact, she'd put on three pounds in two weeks, which only determined her to eat more mushrooms. Now, she was having a cheese and mushroom omelette with a side of mushroom pâté on toast.

"Trust me," she was saying, stuffing a mushroom into her mouth, "women *have* to marry money. But if a man marries money, that's a sign of greed and laziness."

"Max doesn't care about money."

"*Everybody* cares about money."

"He doesn't. Really he doesn't. Sometimes I think he despises it."

"Well, there you are then. He must have Bolshevik sympathies."

Martha wasn't listening. She speared the sea bass with her fork, but she had no appetite now. She was quiet for a moment, regarding the dead fish. Then she looked up at her mother and said, "Sometimes I think he despises me for having it. Or coming from it."

Mrs Webster sighed heavily. "Then he's an idiot or he's a Bolshevik, and I don't know which is worse. Either way, you should never have married him."

Martha was about to tell her mother that marrying Max was the best thing she'd ever done, but she never got the chance.

Everyone's attention was caught by a commotion at the entrance. The maître d' stood with a woman before him, barring her entry to the café on grounds of lacking a reservation. He kept raking through his long dark hair, trying to push it back on to his skull in a proxy, no doubt, for pushing the woman out of the café.

The woman was young and slim and seemed to have limbs that were too long. She wore a shapeless brown coat and a misshapen hat that wasn't doing much good at all. "Stuff your bleedin' reservation," the woman said.

"Please, miss," the maître d' was saying, flattening his hair. "You *must* have a reservation."

"Isn't that your girl?" Mrs Webster said, peering through the pince-nez she held in front of her face.

"Flora?" Martha said. "Oh, Flora."

Flora, seeing her mistress, pushed past the maître d' and rushed forward. Her face was red with effort and emotion. "Ma'am," she said as she reached the table. "Oh, it's awful. Ma'am, sir, coppers, I mean, police, he's… oh…"

"What's wrong with you, girl?" Mrs Webster said.

Flora, apparently noticing Mrs Webster for the first time, burst into tears. "Max… I mean, Mr Max, I mean, your – bugger – I mean, ma'am, sir –"

"Calm down, Flora," Martha said, putting a hand on the girl's arm. "Sit down."

Flora pulled out a seat and sat down, Martha's hand still on her arm.

The maître d' was upon them now, trying simultaneously to maintain his dignity, avoid the embarrassment of a scene and keep his hair in order. He was failing at all three.

"What's wrong?" Mrs Webster asked him firmly. "Can't you see this young girl is overwrought?"

"She doesn't have a reservation," the maître d' said weakly before withdrawing to hide somewhere, taking his hair with him.

Most people in the café watched the small group, although some were determinedly not watching, feeling it was all too emotional and vulgar, especially at lunchtime.

"Flora," Martha said, "please calm down and tell us what's happened."

Flora breathed deeply for a few seconds. Then she looked up at her mistress and said, "It's Mr Dalton, ma'am. He's been arrested."

"I knew it," Mrs Webster said.

"Flora," Martha said, glaring at her mother. "Arrested for what?"

"Murder."

Chapter Four

The room was about fifteen-foot square with walls that were a colour previously unknown to humanity, waxed in a coating of nicotine and dust, and paled by sunlight. There were two desks at right angles to each other, one opposite the door and the other, on the right as you entered, facing the window, which provided a nice view of a brick wall.

The desk opposite the door was cluttered with papers, files, a telephone, a folded map, ashtrays, books, photographs and a dozen other incidental items. At the front of the desk was a wood-mounted brass nameplate announcing that the occupant of the desk was a Detective Sergeant Pierce.

The other desk belonged to Detective Inspector Longford. His desk had as many items, but in a neater order, the blotter parallel to the edge of the desk, the telephone to the right and various files stacked to the left. In a silver frame, behind the telephone, was a photograph of a woman with two young children, taken on the promenade of a beach town, all three of them smiling broadly. An ashtray, a packet of pipe tobacco and a box of matches were at the corner of the blotter, and a rack of pipes stood by itself to one side. This desk, Max thought, was orderly and unimaginative.

Max had been waiting in the office, by himself, for half an hour. When, finally, the door opened and two men entered, Max felt like he knew them both well. Old Longford, reliable and dull, and his dishevelled sidekick, Pierce.

Longford was tall, about the same height as Max, but a little heavier around his torso. He was in his mid-fifties, which made that photograph on his desk a decade or so old. He had a prominent, straight nose, short brown hair and gentle eyes, grey or light blue.

The other man, Pierce, was shorter by four inches, and heavier by four stone. He looked like he'd been carved from the trunk of an ancient oak. Max thought he'd have made a pretty good prop for the British Lions. In fact, judging by his face, he'd been just that since birth, cauliflower ears and scar tissue around his eyes, and a nose that must've been broken a dozen times. But, for all that, his eyes were young and his face was unlined, so Max put him below thirty.

Both men took positions behind their desks, with Longford packing a pipe and lighting it while Pierce took a notebook from a drawer and a pen from his inside jacket pocket.

Longford was the first to speak. He sucked on his pipe, blew the smoke out and said, "I'm sorry to have to bother you with this, Mr Dalton."

He didn't sound sorry, but Max was determined to appear unruffled. "No bother," he said, as casually as he could. "Perhaps you could tell me what all this is about. The detective said it concerned a death."

"A murder, sir," Pierce said. "Not a death."

Max turned to the sergeant, who hadn't taken his eyes from his notebook, and was busy scribbling away. "That's right. I promise you, Inspector," Max said, turning back to Longford, "I haven't murdered anyone for at least two weeks."

Longford smiled thinly.

"May I ask where you were last night, sir?"

"Last night? I was in a pub, The Lion, on the Strand. Why?"

"And before that?"

"My paper. The *News Chronicle*."

"Oh, yes. I understand you're a journalist, sir. Is that right?"

"On occasion. I'm freelance, but I used to work at the *Chronicle* and a friend of mine lets me use his desk when he's not there. So I popped in to check my mail, and to have a word with Features. I fancied an idea about the Berlin Olympics. Should be an interesting contest."

"Features?"

"Yes. Man called Barney Watson. Features editor."

The sergeant made a note of this. The inspector blew smoke out, forming a cloud that hung under the ceiling like fog. Max watched the smoke, remembering years earlier. His eyes became soft and sad.

"Sir?" the inspector said.

Max blinked.

"Um, afterwards, I wandered along to The Lion."

"And what time was that?"

"Seven, half past, something like that. Look, can you tell me what this is about? The detective only said that someone was dead and I might be a witness. If I'd seen anything, don't you think I'd have told you?"

Inspector Longford glanced over at his sergeant. There was something in that look that Max didn't like. It said: 'He doesn't understand what we do.'

"As we mentioned, sir," the inspector said, returning his gaze to Max, "it's about a murder, and you might be a witness without realising it, you see? Now, you were at the pub for how long?"

Longford sucked down some more smoke and blew it out, making the cloud even thicker. The smoke, in this confined room, was making Max feel ill. He wanted to open a window, breathe in fresh air. He felt trapped, somehow. "Few hours. Until last orders, a bit past there."

"And can anyone verify that, sir?"

"Is it important?"

The inspector answered that by smiling vaguely. He did lots of things vaguely, except when it came to being vague, which he did precisely and with the apparent purpose of unsettling Max.

It was working. He hadn't murdered anyone, of course, but, still, he felt that he might be guilty of something, and that the inspector knew what it was, even if Max didn't.

"Were you with anyone, sir?" It was Sergeant Pierce who'd spoken.

Max almost told them about bumping into Burton, but he didn't want them to know about that. He didn't want anyone to know about that. Or, rather, he didn't want them to know about him knowing Burton. It had been a long time ago, certainly, but, still… "I don't recall anyone," Max said. "It's all a bit hazy."

"Do you know anyone called Crawford? John Crawford?"

"No. Is that his name? The dead man?"

"The murdered man," the sergeant said.

"That was his name, sir," Longford said, "when he was alive."

When he finished saying this, the inspector sucked on his pipe, making a dry sound, as if he were drawing a deliberate link between the death of the man and the extinguishing of his pipe. There was no smoke now, though, which was a small relief to Max.

"I've never known anyone called Crawford, as far as I can recall."

The inspector inspected the bowl of his pipe and decided that it was, indeed, dead. He tapped it out in his ashtray and started to refill it, pressing the tobacco down with his thumb.

Longford now sat back and regarded Max for a moment.

Max shifted in his seat. He'd been trying to remember exactly what had happened last night, but it was a bit of a blur. The one thing he was sure of, though, was that he hadn't witnessed anyone being killed. Still…

"Were you ever in the army, sir?" Longford said as he struck a match and put it to his pipe.

The question seemed so casual, and yet Max felt there was significance behind the asking. There had to be. What did they know, these policemen? What could they know? "Yes. '16 to '18."

"Which regiment, sir, if you don't mind my asking?"

"Why should I mind? Grenadier Guards."

"You were an officer?"

Again, the question seemed trivial, but they were digging into Max, bit by bit. He answered the question carefully. "I became an officer, yes."

"And were you conscripted?"

"No."

"You enlisted?"

"Yes."

"Very noble of you," Sergeant Pierce said flatly.

Max turned to him. He was beginning to feel like a bull in an arena, prodded by small men with long swords, each cut making him more fearful, more angry. "What does that mean?"

Pierce didn't reply, but instead glanced at his inspector, who said, "Well, you were young, the war had been going for a couple of years by then. You must've thought you could wait it out, perhaps survive the war without serving. So, it was a noble gesture, volunteering."

"There was nothing noble about it. I thought they'd probably fetch me in the end. If I enlisted, I'd at least get to choose which regiment I served in."

"In which you served," the inspector said quietly, although not quietly enough.

"What?"

"Oh, I beg your pardon, sir," Longford said. "It was just that you ended with a preposition."

Max felt himself redden. "Did I? How unfortunate of me."

"So you chose the Grenadier Guards," Longford said, looking perplexed. "Any reason why?"

"I like red."

"Red?" Longford, still looking perplexed, examined his pipe.

"The dress uniform," Max said. "You must've seen the changing of the Guard at Buckingham Palace."

"I don't get much time to go to Buckingham Palace, I'm afraid."

"Well, they have nice red uniforms. And bearskins."

"And did you find many occasions on which to wear your nice red uniform, sir?"

"The army aren't keen on Guards wearing their dress uniforms at the front. Might get dirty."

"And you received a commission when you enlisted."

The inspector had said that as a statement, even though Max felt it was a question. Should he tell them the truth? But why should he? What difference did it make to a couple of coppers whether he'd been commissioned? He was beginning to feel afraid. "Why all the questions about my war service?" he said.

"Is that when you met Mr Crawford, sir? When you were in the Guards?"

"What?"

"The deceased."

"I told you, I've never heard of anyone called Crawford."

"Ah. It's just that we noticed he was wearing Grenadier Guards cufflinks. Silver, no less."

Max's blood ran cold. He said, "What?"

"Well, you were both in the same regiment, and you were both approximately the same age, and you were both seen in approximately the same place last night, at approximately the same time, and he was murdered and you say you don't know him. So, I wondered whether there was anything in that, in you both serving in the Grenadier Guards."

"Did you know him well, sir?" Pierce said.

Max glanced over at the sergeant, who was leaning over his desk, pen hovering over the notebook, looking at Max, waiting. "Um."

A cold sweat broke out over his body. He shifted in his seat. Longford and Pierce waited, silently, and the silence started to seem to Max a tactic, a trap of some kind. He felt the sweat begin to gather around his collar as the silence got louder. What did it mean? "May I have a glass of water?" he said.

Longford flicked his gaze to Pierce, who stood slowly, as if it were a great effort. He walked casually from the room. "Are you ill, sir?" Longford said, blowing smoke in Max's general direction.

"No, just a bit…" He was about to say 'hungover', but realised with a sudden dread that might imply a blackout or a drunken spat or something. Did he want Longford to know that? Did he want Longford to know anything about the night before? But hadn't he already told them he'd been drinking? Hadn't he already implied that he couldn't remember? Oh, God. This was bad.

"A bit what?"

"Hot."

Longford nodded, but his affirmation was the least affirmative that Max had ever seen. Rather, it was as if Longford were laughing at him. Or so it seemed to Max.

After a few hundred years, Pierce returned and handed Max a glass of lukewarm tap water, which Max received gratefully. "Where... where did he serve? This Crawford?" he said.

"Wouldn't he have served where you served? If he was in the same regiment?"

"Depends which battalion he was in."

Max cursed himself again. Ending with a preposition. How terribly gauche. He felt himself redden, and knew that Longford had noticed.

"We're waiting to hear from the War Office," Longford said. "About the details of Mr Crawford's service."

Max didn't speak, didn't think he could speak without his voice betraying him. He kept thinking of Burton. There were too many coincidences. The pub the night before, the same regiment, the chance meeting.

Longford waited. Pierce waited, pen suspended. Finally, Longford looked at his thumb nail and said, "Oh, there was one other thing, sir."

Max watched Longford as he examined his thumb nail. It was all so casual, all so polite. And yet, there was something in this, the pipe, the glances, the bloody thumb nail.

"What?" Max said, his voice husky.

Longford moved his eyes slowly from his hand to Max. Pierce sniffed. Max felt like that bull in the arena, skewered, bleeding, dying.

Longford opened a drawer in his desk and, with an economy of movement that told Max he'd planned this all along, removed a small book, opening it to a page and holding it out for Max to see. "A notebook, found on the deceased. It contained your address, and the phone number of your workplace. That is your address, isn't it? And your workplace number?"

Max found himself looking at neatly written black words on white paper. He knew the address, and the phone number. He couldn't breathe. He felt his heart hammer in his chest, in his throat. He felt dizzy, light-headed. He felt guilty. He thought, they've got me.

Then the door burst open, and Martha marched in. A small man in a blue suit and glasses trotted behind her and a befuddled-looking police constable brought up the rear.

"Sir," the police constable said, pushing his way to the front, "this lady—"

He didn't get any further because Martha pushed him aside. "Max," she cried, rushing towards him and grasping him around the neck, kissing him on the cheek and lips.

"It's… all… right… Martha," Max said between kisses.

Martha suddenly straightened up, turned to Sergeant Pierce and said, "Inspector, I'd like to know what—"

Pierce pointed to Longford, who cleared his throat. Martha swung around and faced Longford. "Inspector, I'd like to know what the devil's going on here. Why have you arrested my husband? I demand—"

"We haven't arrested him," Longford said.

Martha took a deep breath and said, "Oh."

"I'm a potential witness," Max said. "Although I think I've answered your questions, Inspector."

He stood up, and Martha took his arm possessively. "If you have any further questions, please speak to my solicitor," she nodded to the small man with glasses, "Mr... uh..."

"Mr Bacon," the small man said.

"Bacon?" Martha said. "Are you sure?"

"Quite sure."

With that, Martha marched out, Max in tow. Mr Bacon smiled nervously and followed. Sergeant Pierce glanced at Inspector Longford, who was lamenting another dead pipe.

"What do you think?" Pierce said.

"I think something is rotten in the state of Denmark."

"Eh?"

"He's lying."

Chapter Five

They were silent for a while, sitting in the back of a cab, avoiding talking about what had happened. Max thought about the questions he'd been asked, and knew that there had to be a connection of some kind that he couldn't see. Unless… Unless Burton was Crawford. Things made sense if that were true, but otherwise they made no sense at all. And what of the detectives Longford and Pierce? That had been a strange interview, and unpleasant. He'd felt as if he really had witnessed a murder or, worse, as if he'd had some involvement in one.

Their attitude, from the start, had been to treat him with hostility and not, as they'd maintained, as a witness. He'd been rattled, that was true. He'd been evasive, not wanting to explain about Burton, and that had been stupid, only making them more suspicious. God knows what would've happened if Martha hadn't burst in with that little man.

"Where did you find him?" Max said, turning to his wife.

Martha had been watching the streets of London blur past, losing herself for a while in the anonymity of the city; the dark and grey people, the stone buildings and the tarmac roads, the black cabs, buses and trams liveried in dirt-stained red or green. It all became one thing, each bleeding into the others so that Martha could feel a part of the melee and yet removed from it, watching it through a window.

"Martha?" Max said.

Martha turned, smiled faintly, snapped out of her reverie. "What? Oh, Mr Gammon. He works at Daddy's solicitors."

"And how did you find out where I was?"

"Flora. Made quite a scene at the café."

"Flora," Max said.

"Let's not talk about it now," Martha said, raising her eyebrows at the cabbie.

"Oh. Right."

Martha went back to watching life pass by as the cab rumbled along. It was true she didn't want to talk about things now, but not for the reason she gave. The truth was, she was afraid.

When they entered the flat, Flora was waiting, standing in the sitting room with her arms by her side. She tried to smile as Max winked at her. "Oh, it was awful," she said. Then she burst into tears.

"It's okay, Flora," Max said. "Just a misunderstanding, that's all."

"Compose yourself, Flora," Martha said.

"Oh, sir," Flora said. She attempted to fling her arms around Max, while, at the same time, trying to compose herself. She ended up sticking her elbow in Max's ribs and bursting into tears again.

"Flora, why don't you go and carry on in the kitchen for a bit. We're behind schedule for the dinner tonight."

"Yes, ma'am." Flora, wiping her nose on her sleeve, walked stiffly from the room.

For a moment, Max and Martha looked at each other, not quite knowing what to say. Finally, Martha said, "Oh, hell."

She went to the drinks cabinet and poured them both large Scotches.

"Are we going to carry on with that?" Max said. "The dinner party?"

"Why not?"

Martha handed Max his drink. He looked at it, then at Martha, who was watching him with something like pain in her eyes. Max smiled at her. "It's over now."

"Is it?"

"Yes, of course. Why do you say that?"

Martha didn't answer for a long time. For some reason, she thought of the young couple she'd seen in the café at lunchtime, and the memory of them sank to a point, far inside her, and echoed with a hollow ring. "I was scared," she said finally. "I was actually scared. I can't remember ever being scared before, except when I was a child and my cat ran away."

"Don't worry. I won't run away."

"It came back. My cat."

Max sipped his Scotch. Martha looked at hers, then sat down, pushing herself over to the very edge of the sofa. She put the glass on the coffee table. "Perhaps you'd better tell me about last night."

"There's nothing much to tell."

"Max. Please. I know you. I know you're not telling me something. Was it a woman?"

He didn't even need to answer that.

"Well, all right. But there's something, isn't there?"

Max took another sip of Scotch, then swirled the remaining fluid around in the glass and watched it rotate. Martha watched him watching the Scotch.

"Who was he, Max?"

"What?"

"The man who was killed. It's obvious you knew him. Was he the one you met last night? The one from your regiment?"

Max still wouldn't look at her.

"Max, please," Martha said, her voice almost breaking into a sob.

She took a deep breath, brushed a curl from her forehead. "I saw you when I went into that room. Max, your face was white. You were scared, weren't you? If you can't trust me, who can you trust?"

Max downed the rest of the drink, sat down next to Martha and put his finger gently into her shining brown hair. He pushed a curling lock away from her eyes. "The man I met last night was called Burton, Daniel Burton. I knew him during the war. He was a sergeant in my platoon. I hadn't seen him since the war ended."

"Why did you lie to the police?"

"I didn't. They asked me about someone called Crawford. I don't know anyone by that name. But they told me he had Grenadier Guards cufflinks and I started to get a bad feeling.

And then they said this Crawford had our address and the phone number of the paper. That's when you came in. That's what you saw in my face."

"So you think Burton is Crawford?"

"It might be another man, but if it is, it would be a hell of a coincidence."

Martha thought about that. "Well, let's try to call your friend. You have his number, don't you?"

"No. He didn't give it to me. We just had a few drinks and a chat. I'd already had a few, so I was a bit, um…"

"Blotto."

"Fuzzy. And then he left."

"Hmm." She tried to sound casual, but many emotions were moving around, clashing and colliding into each other. She believed Max, of course, about his friend, and about his fear that it was Burton who was dead. But, still, there was something else that he wasn't telling her.

She put a hand on his arm. "What did you talk about? With your friend, Burton. What did you say? Precisely."

"Um…"

"Oh, Max. Think."

"I'm trying. Let's see. Well, I was in the pub, and I'd had a few. I'd chatted with a couple of fellows from the paper. That's right. Burton came up to the bar and sort of turned and looked at me and then I turned away, you know, like you do when you're casually glancing around. Then I turned back and said, Burton? Dan Burton? And he said, yes. And then it was as if I was looking at my past and I knew him suddenly, instantly. I suppose there are faces you'll never forget. And we had a few drinks, chatted about this and that. I told him I was married, worked at the *Chronicle* now and then. He said he'd read my stuff and liked it. It was busy then, and when it got quieter we talked more, but I can't remember that."

"But what of him? What did he say about himself? Where does he live? Is he married?"

Max thought, tried to remember. He squeezed his mind for any clue, any remembrance, no matter how trivial. He shook his head. "If he told me anything that could help, I can't recall it. I think I'd had more than a few by then."

Martha sighed audibly. She couldn't hide her frustration, but, equally, she couldn't hide her fear. After a moment, though, she started to think about Max, and her anger and annoyance evaporated. "I'm sorry," she said. "If it's your friend who's dead, I'm sorry for that."

"It's strange, though," Max said. "What the police told me about the man having our address and the number of the *Chronicle*. If it is someone called Crawford, why would he have my name? And if it was Burton, then him meeting me wasn't the accident, it seemed."

"Yes, that is strange. So, what exactly happened to this man who was killed, whoever he was?"

"I don't know. They didn't tell me."

"Didn't you ask?"

"I would've done, but then you came marching in with your solicitor."

"Oh. Yes."

"Thanks, by the way."

She smiled, but it was a weak smile, and Max knew it, and knew that she knew he was lying.

Martha stood abruptly, and smoothed her skirt. "Max, we need to find out what happened last night. What if it is your friend?"

"It might be in the morning newspaper. If not, I'll call Joe Pollard on the City desk. He'd know."

"You do that. I'm going to have a word with Flora about dinner tonight."

Max looked through the morning editions and then, failing to find anything about the killing, called the *Chronicle* and spoke to Joe Pollard, who didn't know anything either. He said he'd check and call Max back, which he did.

"They're keeping very quiet about it," Joe said. "Probably means they don't know anything more than you do. Or it could mean they do, and they're not saying yet. I got hold of a contact at the Yard and all he told me was that they were investigating a death."

Max explained all this to Martha.

"That was a waste of time, then. I can call Mr Mutton and ask him to look into it."

"Bacon."

"Yes. Bacon."

"I think we should let the police handle it."

"But they think you're guilty. Don't they?"

Max thought about that for a moment. "Yes," he said, "I think they might."

Chapter Six

Of course, it was Saturday. Martha hadn't considered that. In fact, once she'd sprung Max, as she insisted on putting it, she hadn't thought any more about Mr Gammon, or whatever his name was. Once they'd determined that Max was only a witness, it hadn't seemed necessary to delay Mr Whatsit, who was evidently impatient to get away and enjoy the rest of his weekend.

Now that Max was a suspected murderer, Martha was regretting not taking more notice of the poor little man.

"He kept looking at his watch," she told Max. "Daddy phoned him and he met me at the café, came in a cab. And all the way to Scotland Yard he kept looking at his watch. So, I didn't think to detain him more than was required."

Max nodded. "Why would you? Do you know where he went?"

"Oh, he mentioned something about a villa on a bridge, or near a bridge. Maybe it was Stourbridge. Although I can't imagine why he'd have a villa in Stourbridge. Awful place."

Max thought about that. "What time did you arrive at Scotland Yard?"

"Well, it must've been about an hour after Flora came into the café. That was just after lunchtime, so, about two o'clock or probably half past. Thereabouts."

Max went off in search of the paper, which he found rolled up and stuffed down the side of the sofa. He pulled it out, glanced at the last page. Then he looked at his watch and smiled. "I know exactly where he is," he said.

Martha arched her left eyebrow. "But you don't know him. How could you possibly know where he is?"

"It wasn't a villa near a bridge, or even in Stourbridge. It was Villa at The Bridge."

To Martha, that made less sense than having a villa in Stourbridge. "You're talking in riddles," she announced.

"Aston Villa are playing Chelsea at Stamford Bridge. Three o'clock kick-off. No wonder he was worried about the time. And since it's now twenty minutes past three, I'll lay a pound to a penny that he's surrounded by Chelsea supporters, cheering on his team."

Max smiled again, and felt rather pleased with himself. Martha, meanwhile, seemed shocked.

"Mr Bacon a football supporter? I never would've guessed. He seemed such a decent little chap."

Max's eyes narrowed and he was about to tell Martha that she was being a snob, but he didn't get the chance because she said, "That was very clever of you, Max. Come on, then. Let's go."

And she grabbed her handbag, opened the door and marched out before Max could explain that they'd never be able to find Mr Bacon at a football game.

Chapter Seven

"I don't know how you plan to find him," Max said, as they were bumping along the Fulham Road in a cab. "They had over eighty thousand for the game against Arsenal a few months ago."

"Well, we could go on to the pitch or something, stop the game and demand that Mr Liver come to us."

Max rolled his eyes, but elected to stay silent. Surely even Martha wouldn't try a stunt like that.

"How did you know all that?" Martha asked him. "About Villa and how many people might be at the game?"

"I like football," he said reasonably.

"Since when? I thought you were a cricket man."

"You know, it is possible to like football *and* cricket. Besides, whenever I mention anything about sport, you go into a trance."

Well, Martha thought, that was true enough. "Football *and* cricket," she muttered. "Well, well."

*

"This is an urgent call for Mr Harold Sausage. Would Mr Harold Sausage please make himself known to any member of the ground staff."

Mr Bacon was, at that moment, standing in the Fulham Road End, trying to eat a steak and kidney pie, which was proving hard to do with all the people pressing into him. He'd been forced to miss his lunch on account of the pointless business with that woman and her husband over at Scotland Yard. If it hadn't been for the call from Mr Ronson himself, well, he would've done what he often did on Saturday; have a leisurely meal at a greasy spoon he liked, followed by a pint in one of several pubs, and a nice stroll to the game. Instead, he'd missed lunch, missed his pint, and almost missed the kick-off. In fact, that blasted woman had almost made him miss this, George Mills and Chelsea fighting for something. Imagine if Mills scored and he'd been forced to miss that. Oh, it was too much. George Mills was something of a hero to Mr Bacon. He represented the epitome of Britishness. Mills wasn't one of those spectacular players who could burn brightly for a while, and then fade. He wasn't a big star, hadn't been a high-profile signing. What George Mills was, though, was dependable and loyal and hard-working. What more should a man aspire to?

The announcement was one of the strangest things Mr Bacon had heard at a football game. As the speaker went quiet, Mr Bacon resumed his pie-eating. The game had been flat for most of the time, with both Villa and Chelsea scrapping it out in the middle of the park. But now it looked promising, and it looked as though Mills and Burgess were finally getting the measure of the Villa defence. Tenacity. That's what Mills had.

Just as Mr Bacon was about to take another bite from his pie, the speakers started up again: "Correction. This is an urgent call for Mr Harold Bacon. Would Mr Bacon, not Sausage, please inform a member of our ground staff of his presence. Thank you."

Mr Bacon stared at the pitch, the pie an inch from his gaping mouth.

*

"Ah, there he is," Martha said when a man opened the door and showed Mr Bacon in. "We've found you."

"Mrs, um, Dalton," Mr Bacon said, staring down forlornly at the steak and kidney pie in his hands. "What… uh…"

Max, who had been standing against the wall, pushed himself forward and touched Mr Bacon on the shoulder. "I'm very sorry about all this," he said, pointedly glancing at his wife. "We really didn't mean to spoil your game."

"There'll be other games," Martha said. "You can watch your team any time, but this is far more important."

"Oh," Mr Bacon said, not entirely agreeing with her assessment.

The office was small and had wooden walls and a wooden door with a glass panel at the top. The desk was more like the kind you'd find in a school. On top of the desk was a microphone on a stand, a pencil and a clipboard to which was clipped a piece of paper with some kind of table of statistics being charted.

A man sat at the desk, and viewed the game through a window. Mr Bacon tried to glimpse the game, but didn't have the right angle. "How can I help?" he asked Martha.

"It's all about this dreadful business last night. About that poor man's death. Max and I thought we'd try to find out a little about it, but it's not in the papers and the police aren't revealing any details. We wondered whether, as a member of the bar and so forth, you might have contacts at Scotland Yard."

"Oh," Mr Bacon said. "Um, well, I'm not a member of the bar, you see, but, yes, I could look into it for you, although I wouldn't be able to do much today. I could try, I suppose."

"Splendid," Martha said, handing over a card. "Our address and telephone number. Anything you can do would be wonderful."

At that moment, the small office was rocked by a huge roar from the crowd.

"Mills just scored," the man at the desk said.

Max glanced at Mr Bacon and half-shrugged sheepishly. Martha was also looking at Mr Bacon and wondered if he was ill. He seemed to be suffering some kind of seizure.

Chapter Eight

Max couldn't find his dinner jacket and was starting to believe that Martha had hidden it deliberately, just to send him mad. He'd tried the bedroom and his study, and the dining room and sitting room and bathroom.

He went into the kitchen and interrogated the women, but Martha claimed that she hadn't seen it either, and it fell upon Flora to confess that she'd forgotten to pick it up from the cleaners. "What with all that stuff happening," she said.

"It's all right, Flora," Martha said. "Max, you can wear your navy-blue suit."

"I left the jacket at the paper. On Monday, I think."

"Why would you do that? Surely you didn't go out in just a shirt."

"I wore a coat. I fully intended to collect my jacket, but I went to the pub with Bobby Rollins and—"

"Say no more," Martha said, holding up a hand. "Well, wear your dark grey one, the charcoal one you were wearing this morning, when I found you on the floor. It's the closest you have to black. It'll be creased, but Flora can iron it quickly. With a cold iron, Flora."

"Yes, ma'am."

With that in hand, and most of the food prepared and waiting to be rewarmed and served, Max decided to treat himself to a drink, just to relax a little. In truth, he didn't like this kind of affair. Having a meal with friends was fine, having a drink with friends was better, but this was too close to being formal, and he felt uncomfortable with formalities. Besides which, those who came to the dinners were almost invariably friends and acquaintances of Martha. Max had few close friends, and most of those were at the paper. He invited them sometimes, and sometimes they came, but mostly, as tonight, they didn't.

But Martha liked hosting, and Max didn't want to spoil her fun, so he bore these things with as much good humour as possible, taking his pleasure vicariously from Martha. Besides, it had been his suggestion that they have a dining room in the flat, rather than a second bedroom, which is what it would otherwise have been. He reasoned that if it were a bedroom, it would be used several times a year for guests, but if it were a dining room, it would probably be used once or twice a month. This was sound logic, and Martha agreed, but the real reason Max didn't want a second bedroom was that it would inevitably encourage Martha's mother to visit for days at a time.

"Who's coming tonight?" Max said, trying to sound interested.

"Well, let's see, Rosamunde's coming, with her new beau. Quite a catch, apparently. American, I think she said. Rich too. Or maybe African. Or Australian. And Alice Dunaway, you know, dear old thing, lived near us when we were children, gave us cake…"

Rosamunde was an old school friend of Martha's. However, as far as Max could recall, Martha had never before mentioned to him anyone by the name of Alice or Dunaway, although clearly Martha assumed that she had, and it was easier to say nothing.

"So, now, that's Rosamunde and partner, old Mrs Dunaway, Mr Frost. Oh, and Lindsey, of course…"

"Lindsey?" Max said. "I didn't know he was coming."

"Well, he called up, asked if he could. Probably to say hello."

Max and Flora exchanged glances, with Max crossing his eyes and sticking his tongue into his cheek, and Flora concealing a smile, all of which passed Martha by.

"And Mrs Wilson," Martha was saying. "So, with me and Max—"

"Oh, Gawd," Flora said. "I forgot to tell you."

"Tell us what?" Martha said.

"Mrs Wilson telephoned to say she couldn't make it. She said she was very sorry."

"Damned old bat," Martha said. "I knew she was going to cancel. She's done it deliberately, you know, right at the last minute, and all because we cancelled on her last month. Now we'll be short one woman."

"No, ma'am, 'cos Mr Frost asked if he could bring a friend. Someone called Mr Hart. So you'll be short two women, ma'am."

Martha sighed dramatically. "It'll be a disaster. Now I've said yes to Lindsey, there'll be five men and three women. That means we'll have three single men. And poor Mrs Dunaway will be unaccompanied."

"Quick, Flora," Max said, "notify the government. One unaccompanied old lady. Tell them to send the army."

Martha punched Max on the arm while Flora tried to look genuinely appalled by the idea of poor Mrs Dunaway fending off suitors.

At this point, Max left the women to discuss arrangements and strolled into the sitting room and over to the drinks cabinet, where he mixed himself a large Martini. Then, noting that it was only seven o'clock, he decided he'd better make this his final drink for a while. Until eight o'clock, at least, when their guests would start arriving.

Max considered this for a moment and, realising eight o'clock was a whole hour away, he decided to make another large Martini, which he poured into a different glass, telling himself that it wasn't two drinks at all, but only two halves of a very, very large one.

He was trying to seem cheerful, to tease Martha and joke with Flora. But it wasn't working, and his mind kept sabotaging him and reminding him of Burton. And of the past, when he'd known Burton about as well as he'd ever known anyone.

He didn't hear Martha come into the sitting room, but he knew she was there. He turned and saw her standing, watching him, her eyes large and sad. He didn't know whether she was sad in herself, or whether she was reflecting what he felt.

"I'm sorry," she said. "It's stupid of me to worry so much about a dinner party when, well, your friend…" She went to Max and put her arms around him, pressing her cheek to his chest. He stroked her hair.

"It's not stupid," Max said. "It's just who you are. You live for the moment, and I've always loved that about you. I spend too much of my time in the past."

"And I love that about you," Martha said, the words an inch from his heart. "But you destroy yourself over it, the past."

"Maybe."

"Should we cancel the dinner?"

"No. It's too late now, anyway. We'll just carry on, as normal."

"It might be good for you," Martha said. "Mrs Dunaway was such a lovely creature. I have such fond memories of her when I was a child."

"It's nice to have fond memories," Max said.

Martha pushed herself away from him, looked up into his eyes. "Sometimes I think looking back is the only thing you look forward to."

"It's not."

"Perhaps, one day, you'll tell me about it."

He nodded. "Perhaps. Meanwhile, let's get ready for the party, shall we?"

Chapter Nine

Tony Lindsey was the first to arrive. He came in, hung his coat on the hat stand and collapsed on to the sofa.

"Drink, Tony?" Martha said, already on her way to the drinks cabinet.

"Just a small one. Don't want to have too many."

Max smiled inwardly, knowing that Lindsey would have finished off half the bottles in the flat by the time he left. Lindsey was an old friend of Martha's, and had courted her years before she and Max had even met. He was tall and slim, athletic and handsome. He had straight blonde hair and blue eyes, and a permanent suntan from an apparently endless holiday.

Martha handed Lindsey a Scotch on the rocks and it occurred to Max that she hadn't needed to ask what Lindsey would like.

"How are you, Tony?" Max said.

"Brilliant," Lindsey said. "Just got back from Linz. Couple of weeks ago. Went there for the skiing. Had a very bad fall. Quite serious."

"Did you die?"

"Sprained an ankle. Damned annoying. Off trekking next week."

"When do you find the time to work?"

"Work?"

Next came Alice Dunaway, who was a small lady with glasses and curly grey hair. According to Martha, Mrs Dunaway was in her early seventies, but she seemed older, well past a hundred. It wasn't a physical thing that aged her – she looked as a woman in her early seventies might – but there was an uncertainty and hesitation about her actions, and she walked slowly and with small steps, as if she were in constant danger of being blown over.

When she entered, Lindsey stood and shook her hand and said, "How do you do, madam."

Mrs Dunaway smiled and said, "How nice to meet you, Mr Dalton. Martha has written to me about you and I must say I think you're even more handsome than she said."

When it was explained to her that Lindsey was not married to Martha, but merely an old friend, Mrs Dunaway seemed disappointed. She seemed further disappointed when Max introduced himself as Martha's husband. She made no comment on whether Max was more handsome than she had been led to believe, but she did tell Martha that, indeed, Max was quite tall.

Then came Rosamunde and her American/African/ Australian beau, who turned out to be an Argentinian called Fernando Rojas. It transpired that Rosamunde knew Mrs Dunaway slightly from many years earlier and, of course, she knew Lindsey well. Max was left feeling like a stranger invited to a party in his own home.

The last people to arrive were Alwyn Frost and his companion, who introduced himself as Edward Hart. Frost was a tall straight man with a serious countenance from which a smile seemed unlikely to emanate. Hart, however, was quite short and slight and seemed a jolly person. It was an odd coupling.

Alwyn Frost had been married to Martha's cousin, Dorothy, but she'd run off with an American/Australian/African/Armenian businessman. Or maybe he was Argentinian. Anyway, Martha, on behalf of the family, felt some responsibility towards Frost and tried her best to include him in dinner parties now and then.

Frost greeted Max and Martha with a nod and accepted a drink, as did Hart, who then revealed something surprising. He said, "I've read your work, Mr Dalton. I enjoyed your book on Napoleon's Russian campaign. That's why I asked Alwyn whether I could join you tonight. I hope you don't mind."

"Not at all," Max said, feeling, in fact, elated that he'd finally met someone who'd read one of his books.

"I do hope we're not going to talk about wars," Mrs Dunaway said. "That's a terribly dreary subject."

"Don't worry, Mrs Dunaway," Martha said, "I'm sure we can accommodate your interests. What are they?"

"Well, the church, of course. And, erm…"

Chapter Ten

After they'd had a few drinks (excepting Mrs Dunaway, who only drank very small glasses of sherry with the vicar), the eight people took their seats at the dinner table. Flora entered with a tray of warm soup bowls and left, returning with a tureen, which she placed on the table next to each diner, ladling *consommé aux perles du Japon* (which Flora insisted on calling beef stock with tapioca) into each bowl. While she did this, Max had uncorked a couple of bottles of Sémillon and was moving around the table pouring wine into glasses.

He sat just as Flora had reached the last person to be served, which was Tony Lindsey. There was a sudden yelp, and everyone looked up to see Flora holding the tureen stiffly before her as she walked quickly from the room. Max frowned and glanced at Lindsey, who was busy inspecting his thumb nail.

The wine flowed and the talk talked and there were occasional witticisms from Max and Martha and Lindsey, while Mrs Dunaway expressed her opinions of the world and how it could be improved if only people were more like her and her friend, the Reverend Oliver.

"I think it's a shame that young people these days have moved away from the church. Don't you agree, Mr Lindsey?"

"Don't know what young people do," he said. "Never did, even when I was young. Mystery to me."

This made Mrs Dunaway laugh, for a reason that only she knew.

"Do you happen to know Martha's mother?" Max asked Mrs Dunaway after one of her comments regarding the inevitable demise of Britain as a result of immigration levels.

"Of course I know Martha's mother. We've been friends for years. Even before Martha was born."

"Aha," Max said, triumphantly. "That explains a lot."

Martha smiled at Mrs Dunaway and looked daggers at Max.

Rosamunde mostly spoke of her darling Fernando, saying things like, 'He plays golf, don't you, Fernando?' and 'Fernando's a musician, aren't you, Fernando?'

Occasionally, Fernando said, "Sí." And sometimes he elaborated. But mostly he looked bored.

"If there's one thing Fernando's good at," Rosamunde declared, "it's golf and polo."

"That's two," Mrs Dunaway said.

"Two what?"

Frost and Martha chatted about everything except her family and his ex-wife and anything to do with Americans and Africans and Armenians etc.

Meanwhile, despite Fernando's lack of enthusiasm, conversation had turned to sport, and Hart had asked about the current state of English cricket. Frost, eager to avoid the subject of Americans etc, said, "Well, I think we've been losing games we should've won. I don't know how we lost to South Africa. We certainly wouldn't have done if we'd kept Jardine and Larwood."

This, of course, was a reference to the Ashes series in '33, and the issue of the leg theory of bowling, which then came up as a topic. Frost contested that it was necessary to win at sport, by whatever method was available, provided it was legal.

"Not cricket," Lindsey said.

Hart, an acknowledged sporting innocent, asked what leg theory was.

"Oh," said Rosamunde, "it's when the bowler tries to kill the batsman, or break his leg or something."

"It's nothing of the sort," Frost said. "It's simply a method of bowling close to the line of the batsman in order to curtail his effort and attempt a dismissal from a close field, or by LBW."

"Ah," Hart said, none the wiser.

Even Fernando was aware of the controversy of three years prior, and looked disapprovingly at Frost.

"Is that the purpose of sport?" Martha said. "To win at all costs?"

"Of course," Frost said. "Sport is the test of a country's mettle. It has no other purpose."

"I agree," Hart said. "And if your country is able to win, then it is the best."

This led Max to a lengthy soliloquy, which came from an article he'd submitted to the *Chronicle* back in '33. The article was spiked and Max had long wanted a reason to reprise its content. "Sport," he said, "gives one a fundamental choice, or, rather, creates the situation in which your character displays one or other of two possibilities: whether to play to win – which entails ruthlessness, selfishness, strength, ambition, all the traits that are commonly regarded as reprehensible – or whether to play fairly, which entails all the opposites and which, while possibly winning you plaudits in the short term, leads to failure. Winners are lauded. Hitler knows this. Mussolini knows this."

"Are you comparing Hitler to the English cricket team?" Frost said.

"Um," Max said. "Yes. I think I must be."

"But the Germans don't play cricket, do they?" Rosamunde said.

"Look, what I'm saying is that all the stuff we're taught when we're young – honour and fairness and all that – is precisely what the Australians were practising in '33. And yet you're now saying that they were wrong to do so. It's contradictory. You can't have it both ways, Alwyn."

"What are you saying, Max?" Frost said.

"I'm saying you and all those like you, all the pillars of our so-called civilisation, are false. You tell us how to behave so that we're docile and pliable, so that we won't argue with you, and we'll obey the law. But in reality, you want us to be murderous and cunning and Machiavellian, when it's in your interests. I'm saying it's all a lie."

"We succeed through hard work and duty," Mrs Dunaway said.

But Max was shaking his head. "Talent, hard work, duty, conscientiousness; all these are tangential qualities, incidental. One may have these and succeed if one has ambition, but, equally, one may have these and be ignored if one doesn't possess the ruthless selfishness of ambition."

"You sound bitter, Max," Frost said. "Books not selling?"

"Alwyn!" Martha said. "Max doesn't write books to sell them, do you, darling?"

"Just as well," Lindsey said.

"It would be nice to sell some," Max admitted. "I think I've written more than I've sold, which is quite an achievement."

"What has this to do with Germany playing Australia?" Rosamunde said.

"Look," Max said, "what I mean is that at some point, ambition itself became an asset. The very fact that you wanted advancement was reason enough to be given it. The fact that those who were promoted had nothing else to offer was ignored. I saw it in the army, and I've been seeing it ever since. Consequently, the country has become run by incompetents who are always looking to climb further up the ladder where their incompetence does even more damage."

"Quite a polemic," Lindsey said. "Almost sounds rebellious. Not a communist, are you?"

Mrs Dunaway burst out laughing and was in danger of splitting her sides.

Flora, who had been hovering around the table, shot a withering glance at both Lindsey and Mrs Dunaway.

"You know your trouble, Max?" Frost said. "You hate the world."

"No, Alwyn. Only your world."

"You can't mean that," Frost said.

Max wasn't sure what he meant. His head was beginning to buzz. He had the feeling that he was saying things for the sake of being contrary.

"Are you drunk?" Frost said.

"Not yet," Max said, wishing very much that he were.

After the consommé and a few of the bottles of wine, most of which had ended up inside Lindsey, Max and Mrs Dunaway, who seemed to have forgotten that she was mostly teetotal, it was time for the main course, which was fillet of beef in a red wine sauce, served with vegetables.

Max uncorked a Médoc, as well as a Volnay and a St Julien. For himself, he preferred beer, but that was not suitable for a dinner party such as this. Vitriol and bile seemed preferable.

Having brought in warm plates on a large silver tray and placed them before everyone else at the table, Flora made her way cautiously over to Mr Lindsey, where she put his plate down and thumped him on the head with her tray.

"Oh, I'm terribly sorry, sir," Flora said.

"Flora," Martha said, "please be careful."

"It's quite all right," Lindsey said, vigorously rubbing his head, "my fault entirely."

"You should be careful, Tony," Max said, winking at Flora. "You seem accident-prone at the moment, what with your sprained ankle and all."

"Stupid of me," Lindsey said.

This led to a discussion about various accidents that people had encountered, which became an inventory of injuries, increasingly life-threatening in proportion to the amount of wine consumed. Rosamunde claimed to have been maimed by a hockey stick, and Mrs Dunaway, who was slurring her words a little, had almost been killed by a balloon. Or it might've been a baboon.

Hart then asked Max about his next book, and Max explained that he wasn't sure yet what he wanted to write, but he had an idea for a feature for the *Chronicle* on the Berlin games, which led to a new conversation about the new Germany and the rise of Hitler.

Max, however, was quiet during much of the conversation, listening thoughtfully to the different opinions, which ranged from Mrs Dunaway's undisguised enthusiasm for a new strong Continental power to Fernando's shrug and Rosamunde's admission that she was never really sure what the difference was between Germany and Prussia.

"And as for East Prussia," she said, "I haven't a clue, except it must be East of Prussia."

Fernando rolled his eyes at this.

Only Max and Hart failed to offer an opinion, and Martha, sensing that Max was feeling out of it, said, "Max has been upset about this Rhineland business, haven't you, Max?"

Max put down his knife and fork, took a sip of wine and said, "Upset. Yes."

"What in particular, Mr Dalton?" Hart said.

"In particular? Oh, everything in particular. Especially us, in particular."

"Us?" Frost said.

"You don't mean our country, do you?" Mrs Dunaway said.

"Yes. I do. We're doing nothing to stop these people, one after another."

"What can we do, old thing?" Lindsey said. "We can't go to war over the Rhineland. After all, it *is* German."

"We need to stand up to them. They're taking over the world, and we don't care because it's not us they're seeking to control. Not yet."

Martha was now chewing her lip, thinking she might have made a mistake. She attempted to correct the error by glancing at Max and saying, "And those poor Abyssinians."

"Oh, yes. That seems rather unfair," Rosamunde said, also sensing a tension in the conversation, which was in danger of upsetting her. "I mean, the Italians have guns and ships, and what do the Abyssinians have? Spears or swords or whatever."

"Swords?" Frost said.

"Well, bows and arrows, then."

"All's unfair in love and war," Lindsey said, which made Mrs Dunaway laugh.

"Using mechanised warfare to impose your rule on an independent country seems a little *too* unfair," Max said.

"Not just independent countries. Their own people too," Lindsey said, taking everyone by surprise. "Not cricket," he added.

"That's right," Max said. "The Nazis want to wipe out the Jews and the Gypsies and anyone opposed to them."

"Does that matter?" Mrs Dunaway said. "I mean, does it matter to us?"

"It may not matter to you," Max said, "but it matters to me."

"Are you Jewish?"

"No, I'm Pisces."

"I think he's terrible," Rosamunde said. "Hitler. And Fernando agrees, don't you, darling?"

Fernando looked up from his food and nodded vaguely. "Que es terrible."

"He's getting some of us at the FO hot under the collar," Frost said. "We're all trying to work out what his next move's going to be. The Rhineland was just the start. He's a potential threat, for sure."

Now, in a disastrous attempt to lighten the mood and to bring fractious sides together, Rosamunde said, "They're very smart, though."

Nobody knew what she was talking about, and there followed a brief silence.

"I mean those uniforms," Rosamunde said desperately. "The Germans. The black uniforms. I just mean they look very smart. Black suits them."

"Yes," Lindsey said, "it brings out the colour of their souls."

Mrs Dunaway found this very droll. Even Frost smiled at the comment. Poor old Mr Hart seemed to fail to understand, however, in much the same way he seemed to fail to understand cricket.

Mrs Dunaway said, "It seems to me that our biggest threat is from Stalin and all those communists. I mean, they're everywhere, aren't they? It seems to me that Hitler is actually managing to combat the communists. What do you think, Mr Lindsey?"

"Try not to think, madam," Lindsey said. "Hurts the head."

Mrs Dunaway found this amusing, and became overconfident, saying, "I know for a fact that there are many thousands of communists here. Why, Reverend Oliver told me that most unions are communist. And most working people too."

Flora, who was standing next to Rosamunde and missing her plate with a potato, glared at Mrs Dunaway, although that upright lady was unaware of Flora's glare, or even her existence.

"Communism," Max said, "is either a nice idea ruined by human greed or a bad idea saved by human greed, depending on how rich you are."

There was some silence after this announcement while everyone tried to work out whether Max had been clever. Max was trying to work out the same thing.

"I'm afraid I don't follow your logic," Frost said eventually.

Max wasn't sure himself. But he shrugged away Frost's comment. To be truthful, Max's usually sharp dry wit was becoming soaked in alcohol and the edge had been blunted by melancholia. He decided he'd have to disguise the fact by feigning indifference; so whenever someone threw an acerbic comment his way, he no longer seemed insulted, or amused. He didn't seem anything at all, except indifferent.

"Stalin's terrible," Rosamunde said. "And that moustache."

Fernando, who had a moustache similar to Stalin's, raised an eyebrow and glanced at Rosamunde, but she seemed unaware of her faux pas. In fact, she seemed unaware of almost everything.

Martha attempted to steer conversation towards odd surnames, especially those connected to foodstuffs. However, Mrs Dunaway ploughed through Martha's question regarding why people would possibly be named after parts of a pig, and continued, stupidly confident of her facts, to cite probable communist conspiracies in most areas of working life.

"They're bringing them in from abroad," Mrs Dunaway insisted. "These ideas. Foreigners bring them in. I mean, they're just not English, are they?"

"Do you mean foreigners aren't English?" Martha said, confused.

"I think foreigners are fine," Rosamunde said. "Provided they speak English."

"Sí."

"But, I mean, the working person simply needs to be guided, like a child," Mrs Dunaway was saying. "Otherwise they're liable to believe anything."

"Such as your God," Max said, but too quietly for anyone to notice.

"Always had agitation," Lindsey said. "The English. Always had it. Peasants' Revolt, Cade, Chartists, Levellers, Tolpuddle lot."

"Absolutely," Mrs Dunaway said, perhaps not quite realising Lindsey's point. "We'd probably be much better off if we didn't have so many working-class people."

"I completely agree," Max said, leaning back in his seat.

Inwardly, Martha sighed, knowing that 'I completely agree' meant 'You're an idiot and I intend to prove it'.

"I often used to think," Max was saying, heedless of Martha's discomfiture, "that we should have fought the war entirely without the working class at all. They just kept getting in the way of all those damned bullets, after all. I mean, what was the point of them?"

He paused for effect.

Sometimes when he was like this and raised a rhetorical question, some fool attempted an answer. In this instance, everybody was looking awkward, except for Lindsey, who was looking drunk out of his very small mind, and Flora, who was gazing at Max in the same way she sometimes gazed at Gary Cooper or Robert Taylor. Max and her father were probably the wisest men Flora knew. Oh, and possibly Eric, of course.

Martha was chewing the inside of her cheek and pushing a pea around her plate.

Then Max happened to look over at Hart, expecting that quiet man to be unsettled by the turn the dinner had taken. Instead, Hart was attempting to stifle a smile that his twinkling eyes would've betrayed anyway. The two men exchanged glances, and Max was sure the old gent had winked at him.

Having dished out the main course, Flora put the remaining vegetable dishes on the table so that people could help themselves to more, if they wanted. Then she put the tray under her arm, walked serenely past Mrs Dunaway and bashed her on the head. Mrs Dunaway's head caused the silver tray to ring like a bell.

"Ouch."

"Flora."

"Terribly sorry, ma'am."

"My fault entirely," Lindsey said.

Conversation then became fragmented, several exchanges going on at once, as often happens when people become more drunk and thus unable to follow a multi-line discourse.

Martha, who was agreeing with whatever it was that Mrs Dunaway had said to her, was watching Max, and had determined to cheer him up a little, and take his mind off his poor dead friend. She had, by now, become slightly blotto, or fuzzy, as Max would have it.

After the main course, Flora served the dessert, which was a vanilla and ginger cheesecake with cream. By now, most of the table was in various latter stages of inebriation, with the exception of Frost, who was uncannily sober, and Fernando, who'd been drinking the same glass of wine for the last hour. Lindsey and Mrs Dunaway, in particular, were feeling the effects of Max and Martha's hospitality.

"Tell me about your family," Mrs Dunaway said to Max. "What is your hic-story? Who are you from?"

Talk of his background made Max uncomfortable, something that Martha knew and occasionally played upon, teasing him in the way that someone who knows an unimportant secret might do.

"Max doesn't have family, do you, darling?" she said.

Martha was in that dangerous area beyond sobriety but before the wavering-eye, wobbly-leg state of no return. She had a wicked glint in her eye.

"No."

"What happened to them, Max?" Rosamunde said.

"They died."

"Oh. I'm sorry to hear that."

"The swings and roundabouts of outrageous fortune," Lindsey said.

"I never knew them. I was adopted. They've gone now, too. My adopted parents."

"You're an orphan," Rosamunde said. "How sad. Isn't that sad, Fernando?"

"Muy triste," Fernando agreed.

"I don't think Max ever had a family," Martha said. "I think he was a foundling. A rejected baby. Abandoned for some reason."

"I was an ugly duckling," he said.

"Yes," Martha said, "and you grew into an ugly duck."

"Family is very important," Hart said, "one's roots are what makes one. For example, take us here, obviously we are all from good stock, Anglo-Saxon and—" here raising his glass to Fernando, "of course Spanish. Our civilisations have shaped the world, for the better, I might add. Background is essential. It's *everything*."

"Disagree," Lindsey said. "Take my lot. Hideous examples, mostly."

"I don't agree with you, Lindsey," Frost said. "I think Hart is right, family is extremely important. They're the backbone of a country, a society. And the family one marries into is, perhaps, just as important. Providing," he said, brushing a speck from his jacket sleeve, "they're the right sort."

This was a loaded comment, as far as Martha was concerned, since it was clear to her that Frost was here referencing her own family, especially her cousin who'd unfortunately run off with that American/Albanian/Armenian businessman. But, Max, seeing Martha's unease, came to the rescue, saying, "And what is the 'right sort'? And who decides which sort of sort a person is?"

"Background, breeding."

"Religion," Hart said. "Class, the usual things. One doesn't compare a thoroughbred to a donkey, does one?"

This observation actually received applause from Mrs Dunaway, who said, "How well put, Mr Hart. A thorokey and a whatsit. Very good."

There was some more talk, and a lot more drinking, with Max passing round an Italian dessert wine.

Finally, it was time for everyone to leave. Fernando shook Max's hand and said, in perfect English, "Thank you. I've learned a lot about the British tonight."

Rosamunde held tightly to her lover and whispered to Martha, "Doesn't he have super eyes? And he has oodles of money."

Lindsey and Mrs Dunaway walked – well, staggered – out together, both rubbing their heads. Frost left with a nod, while Hart paused a moment and thanked Max and Martha for a wonderful evening.

"I wonder if I might call on you again," he said. "Perhaps we could discuss the Peninsula Campaign, Mr Dalton. I understand your latest book was on that subject. I have some contacts on the continent. Perhaps a translated volume of your work would sell well."

Max smiled and said, certainly he could call again. Hart handed him a business card, which read "Edward Hart", followed simply by a telephone number.

Then Hart left and it was over and Max let out a long sigh.

"I think that went quite well," Martha said.

Chapter Eleven

Martha mentioned Flora's strange behaviour to Max, saying, "I don't know what's wrong with her. She kept hitting people with the tray and dropping potatoes and carrots all over the place."

"She's probably exhausted," Max said.

"You think so? Oh, poor girl."

Martha then told Flora to go home and to leave the cleaning to her and Max. Flora, surprised, left with her wages and got the bus home, wondering along the way how she might renew her attacks on Mrs Dunaway and Lindsey, should the opportunity ever arise, and even whether she should include Mr Frost and Mr Hart, as a strike for the working cause. She imagined a whole table of massacre and errant vegetables.

Meanwhile, after they'd had some coffee, Max and Martha were in the kitchen, swaying while washing and drying the dishes. Martha had a pinafore over her dress, Max had hung his jacket on the back of a chair and rolled his sleeves up.

They didn't say much, each wondering whether they'd upset the other. Finally, with a dish mop in her hand, Martha turned to Max and said, "I'm sorry about Mrs Dunaway. I always thought she was a harmless old thing. But it's been so long since I last saw her."

"It's not her," Max said. "At least, it's not *only* her."

He abandoned the towel and found his cigarettes, which were in his jacket.

"I know you don't like people smoking in the kitchen," Max said, lighting a cigarette for himself, and one for Martha, which she took, wiping her hands first on the pinafore. She said, "What the hell."

"They're killing us, Martha," Max said. "Can't you feel it? Can't you feel them killing us, amusing us to death with their wit and dryness? It's osmosis in reverse; they're taking the life from us, pulling it down into their dryness so that, for just a while, they don't feel dry, but feel alive. They're feeding on our life, Martha. And we're dying from it."

"I don't know what you mean, Max. Don't you like our friends?"

"They're not friends. They're just people we know. We only know people we know."

"You're not making sense."

"I'm making more sense than I ever have. Except when I asked you to marry me."

"Max. I… I don't understand you."

"No, you don't, do you?" Max said.

They were quiet for a few minutes, each trying to understand what the other felt, what they felt themselves.

"You're upset," Martha said, after a while. "It's been difficult for you, with your friend dying, well, possibly dying, and the police and everything."

Max didn't say anything to that. Martha was right, of course, but he didn't know to what extent she was right. Had he been unfair to their guests that evening? He was the host, after all.

"I'll tell you one thing, though," Martha said, a small glint in her eye. "I'm never going to invite Mrs Dunaway again."

But Max was struggling now to be jocular, and Martha saw it in his expression, which was remote, pained. She knew that every now and then a wave of sadness would roll over Max, knock him down and scrape him along the shingle, threatening to drag him back with it, back to the sea. She didn't know much about these waves, often didn't even see them coming, but she knew this much: they started way off, way back in the deep and cold of the ocean.

Martha took him by the hand. "Let's leave the washing up."

She led him into the sitting room and pushed him down on to the sofa, sitting on his lap. "I wish I knew where you went."

"We went to The Lion."

"That's not what I meant."

"Oh."

"It must've been very terrible."

"Only in parts. Mostly, it was just plain awful."

"Why do you do that? Hide it all beneath that dry wit of yours?"

"I think, because I don't want it to hurt you."

"You must think me terribly weak."

"Only in parts. Mostly I think of you as terribly strong."

Martha put her hand on Max's neck, ran her thumb nail over the bristles on his jaw, her fingers through the short bits of black hair at the base of his skull.

They stayed like that for a long time, each thinking silent thoughts. Then Martha suddenly tensed. "I know what we're going to do," she said, turning herself around on the sofa, drawing her knees up, her ankles together.

She was facing Max now, and there was an excitement in her expression, and Max's heart melted. "You do?" he said.

"Yes. We're going to investigate what happened."

"We are?"

"Yes. We can't rely on the police. We have to do it ourselves."

"Uh, ourselves?"

"Surely. Why not? You're a journalist and I'm well connected. And we have lovely Mr Thingy. He'll probably tell us tomorrow what he's found out." She smiled. "Hey, you know what, we're like Nick and Nora Charles."

"Who?"

"William Powell and Myrna Loy. *The Thin Man* and all that. You've heard of *The Thin Man*, haven't you?"

"Darling, I *am* the Thin Man."

"Well, that's wrong. On both counts. You had far too much pudding."

Then Martha smiled and said, "When Flora told us you'd been arrested for murder, I really believe I saw my mother trying to hide a smile behind her napkin."

Chapter Twelve

Sunday lunch was, as usual, spent with Martha's parents. Max, of course, was reluctant. And Martha, of course, was insistent. "When you get parents of your own," she'd say sometimes, "we'll have lunch with them. Meanwhile, we'll have lunch with mine."

Other times, she'd say, "If I have to do it, you have to do it. That's what marriage is about – mutual suffering."

Of course, after the events of Saturday, they both knew this would be an unusual lunch, and was bound to involve an interrogation. So they plodded along to Mr and Mrs Webster's house in Kensington, walking as slowly as they could.

The roads were quiet and the weather was pleasant, a warm sun and hazy sky. Max and Martha took a long route, walking up Sloane Street and then on to Knightsbridge and Kensington High Street. A couple of young men in suits cycled past them, on their way home from church, perhaps. They were followed by a rattling old green truck with a gold livery advertising a furniture manufacturer.

When they came adjacent to the Albert Memorial, Max and Martha paused for a moment. Martha put her arm in

Max's, and they stood like that, silently, and gazed at the monument, a seated Prince Albert beneath a gothic canopy that reached for heaven and the Albert Hall looming behind them. Nearby, several groups of people were enjoying the spring weather, some seated on the steps smoking or eating sandwiches, some wandering towards Kensington Gardens.

Max and Martha were each thinking different things as they stood there. For Max, the monument was a melancholy sight, for he felt how pointless such beauty has to be, in the end; *sic transit gloria mundi*. For Martha, it was a statement of love, defying, as best as possible, the loss of someone.

They walked on.

When they arrived at the Websters' Georgian townhouse in Phillimore Gardens, their coats and hats were collected by an elderly retainer called Seymour who greeted Martha with a complete lack of recognition, despite having known her for her entire life.

Once Martha and Max had introduced themselves, they followed Seymour into the kitchen, the conservatory, the kitchen again and, finally, the breakfast room where Mr and Mrs Webster were sitting. Seymour attempted to announce Max and Martha, but had forgotten their names and why they'd come. Max and Martha sat at the table. Max lit a cigarette while Mrs Webster gave instructions to Seymour to bring in a new pot of tea.

"I don't understand why anyone would have tea at this time of day," Mr Webster said to nobody.

"Remember," Mrs Webster was saying to Seymour. "Pot. Of. Tea."

"I think he's getting a bit past it," Martha said after Seymour had wandered off. "Shouldn't he retire or something?"

"Retire?" Mr Webster said. "And what will he do when he retires? He wouldn't have a reason to go on living."

Mr Webster was a thin and tidy-looking man with an aquiline nose and neat grey moustache. He was scrutinising his newspaper, trying to do the crossword.

"I'm sure there are reasons for living, other than serving you," Max replied.

Mr Webster chose to ignore this, as he often did when Max said something.

When Seymour returned, with a new pot of tea, Mrs Webster poured it out, and Max and Martha added milk and sugar. "Now," she said, "I think you'd better tell us why you were arrested yesterday, Max."

"He wasn't arrested," Martha said.

"Nevertheless."

Mr Webster was apparently staring at his newspaper, but his eyes hadn't moved across the text.

Max stirred his tea.

"I happened to have seen an old friend on Friday evening," he said to his tea. "And someone was killed nearby at approximately the same time. The police simply wanted to ask me some questions, as a witness."

"Well," Mrs Webster said, smiling, "that's a relief."

This resulted in a stern glare from Martha. But her glare fell on deaf eyes. "It might've been Max's friend who was killed, mother," she said sternly.

Mr Webster lowered his newspaper and said, "That's unfortunate, Max. Naturally, Eleanor and I are sorry for your loss, if it is your friend."

"Thank you, Donald," Max said.

"Yes, of course," Mrs Webster said. "Terrible. Now, what do the police know?"

Max and Martha explained that they were awaiting a report from Mr Bacon.

"But we're going to investigate it ourselves," Martha said.

Mr Webster looked at his daughter over his newspaper.

"We're just going to have a look," Max said. "After all, it can only help the investigation if I can add my point of view, assuming it was Burton who was killed."

"Don't the police know?" Mr Webster said.

"They're… uncertain," Max said.

"And you're going to investigate it?" Mrs Webster said.

"Yes. Like Nick and Nora Charles."

"Oh," Mrs Webster said, trying to recall who they were and whether they were related to Hugo Charles.

"And we want Mr…"

"Bacon," Max said.

"…Bacon to help us. Daddy, you'll speak to your solicitor friend, won't you?"

"I hardly think the firm will spare him for one of your whims, Martha."

"We'd pay, of course."

Mr Webster sighed. Everyone knew that he'd do as Martha asked. He always did. "I'll have a word with them," he said.

"But I still don't understand why you can't let the police deal with it." Mrs Webster said.

"Because they think Max is guilty." Martha, immediately realising her mistake, put her cup to her lips and drank her tea for about two minutes, moving her eyes from her parents to Max.

"Max?" Mrs Webster said. "Guilty?"

"Um," Max said.

"Is that why you want to use Mr Bacon?" Mr Webster said.

"There's just some confusion. That's all. And if the police thought I was in any way involved, they'd have arrested me."

At this moment, Seymour entered the room and announced that dinner was ready. He left. And immediately returned to announce that dinner was ready.

"Lunch, Seymour," Mrs Webster said. "Lunch. Remember?"

Seymour left again.

Mrs Webster then surprised Max and Martha by saying, "Dear old Mrs Dunaway telephoned me this morning to say what a lovely time she had with you last night."

"That's nice," Martha said doubtfully.

"But she said she had a lump on her head and couldn't remember how that happened."

"Hmm," Martha said. "Well, as long as she enjoyed herself."

"Yes," Mrs Webster said, "she said she was especially impressed with Mr Lindsey. Apparently, she thinks he's very handsome."

"I'm surprised she could see Lindsey, the amount of booze she put away," Max said.

"Nonsense. Mrs Dunaway's a teetotaller. Always has been."

Max was about to dispute this, but decided to attempt a conciliatory manner and closed his mouth.

Seymour returned with a tray on which were four plates. Each plate had a slice of bread and butter, and a selection of pickled onions. He placed these before those at the breakfast table and wandered off again.

They all waited for him to come back. After ten minutes or so, Mrs Webster said, "Well, I think we should start."

They made the best of it, commenting now and then on how good the bread was.

"These pickled onions are marvellous," Max said, eliciting various non-verbal responses from the others.

As they struggled through, talk turned again to Mrs Dunaway.

"And she said there was a delightful man called Mr Hart," Mrs Webster was saying. "Who is he?"

Martha and Max looked at each other. "We don't know," Martha said. "He came with Alwyn Frost."

"Well, whoever he is, Mrs Dunaway was most impressed with him. Said he was as intelligent as her vicar, whatever his name is."

"I believe he's called the Reverend Oliver," Max said.

"Is he? Well, apparently this Mr Hart is clearly on par with Reverend Oliver, and even Mr Churchill."

"Churchill?" Mr Webster said. "I'm getting tired of hearing from that man. He made a speech in Birmingham last week, some bash or other. Kept banging on about the League of Nations and process of the law, and saying how this Rhineland business will be the start of a slippery slope."

"Oh," Mrs Webster said, "these days everything is the start of a slippery slope. It's a wonder we haven't all slid off into the sea. And Mr Churchill is scaring everyone silly. As Mrs Dunaway says, it's not the Germans we should worry about."

"Mmmm," Martha said quickly, glancing at Max, "I do like these onions."

"Um…" Max said.

"I don't altogether trust him," Mrs Webster was saying. "Churchill. In the place where he should have integrity, he has ambition."

"I agree," Max said, surprising everyone. "He wants the top job. He might get it."

Mr Webster had now lowered his newspaper and was looking down the table. "He's a heel," he said, having picked up that particular term from some American gangster picture.

Max said, "He made a mistake with Ireland, and now he's making one with India. The empire has gone. We won the war and lost the empire."

This didn't meet with approval from Max's in-laws, but, while Mr Webster simply humphed and went back to his newspaper, Mrs Webster glared with disapproval at Max and said, "I told you, Martha. This is exactly what I meant yesterday."

"Mother thinks you're a Bolshevist or communist or something," Martha said. "Are you?"

"I'm not any kind of -ist."

"Well, that's a relief," Mrs Webster said. "Now, shall we attempt some cake?"

Chapter Thirteen

Mr Bacon had telephoned just before lunchtime, and Flora had explained that Max and Martha would be out until the afternoon. Not deeming it apt to leave a message, and not trusting that Martha wouldn't again track him down and ruin his day, Mr Bacon decided to journey to Pimlico and wait for the return of Mr and Mrs Dalton.

So, after explaining who he was to Flora, Mr Bacon removed his hat and coat, hung them up on the stand, and sat.

He was still waiting, and hadn't seemed to have moved, two hours later when Max and Martha returned.

"Oh, Mr… uh… Onion," Martha said, coming through the doorway.

"Bacon," Mr Bacon said, standing and shaking hands.

"Yes. How are you?"

That was a question that Mr Bacon wasn't keen on answering because he hated mendacity, and he didn't want to be rude to Mrs Dalton, especially as her father was a friend of his boss. He smiled and said, "As well as can be expected."

"Good."

"Has Flora offered you anything?" Max said.

"Yes, thank you. She made me a cup of tea."

Martha offered him another cup of tea, which he now declined, preferring, conspicuously, to conclude his business as quickly as possible, so that he could salvage some kind of a weekend.

"I apologise if we're keeping you from anything," Max said.

The three sat, with Max and Mr Bacon on the sofa, and Martha opposite them in a chair. Mr Bacon pushed his glasses up his nose and said, "I first tried to learn something from the policeman investigating the case. I believe he is an Inspector Longford."

It wasn't a question, but Mr Bacon glanced at Max and waited, apparently seeking affirmation. So Max affirmed.

"Yes, well, it seems the police are not keen on divulging information," Mr Bacon said. "I wasn't able to speak to anyone involved in the case. I had to go to an old friend of mine and wait for him to contact me. So if anyone should ask, it's better if you don't admit to knowing any of this."

"We understand," Martha said solemnly.

"Right," Mr Bacon said, snapping open his brown leather briefcase, flipping over the flap and removing a single piece of paper. He scanned it, nodded to himself. "The pathologist has made some notations but the report is not conclusive, so, I trust, can be considered by us as sub rosa?"

"Absolutely," Martha said, not knowing what on earth he was talking about.

"Then I'll begin with the pathologist's report. Now, let me see. Ah, yes. The deceased was a white male, approximately thirty-five years of age, measuring five feet ten inches, with a number of old wounds on the left side of his torso—"

"Oh, God," Max said.

Mr Bacon stopped and glanced at Max. "Is there something wrong, sir?"

"No," Max said. "No. Please continue."

Martha watched Max, and saw that there was, in fact, something wrong. She could guess what it was – Max knew about those wounds.

"...Measuring five feet ten inches, with a number of old wounds on the left side of his torso, wounds that would approximate those obtained by a fragmentary explosive device, or from the shrapnel."

Now Mr Bacon paused and lowered the paper. He looked at Max and said, "I'm not sure that Mrs Dalton should hear the rest, sir."

Martha's eyebrow arched and her lips thinned. Max said quickly, "My wife's not as delicate as she seems."

Mr Bacon nodded, and continued, while Martha was still trying to work out whether Max had said something insulting.

"There is considerable trauma to the face and head of the victim, and lacerations around the left cheekbone, suggesting he was struck about the face and head, possibly with fists or a simple blunt device such as a blackjack. There is a single, deep penetrative wound, which entered the thoracic cavity at a point between the fifth and sixth ribs, causing considerable incisive trauma to the left ventricle and—"

Max had touched Mr Bacon on the arm. Mr Bacon paused, lowered the paper and followed Max's glance, scrutinising Mrs Dalton through his glasses. Martha was now no longer seated upright, but had sat forward, with her knees together, and was holding her head in her hands. Mr Bacon considered this new situation and decided to summarise the information.

"Well," he said, "in short, the deceased was murdered by a knife or dagger. The pathologist has made a note here that he believes the blade of the weapon to be double-edged, on account of the shape of the wound, but he hasn't officially stated such. Further, he suggests that the victim was most likely accosted about the head and made insensible prior to the fatal wound. Again, this is opinion."

He now replaced the paper in his case and looked at Max. "Not a great deal of information, I'm afraid."

"That was plenty, thank you," Martha said, gradually recovering her colour.

"Did you manage to find out anything else?" Max said, his tone grim. "Anything about the police's inquiry?"

Mr Bacon took another piece of paper from his briefcase and looked at it. "The victim had a copy of Friday's late night final edition of the *Evening Standard* in his jacket pocket, and there was a ticket stub from Peterborough to King's Cross, also from Friday, which was in his hatband. His hat was about eight feet from the victim and police surmise it was knocked from him with the initial blow."

He paused a moment to clear his throat, then, without taking his eyes from the paper, said, "There was found to be a noticeable odour of smoke on the clothes, and a detective constable noticed that there was a stain on the sleeve of the victim's jacket, which, upon inspection, was determined to be beer. From this the detectives concluded that the victim had been in a public house or houses prior to his murder. Inquiries conducted at several produced a witness, the barman of a public house called The Lion…"

While Max was listening to this, Martha was watching him closely. There was a sadness in his eyes. It was almost as if he was unaware of her or Mr Bacon, or anything really, except the terrible thoughts in his mind, or, perhaps, the terrible memories. She wanted very much to hold him, but knew he'd feel embarrassed by the action.

"The police haven't yet been able to find an address for the deceased," Mr Bacon was saying. "And they didn't find a latchkey, or any keys, on the body."

"Wait," Max said, alert suddenly. "Did you say they didn't find a key?"

"That's correct, sir. Does that suggest something to you?"

"I'm not sure," Max said. "But it's unusual, isn't it? Have the police checked hotels?"

"Hotels?" Martha said.

"If you don't have a key, what does that suggest?"

"He didn't have a home to go back to," Mr Bacon said.

"Yes, of course," Martha said. "And if you're staying at a hotel, you'd hand your key into the reception whenever you go out. That's why he hasn't got a key. Max, you're brilliant."

Mr Bacon was scanning his notes. He nodded and said, "Ah. Yes, sir. I'm afraid the police canvassed hotels in and around King's Cross station, and near the area the deceased was found. There was no record of any Mr Crawford."

Max glanced at Martha. Neither spoke for a moment.

"And that's all there is at the moment, sir," Mr Bacon said.

"Thank you," Max said. "You've been very helpful. I'm sorry we've caused you such inconvenience."

"That's all right, sir," Mr Bacon said, trying as hard as possible to chart a verbal path between what he really felt and what he felt obliged to say. "I don't feel particularly inconvenienced today."

"Thank you, Mr Bacon," Martha said.

"Bacon," Mr Bacon said instinctively. "Oh. I mean, you're welcome."

Now that Mr Bacon had successfully concluded his business, he felt, at last, that he could enjoy his weekend, what remained of it. He removed his hat and coat from the stand, folded the coat over his arm, placed his hat squarely on his head and left, happy at last to be free.

After she'd shown Mr Bacon out, Martha turned and said, "Are you thinking what I think you're thinking?"

"I think so," Max said. "The police checked the hotels for someone called Crawford. If it's Burton, which I think it probably is, they wouldn't know that. I think they've missed a trick."

"What are we waiting for, then? Let's find out where your friend was staying."

Max hesitated. He looked at Martha, and it was such a serious look that she found herself dreading its cause. "There's something I have to tell you," Max said.

"Don't," Martha said, terrified now.

"I lied, Martha."

"Lied?"

She seemed, for a moment, distraught. And, of course, she was. Max had never lied to her about anything, and she knew that. And he knew that she knew it. He had to explain, and quickly. He couldn't prolong the pain. He said, "About the pub. About not remembering what Burton and I spoke about."

"Why, Max? Why would you lie?"

"Because I'm ashamed. Because I'm scared."

"Of what?"

"I'm ashamed of what I did, back then, in the war. And I'm scared of telling you."

Martha seemed now like a child, the confusion evident on her face. It was, perhaps, the thing Max loved most about her. She never tried to hide her feelings. It probably had never even occurred to her to dissemble. She had no guile.

There was relief, too. She'd been imagining all sorts of things, her mind racing through the possible reasons that Max would lie. Of course, she knew Max well enough to dismiss them, but, nevertheless, the doubt was sufficient. That's the problem with deceit, it renders all certainties doubtful. She said, "But, you… you said you were talking about Hitler. You were calling him all sorts of names, no doubt."

"Yes," Max said slowly. "Partly. And it's true that I can't remember much of our conversation. But we were remembering. And I remember that."

He stopped for a moment, unsure how to speak of the past to anyone who wasn't there. With Martha, perhaps, Max was finding it particularly difficult. He knew he'd be risking a lot by telling her. What would she think of him? What would he think of himself?

He knew, too, that he'd avoided talking to her about this for years, and not only for selfish reasons. Martha had never known hardship or anything, really, of the world. For her, the loss of her cat as a child had been the most frightening event in her life. How could he destroy that purity of illusion? Hers was a kind of make-believe Britain in which policemen protected the people and the law was a vessel for establishing innocence and the politicians were patrician types who knew how to do things for the best. It was a world in which truth and honesty and decency prevailed. Max might have once believed it himself, had life been a little different. Instead, he knew it was a sham, and he suspected that Martha knew it too, but, because he loved her, he wanted to keep it as it was, to keep up the pretence of not knowing that it was a sham, to keep her from ever having to suffer, or ever having to acknowledge suffering.

Then there was, and always had been, an unspoken acknowledgement between the two that Max would talk about the war only when he felt able. Martha had never once asked him about it, and he'd never once volunteered any information, save a few generalities – the scenery in some part of France, the odd humorous moment, for there had been humorous moments, which alone helped Max to believe in hope.

But now the situation was serious, and Max felt forced to speak of the past. And if he was going to do that, he wanted Martha to know first, and in most detail, the events that occurred. So he took a deep breath while Martha, who had guessed much of what Max was feeling, braced herself, and took a silent oath always to protect Max from his own nightmares. "There was a young soldier," Max said finally, "a boy, really."

Again, he ceased.

A boy. My God. For a moment, he wasn't sure he could continue. But he took another deep breath, unconscious of doing so, and said, "There was a boy—"

But he got no further because of the sudden and urgent pounding on the door. Max and Martha looked at each other, each one with their own fears evident.

"Max," Martha said, moving close to her husband.

He smiled at her, or tried to. It didn't quite work.

Flora scurried past them, her face white. She went to the door and opened it. When she did, she stood back to admit Inspector Longford and Sergeant Pierce. Both men entered, neither one seeing fit to remove their hats.

"More questions, Inspector?" Max said, his face grim and fearful. "Can I answer them here, this time?"

"Yes, more questions," Inspector Longford said. "But you can't answer them here. At the moment, I'd prefer you to accompany me to the Yard voluntarily. But, if you resist, you will be arrested on suspicion of murdering your acquaintance Frederick Rice.'

Chapter Fourteen

For a long time after Max had left with the policemen, Martha didn't know what to do.

Flora had collapsed into tears again, and was on the verge of fetching Eric to help Max escape. Martha managed to calm her, and gave her a strong sweet cup of tea, which Flora put over her apron. "He could never kill no one," Flora kept saying. "Never."

"I know, Flora. That's why we have to help him. We have to find Mr Ham."

"Bacon, ma'am," Flora said.

"Yes, well done. How long was he here, waiting for us?"

Flora wiped her nose on her sleeve. "Well, he come just about lunchtime, ma'am. And he was here till you come. So, about two hours, I reckon."

"And did you talk to him at all in that time?"

"Only a bit, just to be friendly like."

"Good. Did he mention anything about Villas or Bridges?"

"Ma'am?"

"Never mind, that was yesterday. I need you to think, Flora. Did he say anything at all about where he was going or what he was going to do after he'd seen us?"

"Um…"

Flora sniffed and Martha pulled her handkerchief from her sleeve and handed it to the girl.

"It's vitally important," Martha said, giving Flora a few moments to regain herself.

Flora dabbed her eyes. "He said something about going somewhere, I think."

Martha just about managed to stop herself saying something rude. Instead, she put a hand on Flora's shoulder and said, "Just try to think, Flora."

Flora nodded, and tried very hard to think. "Well, I remember that he didn't want anything to eat. I offered him, ma'am, but he said he didn't want to be longer than necessary. I said, 'Are you sure I can't get you nothing' and he said… uh… he said… oh, blimey, what did he say? … Oh, yes. He said he'd buy a pork pie on the way to the pictures."

"Pictures? Where? Which film was he going to see?"

"Where, I don't know, ma'am. But I remember it was something with Norma Shearer."

Martha sprang up and went off to find the newspaper. She brought it back in, sat down next to Flora and turned to the cinema listings. "There's an old Norma Shearer picture at the Plaza Piccadilly. The Barretts of Wimpole Street. Was that it, Flora?"

Flora sniffed, and thought.

Martha tried to conceal her impatience. "Flora?"

"I don't know, ma'am. I can't say he told me what picture it was."

"All right," Martha said. "Let me think. Now, would he go to the West End to watch a film? He might, if he wanted to treat himself. It is Sunday, after all. Now, oh… where does he live? Flora, did he tell you where he lives?"

"No, ma'am."

"Hmm. We met him yesterday at the football game. That was Chelsea, and we asked whether he'd like us to give him a lift home. It was the least we could do. And he said, no, he'll walk. So, he must live in or close to Chelsea."

She scrutinised the newspaper again. "Hammersmith. They're showing a Norma Shearer film there. At the Gaumont. *A Free Soul*."

"That's it," Flora said, jumping up suddenly. "I remember."

"Are you sure?"

"Yes. He kept tapping his feet, like he was impatient or something. And he asked me a few times when you was expected back and I said I dunno and he said he didn't want to miss the film and I asked what film and he said *A Free Soul* with Norma Shearer."

"Brilliant," Martha said, leaning over and kissing Flora on the forehead.

Chapter Fifteen

Max was sitting in front of the inspector's desk again, while Inspector Longford, like an avuncular university don, sat back in his seat and, with an apparent airy disregard for precision, prepared to consider everything Max said.

Sergeant Pierce was at his desk taking notes. Again.

"Major Frederick Rice," Longford said, "is missing."

He waited for Max to say something. He waited a long time.

Max didn't dare utter a word, a sound. Anything, he thought, would give him away. All he could do was stay calm, keep quiet and wait for Martha or Mr Bacon to come and rescue him.

Then he heard a voice and looked up and saw Longford regarding him strangely.

"I'm going now to show you some photographs, sir," Longford was saying. "This is the man who was killed on Friday. The one we think you met. We have men now seeking out any witnesses from that night. The reason we're doing this is that we now think the man we have in the mortuary is not called Crawford. We believe that was a pseudonym. Do you recognise him?"

Then Max was looking at a peculiar face – the flat, dry-eyed, pale mask of someone he'd once known as his friend. "I'd like to speak to my solicitor, please."

Longford and Pierce exchanged glances. And Max knew he could be in very real trouble.

"Very well," Longford said, retrieving the photographs. "Meanwhile, perhaps you'd help us with some further aspects of our investigation."

It wasn't a question, more a challenge.

Max said nothing.

He reached into his jacket for a cigarette. At the same time, Longford took a pipe from the rack at one side of his desktop. He scraped the bowl with a small penknife then tapped the charred remains into the ashtray. He began slowly to fill the pipe with fresh tobacco.

Max lit his cigarette, inhaled deeply and blew smoke out.

It was a cold day now, with a bank of blue-grey clouds obscuring the sun, and a biting northerly wind bringing iciness that seeped into the office through the glass of the window and the cracks in the frame. He could feel the coldness about him, in the tiled floor, in the wooden chair. And yet he was sweating.

When Longford had lit his pipe to his satisfaction, he leaned back in his seat. "I was able to see your service records, sir. Cambrai, Arras, others."

"Passchendaele," Max said, annoyed that Longford was consigning that hideous carnage to 'others'.

"Yes. Terrible battle, that."

Pierce said something then, his voice floating slowly over to Max, soft and low, so that it seemed, for a moment, more like an echo. "'I died in hell'," Pierce's voice said. "'They called it Passchendaele.'"

Max didn't say anything, didn't trust his nerve to hold. Longford and Pierce were silent, waiting. Finally, Longford leaned forward and said, casually, "And of course, you won the Military Cross."

"Brave," Pierce said.

"Do you know what happened to him after the army?" Inspector Longford said, leaning back again, sucking on his pipe. "Major Rice, I mean."

That sudden twist in topic startled Max, as, of course, it was supposed to. "No. Why would I? Last time I saw him was in '18."

Longford looked at Max curiously, and Max glanced over to the other desk and noted that the sergeant too was looking at him.

"Did you know that Mr Rice had been abroad, sir?"

"Again, why would I? Like I told you, I hadn't seen him since 1918. He was injured, shot in the leg, I think."

"I thought you didn't know him that well, sir," Longford said casually, as if he were pointing out that Max had misspelled a word.

"Well, I didn't, but, you know…"

"Not really. I was in the Met during the war. I never served. And Sergeant Pierce here was too young. He was born in 1910."

"Just a babe," Pierce said sadly, apparently lamenting the fact that they wouldn't let him serve at the age of eight.

"Well, you hear things in the trenches," Max said, thinking that Pierce was doing well for someone so young. "You know, news."

Even to Max, that sounded weak. "Still," he said, "I might've been wrong. There were lots of bullets flying around. Lots of injuries. Perhaps it was another officer I was thinking of."

Longford smiled. "Perhaps. Were there any other officers in your regiment who were shot in the leg in 1918?"

"Look, I don't understand this. Why are you questioning me?"

"Because he's missing. I thought I'd explained that. And because I don't like coincidences, and you're drowning in them, sir."

The inspector smiled again, which made Max's insides crawl. He suddenly wanted fresh air.

"But you were right, sir. He had a wound. Rice. We've obtained a full description from the missing person report. Rice's wife reported him missing on Saturday morning. Hadn't seen him since Wednesday afternoon, apparently. She gave our colleagues in Lincoln a detailed description of Major Rice. He had an old scar, consistent with a bullet wound, in his leg. Just as you said."

Chapter Sixteen

Harold Bacon was in love with Norma Shearer, and had been for a number of years. It wasn't that she was beautiful, which she undoubtedly was, and it wasn't that she was intelligent and sophisticated. No, it was more than those things. And yet, if you asked Mr Bacon to explain what it was that made Norma Shearer the perfect woman, he wouldn't have been able to answer you. In a way, the reason was precisely that he couldn't answer the question; she seemed to Mr Bacon to be ethereal, above the ordinary, untouched by a world of crime and politics and armies marching here and there. Yes, Norma Shearer was above the world that Harold Bacon knew.

In fact, now that he came to think about it, Martha Dalton was a lot like Norma Shearer. She looked similar, tall and slim and elegant, with that dark and lustrous and short – but not too short – curly hair, and with those large eyes and serene mouth. Yes, she was similar in looks, and, he had to admit, in sophistication and intelligence too, although he was sure that Norma Shearer wouldn't keep getting his name wrong. But, yes, Mrs Dalton had something about her that affected men, even men like Mr Bacon, who rarely felt anything for women, Norma Shearer excepted, of course.

Sometimes, in moments of reverie, Harold Bacon would imagine going to the wedding of George Mills and Norma Shearer. He would sit at the front, or perhaps he would be the best man, and after George Mills had kissed the bride, he'd give Mr Bacon a slap on the shoulder, and Norma Shearer would give him a peck on the cheek. That would be about perfect.

Why it was that Mr Bacon never featured as the protagonist in these daydreams is uncertain. He never imagined himself as a centre-forward for Chelsea, and never envisioned a life of bliss with Norma Shearer. Perhaps the idea that she would be called Mrs Norma Bacon was too much like dull reality. Perhaps he simply never thought of himself in terms of greatness and stardom. He was not, in truth, an ambitious man, or given to improbable abstract wanderings.

Never mind. He enjoyed the fantasy, and was perfectly happy just to sit in the audience and gaze at the silver and grey image of Norma Shearer.

He'd made his way to the Gaumont in Hammersmith this Sunday afternoon because they were showing one of Norma Shearer's old films, *A Free Soul*, which Mr Bacon had missed upon initial release as a result of a large man standing on his foot at Stamford Bridge and breaking three of his toes.

Being hungry, and having missed his lunch, on account of the Daltons – again, Mr Bacon had bought himself a pork pie and a bag of pork scratchings. Gazing at these items, though, brought an odd nagging fear, which he couldn't identify.

The feature hadn't started, and Mr Bacon was settling himself into his seat, knowing that the film contained some pretty warm scenes, which he'd read about in *Film Weekly*. So, preparing for the first of these moments, and nibbling at his pork pie, Harold Bacon should have felt contentment and some anticipation of joy. Instead, he felt ill at ease. Something was wrong, and he thought hard about what it might be.

It had something to do with Norma Shearer. What could it be? And then, as he was trying to visualise Norma Shearer, images conflated and he realised what was wrong. He was beginning to think of Mrs Dalton in Norma Shearer's place.

Oh, that was terrible. Mrs Dalton was the daughter of one of the firm's best clients. Further, she was married. And now Mr Bacon's fantasies were starting to incorporate her. That wasn't right. It made him feel, well, guilty. No, that wasn't right at all.

He opened the bag of pork scratchings and started to feed them into his mouth, the salty-crunchy-fatty taste filling his senses. Norma Shearer, he thought. Not Mrs Dalton. Norma Dalton. NO! Norma Shearer.

Then the credits appeared, and he saw Norma Shearer's name in a large flourishing typeface, and Mr Bacon started to relax, knowing that he'd soon forget that Mrs Dalton ever existed. He put his hat on the folded coat, which rested across his lap, and he prepared to take a bite of his pork pie.

Then, just as Lionel Barrymore was about to hand some skimpy clothes to Norma Shearer, whose form was silhouetted on the bathroom wall, everything stopped and Mr Bacon suddenly found himself in bright light. He looked around at the other people in the cinema, all of whom were equally perplexed. Then, when he saw an usher move to the front of the theatre with a speaking trumpet, Mr Bacon's heart sank.

"This is an urgent announcement for a Mr Ham. Is there a Mr Harold Ham in the audience?"

*

When Mr Bacon walked into the lobby, he saw Martha Dalton and stopped short. Partly, of course, he was annoyed. Partly, he was expected to be civil to his boss's friend's daughter. Beyond these, though, he became uncomfortably aware that he was now, ever so slightly, in love with her. And, what was worse, he was confused about which part of these contradictions was dominant, and which *should* be dominant.

He felt himself blush, felt his heart flutter. He cleared his throat, and moved forward.

"Mr Pork," Martha said.

"Mrs Shearer," Mr Bacon said.

Martha raised an eyebrow. "Are you all right? What's that in your hand?"

"I'm perfectly well, thank you," Mr Pork said, becoming unsure now who he was and what he was doing. He felt suddenly very hot. "And this is a bacon pie."

"Well, you can eat it on the way."

"Please, Mrs Dalton. This is my only free weekend this month."

For the first time, Martha became aware of what a burden she must've been to Mr Pie. She said, "Oh, my! I… uh…"

And then, because she remembered how Max had behaved when he'd tried to tell her of his past, Martha did something that took both her and Mr Bacon by surprise. She started to cry. "I'm sorry," she said, "but, you see, my husband is in terrible trouble. Max is… Oh, Mr Bacon."

It had been rare in Mr Bacon's life that he'd been faced with a crying woman. He felt absurdly stupid and crass, unsure how to proceed. Should he comfort her? He wanted to, greatly, but how did one do that, especially with a half-eaten pork pie in one's hand? He attempted to pat her on the head, as he'd seen people do sometimes, mostly with pet dogs and such. "I'm sure it isn't all that serious," he said softly, slapping her forehead. "I'm sure we'll be able to get him out first thing tomorrow."

"I'm not worried about him being in jail overnight. I'm worried that he'll confess to something."

Ah, so that was it. Mr Bacon was on firmer ground here. He pushed his spectacles higher up his nose. "I see. Well, the police don't use those kinds of tactics much any more," he said. "I assure you, Norma. And if they do, they don't use them on people such as your husband."

"You don't understand," Martha said desperately. "I'm not afraid they'll force a confession. I'm afraid he'll confess freely. I'm afraid he's guilty of something."

Chapter Seventeen

Longford opened the drawer of his desk and removed some newspaper cuttings. He made a show of perusing them at length.

Max heard Sergeant Pierce sniff and then sigh deeply, probably just to remind Max that he was there, watching, waiting to record everything.

Max shifted in his seat. His back was starting to ache, and he wanted to stand up and stretch his legs. He could've done, he supposed, but the way this was going, any movement would have seemed to Longford a signal of deceit or evasion or something. Probably, if Max had stood, Longford would have taken it as a subconscious desire to escape, which it most likely would've been.

Longford lowered the newspaper clippings, placing them on the desktop. He lit a fresh pipe and said, "I've been reading some of your work, sir. Very good. Very, uh, philosophical, some of it. Above our heads, eh, Sergeant?"

"Way above," Pierce said. "I'm just a simple copper, sir."

Max didn't know if Pierce was talking to him or the inspector, and he decided he didn't care anyway.

"I was especially drawn to a phrase you used in the piece you wrote in '34 about the American gangsters. I quote: 'I kill, therefore I am.' Can you tell me what that means, sir?"

Max again had the feeling he was being manoeuvred, ever so carefully, into a trap. Or perhaps it would be more accurate to say, into a cell. But there was no way out of it. If he failed to answer Longford's question, it would indicate some kind of guilt, wouldn't it? Alone, out of context, the line was damning: I kill, therefore I am.

"You have to exist, don't you, before you can destroy? I merely postulated that an act of destruction is, in and of itself, an act of affirmation," he said.

Max waited for a response but, getting none, continued, "What I mean is, whereas people like Dillinger and Van Meter were professional criminals, for whom killing was an occasional necessity, there were others like Nelson, and Barrow and Parker, for whom the act of killing became a means of escape and empowerment. They were weak and unintelligent and disenfranchised people, poor people who learned that they could become like gods with a sub-machine gun or a pistol."

"Very clever, sir," Max heard Pierce say flatly. "I'm just a simple copper, so I don't understand all this pychological whatnot."

"What my colleague means," Longford said, "is that it's an interesting view, of killing, I mean."

"Is it?" Max said.

"If I understand correctly, sir, you're saying that it's a way for the lower classes, the working classes, shall we say, to find a place in society otherwise denied them. Is that it, sir?"

Max sighed. They were playing games with him. But what could he do? "More or less," he said.

Longford nodded. "Perhaps you'd tell us a little about your own background, sir."

Max didn't speak. How could he? What could he say that wouldn't add to their belief of his guilt?

"Are you all right, sir?" Pierce said. "Would you like some water?"

Max smiled at this. He was beginning to understand how they worked, these detectives, always seeking to unsettle him, to hint, through the use of vagaries and loaded comments, mocking and sarcastic asides, and then the abrupt switch.

There was a knock at the door and Longford made a small movement of his head to Pierce, who stood and left the room. When he came back, he whispered something to Longford. Then returned to his desk.

Max wondered what new information they thought they'd uncovered. It seemed, at times, as though they knew everything about Max. But they couldn't, could they? And then Longford spoke again, and Max knew that they did know. Longford said, "We spoke to a man called General Sir Clifford Monroe, formerly Lieutenant-Colonel Monroe of your regiment. Do you know that name, sir?"

It was evident from the grim look on Max's face that he did know the name of General Sir Clifford Monroe, formerly Lieutenant-Colonel Monroe of his regiment.

Max's hands were cold and damp. He felt more than ever as if he were being guided, slowly and very politely, into that damned cell. Or to the gallows. "Uh…"

The sergeant watched intently, waiting to record a confession or some comment that would turn around and trap Max.

Max gritted his jaw. He felt foolish. They'd used his egotism against him, allowing him to talk his way into condemnation. "Yes. Monroe was my commanding officer."

"At battalion level."

"Yes."

"And now?"

"Now?" Max said. "Now I believe he's Chief of the Imperial General Staff."

Longford gave the nod to Pierce, who again left the room.

Max could hear some distant muttering, and then the door opened and Pierce entered, followed by a tall, straight-backed man in the uniform of a general of the army.

Max felt his stomach fall.

General Monroe had flinty eyes and a moustache that was bushy, but less like Kitchener's and more in the manner of Earl Haig, whom the general was often heard admiring. When anyone pointed out that Haig ordered futile attacks that cost tens of thousands of Allied lives, General Monroe would harrumph and say: "He got the job done, didn't he?"

Max's own opinion of Haig was as forthright, but a little more detailed and considerably more offensive.

Max was about to stand and salute the general, then remembered that he was a civilian now, so to hell with it.

Longford offered the general a chair, which Monroe declined. He stood to Max's left side, creaking in his leather shoes. Pierce had returned to his own desk. Max felt cornered, literally.

"General, thank you for coming down," Longford said. "Sir, do you recognise the name of Crawford, at all?"

"Crawford," Monroe said, his voice seeming to bellow in the small room. "I don't believe so."

"In fact," Longford was saying to Max, "the War Office has responded to our request. Apparently, there was nobody called Crawford on service in your regiment at any time during the war. There was a Lawford, and a Crawley. But no Crawford."

"I never said there was, if you recall," Max said.

"Yes, sir," Longford said, hardly bothering to sound convinced. "General Monroe, do you know this man seated here?"

Max felt the general's eyes piercing him, but stared straight ahead.

"Yes. I recognise him."

"Sir, when I contacted you earlier, I mentioned that Major Frederick Rice was missing. I believe you were aquainted with the major."

"He was a company commander in my battalion during the war. Further than that, I'd known him for years before. We've been friends for years."

"Can you think whether the major might have had any enemies?"

Max started to feel faint. It was a tactic, he knew now, of Longford's to do this; to gradually increase the pressure and observe the results. But knowing the tactic made things worse, because he felt the pressure increase, and fought to maintain an even composure, keeping eye contact with

Longford. But he couldn't hide the physical effects. His heart was hammering so hard he was sure Longford and Pierce must hear it. He tried to keep his breathing shallow, through his nose, when he longed to gulp in lungfuls of oxygen.

"As far as I know," General Monroe said, "Major Rice has no enemies in his lifetime, with one exception: this man, Lieutenant Dalton."

"And why would that be, sir?"

"Rice believes, as do I, that Dalton was responsible for the death of another officer, an old friend of Rice's and mine, in fact. And I'll go further. He believes, as do I, that Dalton committed murder."

Then there was no sound, no movement, save the thumping in Max's chest. Not even the smoke from Longford's pipe was moving now; it was a cloud, a pall over the room, floating there, like Pierce's words earlier: I died in hell. They called it Passchendaele.

Yes, Max thought, *I died in hell*.

And then there was a soft, indecisive knock at the door. They all heard it, but nobody moved, nobody spoke and Max began to wonder whether he'd imagined it.

He wanted desperately to light a cigarette, much as a condemned man has a single last chance to act before the bullets hit. But Max didn't have a cigarette. Besides, he feared his hands, by their trembling, would display his guilt in a way that nothing else could. He waited for someone to speak, to respond to the person at the door.

They waited, and it seemed to Max that this might be another trap, a signal, perhaps. He glanced at Pierce, who was staring straight at him, a cold anger in his eyes. Max held Pierce's gaze for a few seconds, then turned slowly to Longford, who was now filling his pipe with fresh tobacco.

The knock came again, louder this time; bang – bang – bang, like the knocking at the gate, each blow sending a greater shock through Max, each indicating his guilt, each signalling some hidden secret.

Then the door opened slowly, and a uniformed police sergeant peered in and said, "Sir, Mr Dalton's solicitor is here."

And Max almost cried with relief.

Longford said nothing, didn't even acknowledge the sergeant's words. He continued to fill his pipe, to tap the tobacco down and light it.

Max turned fully around in his seat and saw Mr Bacon standing by the sergeant's side. He briefly removed his hat and bowed his head to Max, and the sheer relief that ran through Max was unlike anything he'd experienced since the war had ended.

Then Mr Bacon replaced his hat, turned his attention to Inspector Longford, completely ignoring Pierce and the glowering General Monroe. Mr Bacon's demeanor had changed abruptly from the anonymous, mousy affability to one of hardness and coldness, and yet so subtly had it happened that it seemed to Max he must've imagined it. And then Mr Bacon spoke, and Max realised he hadn't imagined it at all.

"Inspector," Mr Bacon said, "I trust you've finished your interrogation of my client."

"Sir?" Inspector Longford said. "Your client is here because of certain unexplained coincidences."

"He's here," Pierce said, "because he's been lying to us."

Mr Bacon appeared not to have heard these words. Instead, he said, "I've spoken with Mrs Dalton, who told me that you'd threatened my client with arrest if he didn't come here voluntarily to answer questions. Now, as we both know, Inspector, if you'd had enough evidence to arrest my client, you would have done so. Also, I noted that there hasn't been a search of my client's premises. Again, as you're fully aware, any basic investigation following an arrest would certainly require a thorough search of the home of the arrested man. That there has been no such search, and because you would have had to apply to a magistrate for a warrant to search, indicates clearly to me that the magistrate in question declined the application, probably on the clear basis that you do not have sufficient reasons to suspect my client."

Inspector Longford listened to all this quietly, and with no discernible change in his even expression. Sergeant Pierce was affecting boredom, although the greater his affectation became (yawning, for example), the more it became evident that his anger was increasing. General Monroe's face was red, and his sharp cold eyes were fixed on Max.

"Now," Mr Bacon said, "my client is leaving with me."

At that, he tapped Max on the shoulder, and they left together.

Chapter Eighteen

When he came home, Martha was waiting. He entered the sitting room and saw her sitting, her knees together, her hands clasped together in her lap. He stopped short, and just looked at her and saw the anguish in her face. If he'd never known her before this moment, he would've fallen in love with her then and there.

She stood up and walked towards them self-consciously. When she arrived at Mr Bacon, she kissed him on the cheek.

Mr Bacon fumbled in his waistcoat pocket, finally producing a business card, which he handed to Martha, telling her that he'd added his home telephone number.

"Should you ever need to see me," he said. "I mean, uh, should you ever need me. To help. Your husband."

Afterwards, Harold Bacon walked home, very slowly, unaware of what he was doing. When he got back to his small terraced house in West Brompton, he removed his hat and coat, sat down, turned on the wireless and spent the next two hours listening to the music of the BBC orchestra and the Bronkhurst Trio, not hearing a thing.

After Mr Bacon had gone, Martha put her arms around Max, resting her cheek on his chest. "Max," she said softly. "Max."

He kissed her on the top of her head, then gently pushed her away from him.

"What's happening?" Martha said. "I don't understand what's happening."

"There was an old company commander in my battalion," Max said, calmly. "Man called Rice. He's missing. That's why they pulled me in."

"Well, that's ridiculous. Do they think you've hidden him here?"

"It's too coincidental, you see? Something's going on. And they don't know what it is, but I'm the common link. And they're right. And I don't know what's going on."

"We'll find the answer, darling. I promise."

But Martha saw that Max wasn't listening. Instead, that wave from far away, deep out in the deep ocean, was threatening again to drown him.

"Sit down," Max said, his voice dark. "There's something I need to tell you."

"No. No, Max. Not now. Tell me when you're ready. I trust you to tell me some day."

She kissed him quickly, almost as if she were doing so for the first time – nervously, coyly. "Flora's still here," she said. "She said she had to clean the oven, but I don't believe her. I think she couldn't go home without knowing that you were okay."

Max smiled, forlornly, as it seemed to Martha. "Well," he said, "she might've been telling the truth about the oven. But, still, I'll go and see her, send her home."

"Then we'll sit here, together, quietly and listen to music, nothing too jazzy, maybe some Brahms. And tomorrow we'll find that hotel that your friend Burton stayed at, and perhaps things will be all right."

"Perhaps."

Max went into the kitchen, where Flora was half-heartedly mopping some pans. Max cleared his throat and that resulted in Flora flinging a pan halfway across the room, which led to more cursing. But when she turned and saw Max, she started to cry, from relief, mostly.

Max soothed her and sent her home, giving her money for a cab and a half-crown so that she could treat herself to something.

Martha had settled down with a Martini, and had turned on the gramophone. She was listening to the Adagio from Schubert's String Quintet in C. Her eyes were soft, resting on a point in the middle of nowhere.

She often listened to Schubert when she felt sad. It was one of those things that Max knew but of which Martha was unaware, so that even though, as now, she smiled at him, he knew it was a front. Anyway, her eyes told the truth.

Max got a drink for himself, and sat beside her, close to her. They listened to the music for some time, both allowing themselves to hide, for a while, in its melancholy spirit.

Chapter Nineteen

The next day was Monday, and bright.

Martha went to the front window, flung open the curtains and stood for a while, watching bustling life pass beneath. She felt stupidly optimistic, although she wasn't sure why that would be. It was true that she didn't like Sundays. They always seemed so claustrophobic to her, so dull and lifeless. Mondays were infinitely better. She could stand here at the window and watch activity, movement, life. It was as if there were now possibilities open to them, things they could do.

When Max had bathed and shaved and dressed, he went into the kitchen where Martha had already made him coffee and scrambled egg on toast.

"I've been thinking," she said. "We need to be logical about things. That's what's missing – logicality."

"Is that a word?" Max said.

"I don't know. Anyway, that's what we're going to do. Now, where do we start? Where would an investigator start?"

"Well, first, we have to know why Burton's identification was under the name of Crawford. And then we need to know why he had me in his notebook."

"I think the first point is obvious," Martha said. "There's only one reason why someone would use a false name – to disguise criminal activity."

"You know, you're pretty good."

"Yes. I know."

"But it doesn't have to be criminal. What if he were having an affair?"

"Well, let's say illicit activity, then."

"But why me?"

Martha thought about that for a moment, a vertical crease between her eyebrows. "Well," she said, "we know he trusts you. Perhaps he wasn't sure who else he could trust. And he must know you're a journalist, so maybe he had a story to tell. If only you could remember."

Martha frowned and put that crease between her eyebrows again. She continued, "First thing is the hotel. We need to find out where your friend was staying. We can do that because we know his real name. The police might not know that yet, so we can go and search his room and leave without anyone finding out."

"Are you sure about this? Shouldn't we—"

"Yes. I'm sure. First thing."

"Okay."

"Then we'll go to The Lion and see what we can find out about your visit on Friday."

So that was what they did.

It took half an hour of telephoning before they finally located the hotel, which was called the Alderney, a middle-range place on Ebury Street.

As Martha was collecting her coat and handbag, Max was thinking. "How will we get into the room?" he said.

Martha, who had also been thinking, smiled and said, "Trust me."

Chapter Twenty

A few minutes after Max and Martha had left their building and departed in a cab, two men crossed the road and walked through the open street door. They quickly climbed the few flights of stairs. When they exited the stairwell, they glanced up and down the corridor and, without speaking, moved towards the left and walked slowly until they were in front of number eighteen.

A short time later, a dark-haired, slightly overweight young man finished climbing the stairs, sweating heavily in his thick woollen suit. He took a moment to get some breath back into his lungs and to wipe his face with a handkerchief.

The young man's name was Eric Thorpe and he worked as an assistant butcher to Mr Stone. He hoped, one day, to be a butcher himself, and to rent a shop somewhere nice and quiet, maybe even outside of London. As a boy, he'd once been to Southend for a trip to the sea, and thereafter regarded the place as about the nearest to Eden he could imagine – people on days out, having fun; a promenade by the sea; fish and chips and pubs; even a pier.

As he padded down the carpeted hallway, imagining a happy life in Southend with Flora, Eric noticed two men standing outside a door. One man was leaning against the wall, his back to Eric, while the other was bent over, and seemed to be peeping through the keyhole. Eric stopped for a moment to consider what he was looking at. Then the man who was standing reached into his pocket and pulled something out. It took Eric a moment to understand what the object was, at which point he said, "Oi."

The two men stood upright and turned, and Eric saw he'd made a terrible mistake.

The man who'd been leaning against the wall was tall and lean, with a sharp-edged face and hard eyes and the kind of lithe, sinewy body that immediately made him seem dangerous. His companion was shorter and broad, with very short blonde hair and a face that was too pale, even allowing for the British winter just past. He had a blank look in his eyes.

The tall man pressed a stud and the flick knife's blade snapped out, gleaming silver, cold and merciless.

"Go away," the blonde man said in a soft, even voice.

Eric was suddenly filled with rage. He charged forward and reached the thin man in less time than he would've thought possible. Using his weight and momentum, he butted the man on his chin. The two of them crashed to the ground, Eric landing on top and slamming his fist into the man's head as fast and often as he could.

Beneath him, the man struggled but couldn't get purchase. He cursed and kicked and snarled and spat venom, but Eric was heavy, and had the man pinned.

Then Eric felt a jolt of electric pain hit him in the ribs and ride around his body in a spasm. He struggled to breathe and felt himself being hoisted up and thrown aside. He hit the floor heavily, the air leaving his lungs in a gasp. He felt something wet on his chest, and an ache that went through his stomach and came out at his spine.

He tried to stand, fearing an attack now would leave him defenceless. He managed to get up in stages, and only then realised he was alone. He tried to knock on the door of number eighteen, but didn't make it, slumping instead to the floor and resting with his back to the wall. He felt dizzy and sick, and was struggling to breathe.

Flora, who'd heard the commotion, opened the door and gasped when she saw Eric outside. He tried to smile to her, but what appeared on his face was more frightening than comforting. Then Flora saw a brown-red stain on Eric's white shirt. Unable to speak, she pointed to it.

"Bugger," Eric said. "They've cut up me heart."

When Flora heard her (almost) beloved say that, her face went a strange pale colour. Eric looked up to see her collapse in a heap and wondered what on earth was happening. He reached into his inside jacket pocket and removed the pig's heart, which was wrapped in paper and was now probably ruined. He stuffed it back in his pocket and went about reviving Flora.

Chapter Twenty-One

The young man at reception was polite, but insistent. "I'm sorry," he said, "but I can't allow anyone into a room if they're not registered."

"Oh," Martha said. "But it's really important."

"I'm very sorry, miss. Perhaps you could try later, or take it to his home."

Max had been waiting outside, smoking a cigarette. When Martha emerged from the hotel, she shook her head and shrugged.

Max said, "I thought you said your sex appeal would win over any man."

"Any normal run-of-the-mill simple man."

"Very simple, I should imagine."

"It worked on you, didn't it?"

Max, having trapped himself, didn't have anything to say to that.

"I did discover which room he's in, though," Martha was saying. "I pretended to write a note to leave for Mr Burton and the receptionist put it into the pigeon hole for number twenty-one."

"That's clever."

"I saw it in a film."

"While you were in there, I had an idea."

"Really?" Martha said, sounding a little too surprised.

"Yes. Look, you go back and tell the receptionist that you have to see Mr Burton personally. Then you'll give him your telephone number and describe me and ask him to hand this card to Mr Burton when he arrives. Then I'll give you a minute and go in and ask for the key to room twenty-one and you'll say 'Oh, Mr Burton, I'm so glad to catch you' or something. The receptionist will see that I match your description of me, ergo, I must be Burton. He won't think otherwise."

"Unless he knows what Burton looks like."

"No. Think about it. We know Burton got in on Friday evening, late, probably."

"Why do we know that?"

"Think, Martha. Mr Bacon told us that the police had found a late night final edition of the *Standard* rolled up in his jacket pocket. That goes to print at five o'clock, just in time for people going home from work. And we know Burton arrived at King's Cross from Peterborough on Friday, because he had the ticket that said so."

Martha looked at Max as if he were explaining to her the difference between Einstein's theories of relativity. She said, "Oh. Uh."

"Let me explain it in simpler terms. It's likely he bought the paper at King's Cross Station. After all, you would, wouldn't you? You'd get out of the train and buy a copy of the *Standard*, and if he had the final edition he must've got to

King's Cross in the evening. And if so, he would've checked into the hotel in the evening."

"So?"

"So, my darling, there are different staff on in the evenings in hotels. There's a night manager and night staff just starting their shift. Now, it's daytime, so I'd imagine the receptionist hasn't met Burton. In which case, I can be Burton. You understand?"

"Yes," Martha said slowly. "Unless the staff alternate…"

"Oh."

"…and unless Burton checked in earlier and bought the paper later, en route to meeting you, say."

"Uh."

"And besides, it won't work. I've seen you lying, and you're hopeless."

Chapter Twenty-Two

Max knocked on the door to room twenty-one. He and Martha waited, listening for any signs of life inside. After a moment, Max knocked again, the bangs sounding flat and dull. Then he unlocked the door and opened it slowly, and they entered.

The room was dark and cool, the heavy curtains drawn, and the few items of furniture were no more than vague shadows. It was a twin room, two single beds along the left-side wall, with a small bedside cabinet between them.

But the most obvious thing about the place was the faint smell, organic and rotten and with an oozing sweetness to it.

Both of them instinctively covered their mouths and noses. Max knew the smell straight away. His body went stiff, with a kind of reflex action. Martha didn't understand immediately, but realised from Max's reaction that it was bad.

They stood for a moment, silently, as if they feared to go further, but were drawn to anyway.

Max closed the door, turned on the light and walked towards the beds.

Then he stopped and stared at the floor where the body of a man was lying face down in a dark, almost black pool. Max instinctively turned to Martha, trying to prevent her from seeing the body, but it was too late. She gasped, staggered back a few paces, her hand to her mouth, her eyes wide in shock.

"My God," she said, closing her eyes and turning sharply away from the sight.

Max went over to the corpse and knelt down beside it. The dead figure had once been a man, and quite old, with grey hair, neatly cut and thinning. He was wearing a decent suit and good-quality black leather Oxfords with leather soles, hand stitched, Max thought.

Max placed the back of his hand on the face, then lifted one of the arms, putting it down again gently.

Martha had now recovered a little and was watching Max from a distance, as if she were scared the body would jump up and attack her.

Max stood, glanced around the room, spotted the radiator and went over to feel it. "It's cold," he said, mostly to himself. He then opened the wardrobe and saw a man's overcoat, which he checked, searching the pockets, which were empty. He went back to the body and carefully felt inside the jacket pockets. There his fingers met nothing.

Next, Max checked the chest of drawers; these were also empty. Finally, he went to the small cabinet between the beds. Again, there was nothing.

He went back to the body. "Don't look," he said to Martha.

He took a gulp of air and slowly put his hands under the body, rolled it over and stared at the face of the dead man, the skin bluish-pale and marbled, the eyes bulging, protruded.

Max stood quickly, backed away from the corpse. "We have to go," he said, his voice low and trembling.

"Shouldn't we tell someone? Call the police?"

"No. We just go."

He continued to stare at the dead man's face, frozen for ever.

"Max? What is it? What's wrong? Max?"

Finally, Max looked away from the body. He looked at Martha, and he was white.

"Max," Martha said.

"I'm in trouble."

"Why? What's wrong?"

"I know him. I know who he is."

Chapter Twenty-Three

Anyone casually glancing at Max and Martha leaving the hotel would have assumed they were a young couple, handsome and beautiful and rich. They would have seen two privileged carefree people strolling together in the weak spring sunshine.

But had anyone scrutinised them more completely, they might have seen that the woman was walking unsteadily, and that she had to cling tightly to the man just to make it a few yards. And they would have seen that the man's face was ashen and grim, his eyes dark with some kind of fury.

Martha wanted to get a cab, but Max told her that the police would inquire of cab firms whether anyone had been collected from the hotel recently. They might even show photographs of Max and Martha to the cab drivers. Somebody would remember, and that would place them at the scene.

"But the hotel staff saw us," Martha said.

"We can't help that. We need to walk and seem normal. And we need to go north or west or east. Not south, not back towards Pimlico."

So they walked, and held each other tightly, and said nothing. After twenty minutes or so, when they were just two of hundreds of people jostling along Piccadilly, they entered a tea shop and took a seat at a table in the corner, a long way from the window and other occupied tables. The waitress came over and Max ordered a pot of tea, and Martha went into the ladies' room and was sick.

When she came back, Max lit a cigarette for her and himself, and poured the tea.

"We're just an ordinary couple," he said. "We've come to pick up a book from Hatchards, something I need for research, and maybe we'll go to the pictures or maybe a gallery. All right?"

Martha nodded, although she wasn't really listening. "I don't understand what's going on," she said. "Max, my God, that man—"

"I know," he said. "Try not to think about it."

"What are we going to do?"

"I don't know."

"You said you knew him. How?"

"Let's drink our tea," Max said. "Then we'll go for a stroll in the park. Green Park should be fine. Then I'll tell you a story."

He put his hand on Martha's, which was deathly cold. This thing he'd always been scared of had happened. The thing he'd always feared had come true; Martha, his beloved wife, had seen death, and would know of his part in it.

"Who was he, Max? That… that body?"

"He was a company CO in my old battalion. Major Rice. He's the one who was reported missing. The police know I was connected to him, and now they're going to think I've killed him."

Chapter Twenty-Four

They were sitting beside each other on a bench, along a promenade lined with trees. Above them, a London plane tree was just coming to life after the winter. Small, bright, fresh green leaves were letting themselves be known along the wide branches and on the small twigs of the broad ancient tree.

Martha held her coat about her tightly. Max, leaning forward, drew on a cigarette. "We were in a shell hole," he said, his voice low, monotone, "half filled with foul, stinking water, up to our knees in mud. We'd been given the order to advance, but the barrage was late and when it got started most of us were already halfway across. It was supposed to be a creeping barrage, you see."

He left it at that, hoping Martha would understand what he was implying. But when he turned his head to see her, she looked at him blankly and shook her head very slightly, as if she had to tell him that she didn't understand, but was fearful that he'd explain.

Max nodded slowly, took a drag from the cigarette. He told Martha that the British army had learned that a sustained artillery bombardment − a barrage − of the German lines didn't have much effect. "The Germans were well dug in, so they just sat below and waited it out," he said. "When the order to advance would come, the Germans would be back up, back in their machine gun nests, and our soldiers would be mowed down. So our lot developed the creeping barrage."

With a creeping barrage, Max explained, the artillery would aim at a point in the middle of no man's land, and the infantry would advance as the barrage moved slowly ahead, the idea being that the shells would hit the Germans, who'd have to take cover, and would be followed quickly by the British troops, denying the enemy a chance to get back to a firing position. "It worked well," he said. "In some cases."

"But it was late," Martha said, and Max could see that she now understood the horror of that.

"Yes. It was late. The distance between trenches wasn't uniform, you see. It changed from one sector to the other. Ours was closer than most, so the powers-that-be had worked out a varied timetable for the bombardments to begin."

He flicked some ash away, watched it scatter on the light wind. "But somebody fouled up. I don't know why. And the batteries behind us were late. And nobody told them to stop. And nobody told us to wait. So when we got the order to advance, we had no artillery cover. That wasn't too bad. The Germans knew what was coming and were keeping their heads down."

Max paused for a moment, and took a long drag on his cigarette, letting the smoke out slowly, watching it as it was spread into nothing by the breeze. "We were about halfway across when the artillery started, and slammed right into us."

He felt Martha shiver, and he wanted to put his arm around her, hold her tightly and tell her the world wasn't so bad. But he couldn't do that, not right then. He didn't trust himself to make it sound convincing. And he didn't want her seeing what his face might be betraying at that moment. "Our artillery were using shrapnel and high-explosive rounds."

"Shrapnel?"

"Canister. Case shot."

"I see," Martha said quietly.

"They were supposed to cut the barbed wire, and wipe out forward German positions."

There was a rustling sound as the wind strengthened for a moment. Max looked up, as if he had only just become aware of his surroundings. In the distance, a family were walking slowly, the woman holding the hands of two small children while the man ambled ahead. The children were sucking on lollipops, the man was sucking on a cigarette. Further on, an elderly man walked with a cane, while a younger woman – his daughter, perhaps – held on to him.

"They burst in the air," Max said, "shrapnel shells. They're beautiful to watch, in some ways, they're like small clouds being born, and they raise the earth up like waves. But they weren't beautiful then, not when my own battalion was being cut in half by them."

He paused again. Martha put her hand on his back, felt the shivering of his body. He didn't seem aware of her touch, or even of her presence. "And then the barrage stopped," he said. "Somebody must've told the artillery what had happened. It should've taken us to within a hundred yards of the lines so that we could charge it and give the Germans no time to recover from the artillery fire. Instead, we were caught in the open. We were sitting ducks. Our entire battalion was stuck in mud in the middle of no man's land, half of us dead or wounded, while the Germans calmly went back to their posts. They'd had plenty of practice. It was a slaughter. Another one. I was with three others from my company. We couldn't go ahead. We couldn't go back."

A man in a pin-striped suit and bowler hat walked towards them, his attention fully on the newspaper in front of his face. Max waited until he'd gone by, and then waited some more.

"We were strung out," he said, "and everyone took cover as best they could. I and those nearest me threw ourselves into a shell hole. Burton was one of the ones there. He was a sergeant in my platoon, I told you that, didn't I? We'd become quite good friends. And our company commander was there too, man called Captain Palgrave. And a young private. I can't remember his name. He hadn't been with us long."

He took another drag on his cigarette. "And then the gas came. You'd think it would be like fog, this gas. But it's not. It's heavier and slower, and it's an ugly pale yellow-green colour, like the slime you find in stagnant ponds. Or maybe it only seemed like that because you had to look at it through the glass in your gas mask. It's not even like a gas at all, it's more like a living thing."

He heard Martha sniff, and knew she was crying softly, and trying to keep it to herself. He wanted to hold her. But he wasn't finished, and it had to be told now. It had to be. So he said, "If you're lucky, and you're in a trench or a shell hole, and there's a breeze, you can watch it float over your head. But it's heavy stuff, dense. Well, there was no breeze on this day and we watched as the gas came crawling down the sides of the crater, as if it were seeking us out, one by one, and clinging to our bodies."

"But… but you had gas masks," Martha said desperately. "You must've done."

"Yes," Max said. "We had gas masks. We had three of them. The problem was, there were four of us in that damned hole."

Martha gasped and threw a hand up to her mouth. She didn't trust herself to speak, except to utter two words. "Oh, Max."

"You see, our company CO had lost his as he'd run back to our lines. We'd all been running flat out, hundreds of us. Well, the hundreds who were able to run—"

He shrugged, and was quiet for a moment.

"Captain Palgrave," he said finally. "Our company commander. Our leader. Captain Richard Palgrave. And he'd lost his bloody gas mask. And the gas was coming and we all knew what it meant. We'd all seen men choking their lungs up, coughing blood and bile, their hands ripping at their throats, trying to get oxygen in, tearing at their own flesh, just to free them from this bloody burning gas."

Max was quiet for a long time. In fact, because it was so long, Martha eventually said, "Is that it, Max? Is that what you want to tell me?"

He shook his head, and over his shoulder he said, "No, there's more. But I need a drink before I tell you."

Chapter Twenty-Five

They strolled back towards the Embankment, slowly and without words, avoiding Victoria, close to where the Alderney Hotel was located, but otherwise not taking much note of where they were. Max kept turning down side streets every time they came to a main road, and Martha simply followed.

After a while, Max looked up and glanced around. He saw a pub called The Falcon and headed that way.

They took a seat at a corner table in the lounge, Martha with half a stout and Max with a pint of bitter. The public bar was busy, and they could hear much chatter and laughter coming over the wooden partition, but the lounge was almost empty, only a couple of elderly ladies jabbering away at the other end.

Max drank deeply from his glass, then wiped his hand over his mouth. He lit another cigarette with his silver lighter. The smoke caught in a burst of sunlight that sent rays down to the ground and lit up patches of the dirty, dusty wooden floor.

Martha sipped her stout, then put the glass down and pushed it away from her. She waited.

Max wasn't looking at her. Instead, he watched the motes of dust trapped by that sunlight.

"The gas," he said. "That bloody awful stuff. It came into the shell hole, and we put our gas masks on – Burton and I, and this young private. Wish I could remember his name. And our CO, Captain Palgrave, watched the gas getting closer, and he backed away from it as far as he could, and his feet were slipping in the mud and splashing the water and all the while he was trying to cover his face with his jacket, but we all knew that was useless, and he did too. And he panicked."

He took another gulp of his beer, and another drag of his cigarette, as if they alone were keeping him from breaking apart entirely. Then he smiled, but it wasn't like any kind of smile Martha had ever seen before. It was bitter and angry and as full of sadness as anything Martha had ever seen, except, perhaps, for Max's eyes sometimes. "Avery," he said.

"What?"

"That was his name. The boy. Private Avery."

"Oh."

"Palgrave took the service pistol from his holster, and he looked at us, at Burton and me and Avery. I knew what he was going to do, and I didn't stop him. He ordered Avery to remove his gas mask, and Burton and I did nothing. What could we do? Palgrave was our commanding officer. But it was murder, no matter what Palgrave was. I can see Avery looking at us, at Burton and me, but mostly at me because I was the only other officer there. And I did nothing. And Avery refused, and Palgrave shouted at him to remove his mask, and Avery's eyes were huge with fear, and then

Palgrave shot him dead and removed the gas mask and he survived. A few hours later, under cover of dark, we crawled back to our trench."

"God," Martha said. "Max, that's—"

"Wait, Martha. I haven't finished yet. There's a lot more to tell, and it's relevant to what's happening."

But he didn't continue. Martha moved her chair closer and put her hands out to cover the one that Max had put on the table. She was trying to stop his hand shaking. "Max," she said.

She didn't say any more. She didn't trust herself to say any more without sobbing.

He stubbed out his cigarette and placed his hand on hers. They were cold, her hands, and soft and delicate. They were serene, unsullied, and the only thing Max wanted to do was hold her hands and forget everything that had once happened. But he pulled his hand away.

He stood and went to the bar and bought another pint. When he brought it back, he sat down again, and leaned back from the table. He lit another cigarette, his third in five minutes.

"Palgrave handed in a list of known casualties, including Avery. I didn't contest it, didn't report it. Things back then were… different. When two million men a few hundred yards away are trying to kill you, law is subjective. Burton and I never talked about it. But Palgrave must've feared we'd say something because he started sending us on these patrols, always my platoon, always Burton's section with me commanding. We had to go out and repair telephone wires, plant mines, cut barbed wire. He'd send us on any reconnaissance or intelligence mission that battalion or brigade HQ wanted. We knew what he was doing, of course – he was trying to kill us. But we just kept coming back, sometimes with casualties, but we kept coming back. Trench raids were the worst. The men couldn't use their rifles in the German trenches; there wasn't enough room. I had a pistol, of course, and we carried grenades, but we had to be as quiet as possible, so most of the fighting was hand to hand, brutal, medieval. We used bayonets and home-made clubs and maces."

Max lifted his glass with trembling hands and downed half the pint in one go. He smoked some more of his smoke, drank more of his drink and put the glass back slowly. "But it kept on," he said, "and I knew that our time would run out one day, and Burton and I wouldn't come back from a patrol. And I made a mistake."

He finished his drink, and sat awhile, holding the empty glass, and his mind seemed to wander so that Martha had to bite her tongue. Let him tell it in his own way, she thought. Let him tell it in his own time. He's had half a lifetime to remember, to keep this to himself, and now he's talking, so let him have a few minutes more.

"I went to our battalion commander and told him what'd happened," Max said. "A man called Monroe, Lieutenant-Colonel Monroe as he was then. He's an important man now, and a general to boot. Anyway, Monroe and Palgrave were tight. They'd been regulars in the Guards, had seen a lot of action while most of us were still civvies. So I spoke to Monroe, told him what had happened in that shell hole, told him about Avery. And he wouldn't believe me, of course, but he called in Palgrave and Burton. And Palgrave admitted shooting Avery but said it was necessary because Avery was panicking and threatening all of them. Burton didn't know what to say, and I don't blame him for that, but Monroe pushed him and he agreed that it might've been justified. That left me, and I maintained it was murder, but now I was alone and the thing was dropped. The patrols went on, but now with Monroe's knowledge, which made it worse. They'd closed ranks, see. The old boy network and all that."

Here Max's voice had become bitter and dark, like the mud and night of no man's land. "And then, one day, we had another big push. And I was half mad with fury, like nothing you could imagine, just this awful suicidal rage, gnawing at my guts and my mind. But not for the Germans, not them. They were just doing what we were doing; we were told to kill them, and they were told to kill us. We respected them. No, my anger now was against my own officers, the ones who should've been on our side but who were intent on preserving themselves at the cost of anything – the enemy, us, principles, honour. And I raced towards the German lines, not caring about a thing except that I had this burning desire to destroy everything."

Whenever he paused, it felt to Martha as if a hole had opened up in the world and taken everyone else away. Max was her centre and everything else diminished in proportion to distance from him. There was Max's voice, and all other noises were just the faraway mutterings of other people who weren't real, or didn't seem to be.

His voice, when he spoke again, was like thunder in the silence. Like thunder, or like a shell blasting deep into the dark earth. "And there was an explosion," he said, "and I felt the shock wave blast me sideways. When I came to, I was in a shell hole with three other British soldiers. Two of them were dead and the third had a gut wound. And I looked up and saw that the man with the wound was Palgrave. Captain Palgrave and me in a shell hole. Again. He was staring at me, and I stared at him, into his eyes that were like dark holes in a white mask, blood caked to his skin."

He hadn't looked at Martha for a long time. He watched the dreg of cloudy beer in his glass, rolled it around a bit. "And I kept thinking about that boy," he said, "the private, what was his name? What was his bloody name? Avery. Yes. I kept thinking about him, and about what Palgrave had done, and what I'd allowed Palgrave to do. And I started to imagine that we were dead, Palgrave and I, and that we were stuck there in some kind of purgatory, each trapped with the other, locked by a shared guilt, each one accusing the other, not with words but with the mere fact of our presence."

"I knew I should've done something to help Palgrave, of course. I'd have done it for anyone. Most of us would've. Even him, probably. But I just sat there and he just sat there and his lips moved now and then and I thought he was asking me to help him. But I kept thinking of that kid, of Avery, and I did nothing. It might've been minutes. It seemed like hours. It was getting near dusk and there was a fog or mist or something. It might've been smoke. For all I knew it was more of that bloody gas, only now neither of us would get away from it. And then his lips moved again, and this time I heard the word. Just one word: 'Traitor.'"

"That word, it cut me in half. It destroyed me. It was the worst word a man could hurl my way, worse even than coward or murderer. I couldn't speak. I tried, but my mouth wouldn't work. I just looked at him. I admit, at that moment I wanted him to die. But he didn't. Then I thought about Palgrave's family, and I suddenly snapped to. Nobody deserved to die alone, like that, in a bloody hole in the middle of that carnage. So I grabbed Palgrave by the back of his collar, and I slid out of the hole, hauling him behind me, and used the gloom and the mist as cover, moving slowly through the mud and rainwater and blood and dead bodies. I crawled for ever, and then I crawled some more. And I finally made it back to the British line and fell into the trench, bringing his body with me. He was dead, had been so for half an hour or more."

Finally, he glanced up at his wife, and saw in her eyes the pain that he knew was a reflection of his own.

The elderly ladies were still talking, complaining of the price of this and that, the quality of this and that, and the laughter and chatter from the public bar came through the divide, but the table where Max and Martha were seated was surrounded by that hole, by that memory and those horrors.

"Max," she said. "Oh, Max. Why couldn't you have told me this?"

"It was murder, Martha. How could I?"

"You didn't kill him, darling. It wasn't your fault."

"There's murder and murder. You can kill a man with a command, or with a bayonet or with the turning away of your eyes. It was murder, whatever else anyone may call it. The British army doesn't like murderers. They especially don't like commissioned murderers, unless they're high-ranking commissioned murderers, in which case they seem to like them very much. But shoving me up against a wall and shooting me wouldn't have made good copy. So they gave me an MC instead. I fail to wear it with pride."

"And what about that man in the hotel room? Major Rice – what does he have to do with all that?"

"He and Palgrave were friends. He'd been a regular too, became a company commander. Palgrave and Monroe and Rice, all of them old soldiers, regulars, officers, friends. And me, an interloper, makes an accusation of cowardice and murder. They must've hated me."

"But nobody knows, Max. You said it yourself, it was just the two of you in that hole, just you and Palgrave."

"Rice knew, I'm sure he did. He never said anything, but he used to look at me sometimes with utter loathing. And maybe he found something out. Maybe that's why he was here, in London. And now he's dead, and I'm in trouble."

"But you didn't kill him."

"Can you prove that? And does it matter if nobody can prove I didn't kill Rice, or Burton? People will suspect I had a reason to kill them, and then they'll start to wonder what happened at Passchendaele."

"So what if they do? I don't care what anyone thinks. I only care what I know, and I know you're the most honourable, decent, kind person I've ever known. And I know I love you, and always will."

Max smiled weakly. "The thing is, old girl," he said, "I know. I know what happened, what I did, what I didn't do. Funny thing, though. I don't care what happened with Palgrave… but that kid, that private. We watched him being murdered, and we did nothing."

"Max, you were so young. You were a boy."

"We were all boys," Max said, "apart from the men who killed us."

He stubbed out his cigarette, put a hand through his hair. "I don't understand all this, Martha. It has to be something to do with the war, and that frightens me. What if it's to do with Palgrave? What if I'm guilty? Not now, but then?"

Martha stood and walked to Max, standing behind him. She leaned over, rested her cheek on his, her hands on his shoulders. "We're going to find out what happened to your friend," she said. "Nick and Nora Charles, remember?"

"*The Thin Man*."

"Yes. And, by the way, you're more handsome than William Powell."

"Good. What about Clark Gable?"

"Don't push it."

Chapter Twenty-Six

They walked slowly back to Pimlico, hand in hand. They didn't speak a great deal, but every now and then Max would slow his steps and crease his brow in thought.

"I wonder," he said as they passed a couple of workmen who were sitting behind a red and white wooden barrier and smoking, their feet dangling in the hole they'd dug in the road.

"What?"

"Oh, I was just thinking about that newspaper in Burton's pocket. You might be right about him buying it on the way to see me. If not, he must've bought it before he got to the hotel. Either way, it's interesting."

"How so?"

"Well, why did he have it on him when he met me in The Lion? Either he would've bought it before going to the hotel, in which case he'd have dumped it in his room. Or he'd have bought it – like you said – on his way to meeting me, in which case, why? I mean, whatever he wanted to see me about must've been important, urgent, even, so why would he pause just to buy a newspaper? It doesn't fit."

Martha wasn't sure that Max's logic was correct, but she had to acknowledge that it was odd behaviour if he'd bought it on the way to see Max. That certainly didn't seem to fit. Unless…

"Unless there was something in the paper that was important," she said.

"Exactly. If he'd been bringing the paper specifically to the meeting with me, then there must've been a reason."

"Right. We need to see a copy of Friday's *Standard*, then."

"Yes. And I'd still like to know what the papers are making of Burton's murder."

"Call Sherry," Martha said. "Would he know anything?"

"He's deputy editor these days, but they've moved him over to the Foreign desk. Still, he'd be able to chat to some people, I think. Quietly."

"Well, go on then. Call him. He'd be pleased to help. You know how much he likes you."

"It's not me he likes. It's my gorgeous wife."

"Oh," Martha said, smiling a little.

They continued in that fashion for a while, Max throwing out the odd question, such as, why hadn't anyone at the hotel found Rice?

"That's easy," Martha said, in a position of out-logicking Max, if that was even a word. "Didn't you see the 'Do Not Disturb' sign? Nobody would dare go in there while that was up. And, since Burton didn't check out, they must assume he'll come back."

That made sense.

"Why a twin room, Max?"

"I think for protection."

That also made sense. Still, there was something else plaguing Max. He thought about things, clicking his tongue now and then, as he was wont to do when trying to write. Then he realised what it was that was worrying him. He stopped, and Martha stopped and looked at him. "It's Monday," he said.

Martha waited for him to say something else, and when he didn't, she said, "Yes."

"There was lividity in Rice's body, and the room temperature was cool. I checked the radiator, which was cold."

He started walking again, but slowly, thinking. Martha, her hand still in Max's, walked slowly with him, and waited. "No rigor," Max said, "and some smell."

"What does that mean?"

"Well, we know Burton was killed on Friday evening. I'd say that Rice was likely killed around then."

"How do you know so much about dead bodies?"

"There are a few million of us who know more than we'd ever wanted to know about dead bodies."

"Oh. Yes."

"Still, it tells us a few things. I think we need to speak to someone at The Lion."

"Let's go home first. We both need a nice cup of tea."

Max smiled. He shouldn't have worried so much about Martha seeing a dead body. What was it he'd said to Mr Bacon? She's not as delicate as she seems. No, indeed she wasn't. His old girl had strength all right.

Chapter Twenty-Seven

Upon entering the flat, Max and Martha were met by a strange sight. A young, pink-faced, slightly portly chap in a dark woollen suit was sitting on the sofa staring at the large feet of a large police constable.

Max and Martha stopped short and glanced at each other. Max shrugged. Martha said, "Well, this is interesting."

The policeman looked over at them. "Mr and Mrs Dalton?"

"Yes," Martha said.

"Eric?" Max said, only now recognising their guest.

"This young man deserves your thanks, I believe."

It took a few minutes for the policeman to explain what had happened and to tell Max and Martha how Eric had come along at an appropriate moment, preventing the two would-be burglars, who were probably miles away by now. He further explained that it was unlikely they'd be able to catch the miscreants, and that, since nothing was taken and nobody was injured, it would probably not be taken much further, but that he, the police constable, would personally do as much as he could, until this evening, anyway, when he had an important darts match.

By now, Flora had also appeared and added to the account, describing Eric's role and her role and the role of the villains, who had evolved diabolical menace.

During this time, Eric had said nothing. Indeed, he had done nothing except try his hardest not to stare at Martha, and, most particularly, at her legs, in which effort he was pointedly failing, as everyone, except apparently Martha, could see.

The policeman took his leave and Max lit a cigarette. "Blimey," he said.

"He was heroic, I reckon," Flora was saying, glaring at Eric, whose mouth was hanging open.

Eric reddened and smiled broadly, and his eyes swam with delight that Flora could possibly see him as a hero. "It weren't nothin'," he said, shrugging.

"It wasn't not nothing at all," Martha said, surrounding herself in negatives and becoming confused by them. "I mean, it was something, Eric. It *was* heroic. Well done."

Flora calling him heroic was a wonderful thing, but with Martha doing it too, and with those legs, Eric became overwhelmed and blushed even more and became stupidly cumbersome. "'Alf a pound, ma'am," he said, to which the others looked completely baffled. "I mean, er, giblets."

"Giblets?" Martha said.

"It's shock," Max said. "Delayed shock."

"Yes," Flora said. "I'll make a cuppa."

"Sit down, Flora," Martha said. "You've had a shock too. I'll make us all one."

She departed and Eric seemed suddenly to become aware of his surroundings, particularly when Flora sat next to him and nudged him with her elbow. He politely took a cigarette, when offered one by Max, and lit it with a match, which he snapped out and dropped on the carpet. Flora cleared her throat very loudly and Eric immediately collected the match and begged everyone's pardon.

Max then lit a cigarette for Flora and handed it to her, and passed them both an ashtray. Martha came back with a trolley on which were a pot of tea, cups and saucers, and a plate of biscuits, which greatly perked everyone up.

"What I don't get," Eric said, munching a custard cream, "is why they was tryna rob this gaff."

Flora stuck her elbow in Eric's ribs.

"Ow, bugger," he said. "I mean – er – giblets."

"It's a flat, Eric," Flora said. "Not a 'gaff'."

But what Eric had said struck a chord with Max. "What do you mean?"

"Well, sir, why bother tryna knock off a… a flat up here, when there's plenty of easier pickings downstairs?"

"That's a very good question," Martha said. "We're on the third floor, so they would've had to pass a dozen other flats, all of which are just as robbable as ours. Unless…"

She looked at Max, and her face was white. "Max."

But he was already ahead of her. "Oh, God," he said. "It can't be a coincidence."

Eric, unaware of the sudden tension in the air, stuffed another custard cream into his mouth. "I tell you what," he said pointedly, "you don't get crime like this in Southend."

"What do you think they wanted?" Martha said.

"Flora, when did they try to break in?"

CHAPTER TWENTY-SEVEN

"Must've been, uh, well, it was only a few minutes after you left, sir."

"Few minutes after? Hmm."

"Max?"

"I wonder. Eric, did either man have any weapon, aside from the knife?"

"I dunno, sir. I didn't see one."

"Could've been concealed, I suppose," Max said to himself.

He thought about the timing, and about the man with the knife standing guard while his partner was attempting to pick the lock of their front door. They were in daylight, so there must've been a greater risk of discovery, which, indeed, was what occurred when Eric came along.

"What are you thinking, Max?" Martha said.

He looked up to see three faces, eagerly watching his. "I was thinking that they were probably not trying to threaten or harm us. If they were, why do so in the day when they had greater chance of being witnessed, and when there was a greater chance that we'd be out, which we were? And it's too coincidental that they tried to break in so soon after we'd left."

He paused for effect, plainly enjoying this role of detective.

"Well?"

"Well, I think they waited for us to leave, probably waiting over the road, perhaps in a car."

"Flora," Eric said loudly. "They wanted Flora." His face was red with excitement and anger. He stood and flexed his fist as if the men were there at that moment.

"I don't think so," Max said calmly. "Otherwise they'd have simply knocked. No, I think they waited for Martha and

I to leave, and then, assuming the flat was empty, they made their attempt to break in."

"Perhaps they were going to lie in wait for us," Martha said.

"No. Because they wouldn't have known how long we'd be, and whether we'd return by ourselves. So, that leaves one thing: they were here to search the place."

Here he paused again, only now it was because he was trying to think what on earth they might be searching for. "We need to go to The Lion," he said. "And I'll phone Sherry."

Meanwhile, Martha was detecting all by herself. Thinking about things, she said, "What kind of knife was it, Eric, that this man had?"

"Flick knife."

"That's a type of dagger, isn't it? I mean, it has two edges."

"Yes, ma'am. Two bloody sharp – I mean, yeah, two edges."

"A twin-bladed weapon," Martha said, glancing at Max. "Just like the weapon that killed Burton."

Chapter Twenty-Eight

After Eric had been rewarded sufficiently with custard creams and ginger nuts, which, to Flora's horror, he dunked in his tea, he remembered that he was supposed to be at work and ran all the way back to Stone's butcher shop.

Max telephoned the *Chronicle* and got the switchboard to put him through to Sheridan Lyle. "Sherry, it's Max Dalton."

"Max? I bumped into Joe Barnes earlier. He said you were trying to find out about some murder. What the hell's going on? There's all sorts of rumours over here."

"I was hoping you could tell me. I thought you might make some enquiries, ask a few questions."

There was a pause on the phone line, and Max wondered whether Lyle was worried about being overheard by the switchboard. His next words confirmed Max's suspicion. Lyle said, "Sorry, Max. There's nothing I can help you with. Don't know anything. But I'll be free for a drink later, if you'll be home. Around six, say? I'd like to see Martha. Haven't seen her for ages."

"Sure. Oh, and see if you can pick up a copy of Friday's *Standard*, will you? Late edition."

"I'll see what I can do."

Max rang off. "He'll do what he can," he said to Martha. "But it sounds like he's worried about being involved, and that's worrying me."

"When will he be here?"

"Six, or thereabouts."

"That gives us time to go to The Lion."

So, with Flora under orders to securely bolt the front door, Max and Martha headed east, to The Lion pub.

A dray was outside the pub as they arrived. The muscular drayman, his sleeves rolled up and his cap pushed back on his head, was rolling barrels off the back of the dray, while another man was lifting them down to someone in the cellar.

Max asked this second man if Jack Connor was around.

"Down there," the man said.

At that moment, Connor's brown and sweating face appeared from the cellar and said, "Another couple of mild, Harry."

"Righto," the drayman said.

"Jack," Max called out.

"Hello, Mr Dalton. Not open yet, afraid."

"Just wanted a word, Jack."

Connor wiped some sweat from his forehead, then nodded. "Go in. It's open. I'll be another ten minutes."

Max and Martha went into the pub and took seats at the counter. Max lit a cigarette and dragged an ashtray towards him.

There was only one bar in The Lion, but it was a large room filled with black-painted wrought iron tables that were probably fifty years old. There was a dark burgundy carpet, threadbare in places, and flock wallpaper, which once had been red but now was closer to brown.

Framed photographs of warships decorated the room, along with some mementoes from Connor's time in the Royal Navy.

The Lion was a free house, which made Jack Connor a respected man, boss of his own place. Legend had it that Connor's great-grandfather was the great Tom Molineaux, who'd been a celebrated black bare-knuckle fighter in the early nineteenth century.

Few people believed it, least of all Jack. "My grandma was bonkers," he'd say. "She told everyone her old man had been Molineaux but she didn't know who it was. Likely he was a sailor out of Africa."

Nevertheless, there was a framed etching behind the bar depicting the famous Black Ajax in fighting pose, and Max believed that Jack secretly enjoyed the story, which, no doubt, came in handy sometimes.

"What do you think those men wanted?" Martha said. "The ones who broke in."

"I don't know. I've been trying to work it out. They weren't there to hurt us, otherwise, as I said, they would've made sure we were home. And if they were trying to break in, they must've assumed the place was empty. So, they were definitely after something they think we have. Or, rather, *I* have."

"But why? What could you possibly have? And where would you have got it?"

"I don't know, Martha. That's one of the reasons we're here."

"But you'd agree that the man with the flick dagger might've killed Burton?"

"It's possible."

"It's likely."

"It could be a coincidence."

"You don't believe that."

Max was quiet for a while, smoking, letting his eyes roam over the bottles of beer on the far side of the counter. "I don't know what to believe," he said finally.

A door opened behind the bar and Jack Connor walked in. He used a Worthington's bar towel to wipe the sweat from his face, then he grabbed a pint glass and filled it from one of the taps. The glass looked small in his hands. He gulped the beer down, set the glass on the counter and said, "Right, what can I do for you two?"

"It's about Friday night," Max said. "I was in here till quite late."

"Yeah. I remember. So?"

"I was with a bloke."

Connor pulled another pint in the same mug. "You two want one?"

"No, thanks."

"I'm fine, thank you," Martha said. "I'm Mrs Dalton, by the way."

She glared at Max, who raised an eyebrow. "This is Martha," he said to Connor.

Connor nodded. "I remember you were talking to a couple of blokes," he said.

"Yes, earlier. But this was later. Say, eight or so."

Connor downed half his pint and said, "Medium height, dark hair, early forties?"

"That's him. Do you remember anything about him?"

"I remember he owed me three-and-six," Connor said.

"He what?"

"He left and never come back. So, he still owes me three-and-six."

Max was silent for a moment, thinking about Connor's words. Then he said, "He was an honest man."

Connor shrugged. "Probably meant to come back," he said.

"I wonder," Max said softly.

"He was a bit upset, I recall," Connor said. "I had to tell that to the Old Bill. They kept asking me, was he upset, did you argue, stuff like that."

"Upset how? About what?"

"Dunno. But you was talking about the war."

"What about it? Please, Jack. This is important."

"Look, Mr Dalton, I don't make a habit of eavesdropping."

"I know, I know. But, you see, I can't remember what it was about."

"That don't surprise me. You'd already had a few when he come in. Then you had a few more. A lot more. You fell asleep at one point, propped up over there."

Connor nodded to a corner of the pub. "You was both at that table, and you was talking, or he was."

"What do you mean?"

"Well, he kept saying something like 'Do you remember, Max. Do you remember?' Something like that. But I don't know what it was about. He was getting a bit heated, though. I had to tell him to calm down."

"Why?" Martha said.

"He slammed his fist on the tabletop. I don't mind a bit of arguing and stuff, but I don't like it getting out of hand."

"So, you were reminiscing?" Martha said to Max.

He wasn't listening. Something Connor had said rang a bell at the back of his head, and now he was trying to crawl in there to see what it was.

"Max?" Martha said.

"Hmm?"

"You were reminiscing. About the war. Is that right?"

"No. Not exactly. I can't put my finger on it, but it was something else."

"You were too drunk," Connor said. "That's why he was getting angry. You just kept saying, 'No, it wasn't me'. Over and over.'"

"Did you tell the police this?"

"No."

"Why not?"

"They didn't ask me. Asked me if I knew what you'd been talking about. I didn't. And I still don't. What's more, I don't care what you were talking about. I only care that I didn't get my three-and-bloody-six."

Max reached into his left trouser pocket and pulled out some coins. He counted out three shillings and sixpence, and added another sixpence, putting the money on the bar counter.

"Ta."

"He left suddenly," Martha said. "Otherwise he would've paid the bill, wouldn't he?"

Connor shrugged. "I don't remember him leaving. I looked over and you were sleeping and he was there, then later you was still sleeping and he was gone."

"And did you tell the police that Max was asleep when this other man left?"

"Yeah. But they kept asking if it was possible you were going to meet him later. I told them I couldn't answer that."

Connor seemed unsure of himself for a moment, as if fearing he'd placed himself in a difficult position. He didn't like odd things happening in his pub. That bloke on Friday night and then the coppers and now this, these two cross-examining him like he was to blame for things.

He pulled a damp cloth from below the bar and began to wipe the wooden counter down, hoping that these people would get the message and leave him to get on with his work.

"What, though?" Martha said. "Why would he be doing that? What was it he wanted you to remember?"

"I can't remember."

Martha made a noise that was part growl of frustration, part scream and part sigh of despair. It was a noise Max knew; he often heard it when Flora had burned something in the oven or when Martha's mother said something.

Connor was back to wiping the bar. Max stood up to leave. Then he said, "Did he have a paper? The *Standard*?"

"A paper? We're twenty yards from Fleet Street. Everybody had a bloody paper."

Chapter Twenty-Nine

Sheridan Lyle was one of those middle-aged men who retained a youthful charm and energy, even while time was clearly winning the physical battle. He had short and thinning silver hair, oiled to his scalp, a jowly, avuncular face and sharp blue eyes.

He slung his coat over the back of the chair, sat and accepted a Scotch on the rocks from Martha, telling her she looked as beautiful as ever and asking her why she was still married to a washed-up journalist.

"Oh, you know how it is, Sherry," she said, "you get used to a pair of slippers, no matter how scruffy."

"You've put on weight, Sherry," Max said, feeling ever so slightly slighted. "And you're losing your hair at a rate of knots."

"That's from worrying about all you dilettante journos."

"Hmm."

"We're sorry to bother you with this, Sherry," Martha said. "But it's urgent, and we need help."

"Of course, dear lady. Now…"

Here Lyle paused a moment, scratched his cheek and said, "Talking of urgent, did your friend find you?"

"Friend?"

"Fellow came by the paper on Friday. He was looking for you. It was urgent, apparently."

Max and Martha looked at each other. Max's mouth felt dry. He could feel his heart speeding up. "Go on," he said.

Lyle could feel the sudden tension. He became cagey, no longer feeling the ease of chatting with a friend. "Friday evening, about eight, a man came into the office. He asked someone if you were around and was sent to me. He told me you were an old friend and he needed to find you urgently. He'd telephoned your place, he said. I told him you'd been in earlier and suggested he should try The Lion. Did you see him?"

"Yes," Max said. "I saw him."

"Are you all right?"

"I think the man you met on Friday was called Burton. He was killed later that evening."

Lyle didn't answer for a moment. He swallowed some of his Scotch. "God," he said, putting the glass down on the side table.

Then, sitting forward, he said, "Before we go any further, you'd better tell me what the hell's going on. All right?"

"All right."

Max told Lyle as much as he could, without going into the details of the distant past, which, surely, would only have served to cloud the issue. So he told Lyle about meeting Burton, and how Burton had left The Lion and had been murdered shortly after, while Max had gone home and been questioned by the police the next day.

When he finished, Lyle picked up his drink and swirled it around, letting the ice cubes ding each other.

"So, what did you find out?" Max said.

"Very little, I'm afraid. When Joe told me you'd been asking about a murder on Friday, it never occurred to me you might know the man. Let alone that it was the fellow I saw."

"Anything, Sherry. Anything at all."

"I don't know, Max. I'm only a deputy bloody editor. But something's going on, and it's well above me, but I'm out in the cold on this one. Our lord and master has nixed it."

"What?" Martha said.

"Our proprietor, my dear. He's killed the story."

"I don't understand. Why would the paper, any paper, not print about a murder?"

"Well, I can only think the old boy's got scared by something. Don't know what."

"I do," Max said. "If I'm somehow a suspect, then my employment at the paper becomes embarrassing."

"But other papers would print it, wouldn't they?" Martha said.

"Maybe, but they might not have enough. By the way," Max said, turning to Lyle, "did you get a copy of the *Standard* from Friday?"

Lyle reached behind him, into his coat pocket, and pulled out a folded paper, handing it to Max. "What did you want it for?"

Max unfolded the paper and began to scan through. There was mention of Eden's address to the House, earlier that afternoon, regarding Germany's violation of the Treaty of Locarno. There was nothing of any note in the article. There were a few smaller items of news, each only a few inches of column: flooding in the United States; a man and woman killed by a car in Stratford; illegal strike action at the Bow railway works; investigation into bank corruption. "Burton had a copy on him when he came to meet me," Max said to Lyle as he flicked over to another page. "I think there must've been a reason."

Max went through the paper, scrutinising each page, turning over to a new one with more and more annoyance. He paid particular attention to any reports of crimes, but these were proving as frustrating as everything else: the body of an unidentified man had been dragged from the canal close to Enfield Lock, on the Lee; a Danish man had been arrested for the murder of a woman in Streatham; a male and female, both young, names unknown, were being sought by police for an armed robbery on a jewellery shop in Brent; an elderly man had been assaulted and seriously injured by two others, following an argument outside a pawnbroker's in Lewisham.

Finally, Max sighed and tossed the paper aside.

"Is there anything?" Martha said.

Max shook his head. "The trouble is," he said, "I don't know what I'm looking for."

Lyle stood and helped himself to another drink. "So, it might be there, then," he said. "I mean, if you don't know what you're after, something there might be important, it's just that you don't know what it is, yet."

Max sighed again. "Sure. It might be there. Maybe Eden's speech about Locarno is the key. Maybe the price of carrots is of vital concern."

"Max," Martha said sharply. "It's not Sherry's fault."

"Sorry, Sherry," Max said. "I'm just… I'm scared."

"You know," Lyle said slowly, "if I were a journalist who'd been assigned to look into a murder, I might start with the victim's background. Your friend's home, for instance."

Martha glanced at Max. Looking back at Lyle, she said, "Would we be allowed to do that? I mean, if there's this secrecy about it all?"

"Well, let's put it this way. I, as an editor at the *Chronicle*, could reasonably ask Max, as one of our journalists, to dig a little. I could do that, couldn't I? Nothing illegal there."

"You're right," Max said. "But I don't know where he lived. He had a ticket stub from Peterborough, but other than that—"

"Ahem," Martha exclaimed. "I have his address."

"You do?"

"Yes, from the hotel. When I pretended to have a message for him, the receptionist suggested I mail it to him. So he gave me Burton's home address, which was in the registration book."

She reached into her coat pocket and produced a piece of paper.

"You're a genius," Max said.

"I know."

Chapter Thirty

It was early evening by the time Max and Martha alighted the train at Peterborough. They'd packed for a couple of nights away, Max carrying the leather grip and suitcase, and complaining that Martha really didn't need three dresses *and* a trouser suit.

"You never know what the future might bring," she said.

They booked into the Great Northern Hotel, which was next to the station. After unpacking, they went down to the front desk and asked the young male receptionist to order them a cab to Wisbech.

"Are you sure, sir?"

"Yes."

The receptionist made no response except to seem a little alarmed that anyone would go to Wisbech voluntarily.

The cab driver, unusually, didn't have much to say on the journey, and Max and Martha were quiet too, rattling along the causeway towards Wisbech, now passing through high-hedged roads, now through the flat fenland that seemed dark and empty in the early evening dusk. They passed small farms, the odd light in a window and pale smoke rising straight from chimneys. They passed a farmer leading his team of plough horses back home. They passed a couple of windmills, survivors from an old age, slow and silent and solemn, like the passing of time itself. They passed groups of farm workers, ghostly visions of shade against the rich dark soil.

Mud. Lots and lots of dark, dank, clinging mud. When Martha looked at it all, she thought of the seasons and the cycles of life, and of the history of toil for people who were doing here what their ancestors had done for hundreds of years. These were people from a Hardy or Lawrence novel.

But when Max looked at the mud, he saw it quite differently: a sea of dark fecund land in which generations would be buried.

The cab slowed at one point and turned on to another road, and they passed a group of men tramping home, spades slung over their shoulders, wellington boots thick with the slimy mud, the peaks of their flat caps pulled low. Max saw them for a moment as soldiers on their way to the front. More ghosts.

Finally, the cab pulled up and Max paid the driver and asked him to wait for them. Then he and Martha walked through the wrought iron gate, along the small garden path to the door of number forty-six.

The house was a red-brick two-up two-down, one of a short terrace, identical to the one opposite and all the others around.

There was a light on behind the door, a yellow line at the top.

Max braced himself, glanced at Martha, and knocked.

A thin woman of medium height opened the door and stared out at them. She was somewhere in her mid-forties, Max thought, but seemed older by decades, toil and pain evident in her eyes and the lines on her face. But there was a kind of grace and strength in her bearing, which was erect, almost belligerent.

"Mrs Burton?" Max said.

She glanced fiercely at him, then at Martha, moving a wisp of greying hair from her eyes in a subconscious act of self-consciousness, if such a thing could exist.

Martha felt exposed in some way, as if the woman before her had described an obvious flaw in Martha's character. She felt awkward, embarrassed. Or was it something else? It felt more like guilt.

And then she remembered what she never should've forgotten: this woman's husband had been murdered.

"I'm sorry," Martha said, her voice low. "For your loss. I'm sorry."

Max glanced at her, never having heard her speak in such a soft, uncertain manner. He looked back at Mrs Burton. "My name's—"

"I know who you are," Mrs Burton said. "You're Lieutenant Dalton. You were in Dan's company."

"Yes."

"And now you're here. And I've already had the local police come and tell me my husband's dead and asking about you and him."

"Yes," Max said again.

"We wondered if you'd talk to us," Martha said.

"Why would I do that? What do I care about you and him?"

"I didn't kill him, Mrs Burton," Max said.

"So what if you didn't? He's still gone from me, from us."

Max didn't know what he could say to that.

There was a silence, which seemed to grow louder to Max as it stretched beyond a few seconds.

Martha, still quietly, said, "My name's Martha. And this is Max. Your husband was called Daniel, wasn't he?"

Then Mrs Burton seemed to fade, very slightly, and her bearing diminished, as it seemed to Max.

"We think your husband had something important to tell Max," Martha was saying. "We think he was killed for it. We want to find out what it was, and why it was so important."

"Well," Mrs Burton said, "I don't know anything about that. You've wasted your time coming here. Still, you're here." Then she turned and walked from them, leaving the door open. "You might as well come in," she said over her shoulder.

They followed Mrs Burton along a narrow hallway, stairs to one side, kitchen at the end, and into the small parlour. Mrs Burton pressed a switch on a floor lamp and a dim bulb emitted its orange light.

There was a black ribbon around the fireplace – which was unlit – and around a photograph on the mantelpiece. Max looked at the photograph and saw that it was Daniel Burton, as a very young recruit in the Guards. He looked like a boy. Most probably, he was.

It was a dark place, the parlour. The wallpaper was mostly brown with small white flowers, and the heavy curtains had been drawn. The furniture was solid, all in dark woods like mahogany or stained oak. There was a brown sofa and a matching chair opposite, both around the fireplace. In the winter, and with a family, it would've been cosy and warm and intimate. Now, it seemed austere and oppressive. Funereal, Max was thinking, which was precisely as it should be.

Mrs Burton stood in the middle of the room, on a dark red and blue Axminster, patterned like a Persian or Indian rug. She was unsure of herself, her arms tight by her side and her eyes flicking around.

Martha, seeing this, said, "May I ask what your first name is?"

Mrs Burton sat in the armchair, one hand clutching the other. Martha nudged Max, and nodded to the sofa. She sat, and Max sat, letting his wife do what he knew she was good at: connecting with people.

"My name's Lillian," Mrs Burton was saying. "But everyone calls me Lilly."

"Lilly, do you have any children?"

"We got two boys. One at school and one at the brewery as an apprentice. That's where Dan…" Mrs Burton paused. Her lips closed and tightened. Then she took a breath and said, "They're with my sister while arrangements are made."

Max felt Martha tense. He put his hand over hers.

Another silence fell, another pall over the atmosphere.

Max cleared his throat. Mrs Burton looked at him, a mixture of fear and pain in her eyes. "Mrs Burton," Max said, "Dan was my friend. I hadn't seen him since shortly after the war, but I always knew he was there if ever I was in trouble, and he knew the same of me. I think he must've been in some kind of trouble for him to come down on Friday. I think—"

"Friday?" Mrs Burton said abruptly.

"Uh, yes. He came to London on Friday. We have… that is, the police have a train ticket. Peterborough to London. He booked into a hotel on Friday evening."

Now Mrs Burton's eyes weren't betraying fear or pain or grief. Now they were showing incomprehension. "He left on Thursday. In the morning. He was supposed to go to work, but he told me he had something to do and he'd be back as soon as possible. I had his manager here on Thursday afternoon looking for him. He hadn't even told them he wouldn't be at work. He worked at the brewery. They've had to lay off a lot of workers in the last couple of years, and Dan can't afford to… I mean, he couldn't afford to lose his job. He's lost it now, though."

For a moment, Mrs Burton didn't say anything. Max and Martha glanced at each other, neither one willing to break the silence.

But then Mrs Burton broke it herself. She said, "What's gonna happen to us now? Who's gonna bring the money in?"

"We can help you," Martha said. "I'm sure it's been terrible for you."

"Terrible? What would you people know about it?" Mrs Burton said coldly. "I bet you've never had to cut back on food and coal, just so you can pay the rent. And I don't want no charity."

Martha's face paled.

"Actually," Max said softly, "I came from a place like this. In East London. My father was killed when I was young. So I do understand."

Mrs Burton wouldn't meet his eye, but her silence was, in itself, enough. Then a crease appeared between her brows and she looked up at Max. "Peterborough?" she said.

"Pardon?"

"You said he took the train from Peterborough, on Friday. Why would he do that? He would've got it from here. Station's not far."

"What happened? Why did he suddenly decide to go? What was he after?"

Mrs Burton shook her head. "I don't know. I don't understand it. There was a man here on Wednesday night, but I don't know who he was or what they talked about."

"A man? Can you describe him?"

"He was an older man, above sixty, I'd say. Quite tall. Posh."

"Posh?" Max said.

"Well spoken, like you. And rich, I'd say, judging by his clothes. Nice suit and Crombie. Expensive, like. And good shoes."

Martha sensed Max tense. "Can you tell us what happened?" she said. "When this man came?"

"I don't know any more than that. There was a knock at the door in the evening and we was in the kitchen, and Dan got up and went to see who it was. I could hear them talking for a few minutes. Then Dan comes back and he looks… I dunno, different. Then there's this tall man behind him, in the hallway, and he looks in and says, 'I'm sorry to inconvenience you, Mrs Burton'. Then he and Dan come into here and shut the door, and I'm in the kitchen, ironing. They're in here for about an hour, talking. One time Dan comes out and says, 'cuppa tea would be nice, love', so I made them the tea and took it in, and this gentleman is sitting right where I am now, and that's when I see him closer, and see his shoes, and I knew they was expensive."

"Brown leather Oxfords?" Max said.

"Yeah, that's right."

"And the man had grey hair, well cut."

"You know him?"

"I think he was called Rice."

"Rice?" Mrs Burton said. "Major Rice?"

"Yes. Did Dan ever mention him?"

"He was in your battalion, wasn't he? But I didn't know I'd ever meet him. And Dan didn't introduce him to me. I don't understand that."

"And Dan didn't say anything about this man's visit?"

"No, sir. Nothing. Next day, Thursday morning, he kissed me on the cheek, like he did every day. He said he had to do something and he'd be back first thing. Then I gets a visit from the police on Sunday and they tell me they think my husband's dead, and they show me a photograph. They asked me some questions, but I couldn't answer them."

"Does the name John Crawford mean anything to you?"

Mrs Burton shook her head. "Should it?"

"Apparently Dan was carrying a driving licence in that name."

"I never heard of anyone called Crawford."

"Did Dan take anything with him when he left?"

"No, sir. He wore his good suit, though."

"His good suit?" Martha said.

"He had two suits – one he wears to work and his Sunday best. He was wearing that when he went."

"And cufflinks?" Max said. "The police said he had silver Guards cufflinks."

"He did, sir. Although, in truth, they were silver-plate. I didn't know he'd worn them, though. I bought 'em for him for Christmas one year."

Mrs Burton had been staring at the floor as she'd said this, almost as if she'd been reciting it from memory, the words merely functions of thought. But now she looked up at Max, and he could see the depth of grief there, and the fear of her loss. "They told me you was likely the last person to see Dan alive. They told me there was a witness who said you'd had an argument, and that Dan had been acting violently, angrily."

"That's not how it was. It wasn't an argument. I… I was drunk, and Dan was trying to tell me something important, something that got him killed. And I don't know what it was. That's why I'm here."

"What's it all about, sir?" she said. "Why would he leave me?"

"Lilly, I wish I could tell you. But I think he wouldn't have done anything to hurt you. I think he was doing something important. That's how I always knew him, anyway. Honourable."

Lilly nodded, but said nothing.

"It doesn't make sense," Max was saying. "Rice – if it was Rice – came here on Wednesday evening. He and Dan talked and first thing the next day, Dan left. Then he arrived in London on Friday evening, probably meets Rice again, and is killed later that same day."

"So what was he doing from Thursday morning until Friday evening?" Martha said.

"Yes," Max said. "What?"

He turned to Mrs Burton and said, "Did he ever talk about the war?"

Mrs Burton sniffed, took a small lace handkerchief that had been tucked into her sleeve, and dabbed her eyes, wiped her nose. "He never told me about the war," she said. "Never mentioned anything about it, really, except now and then when he'd had a few. Then he'd talk about you, Mr Dalton. And sometimes about other things. I never knew him then, see. I didn't meet him until nineteen and twenty-two. I remember one thing he told me, about nineteen seventeen. Passchendaele, wasn't it?"

"Yes."

"I remember he told me how so many men died and were buried. Not in funerals, but by the mud, by others just treading 'em into the mud. And then he told me about times when you'd be marching on them wooden things—"

"Duckboards," Max said.

"Yeah. Duckboards. And he told me how they was covered in slime and you slipped off as much as you walked. And he told me how, sometimes…"

Here she started to cry.

"Sometimes," Max said, "we'd see fellows slide off and into liquid mud. They usually disappeared beneath the surface. Most of them are still there, entombed in that damned stuff."

Mrs Burton dried her eyes. Martha couldn't bring herself to look at either of them.

"You was with him a lot, sir?"

"Yes," Max said, his voice hoarse.

Mrs Burton sniffed and said, "One day, he'd been at the allotment. He loved it there, I don't know why. Sometimes, in the summer, he spent hours of an evening just working on the allotment. One day he went there, and he didn't come back. So I went to find him. It was June and it'd been raining for bloomin' weeks, and his salads weren't doing too good. When I got there, he was sitting on the little seat he had, and he was staring at the dirt, just staring at it. And I never saw anything as frightening in me life. I mean, it wasn't him, least, not as I knows him. It was like he was a ghost, didn't even know I was there. He just stared and stared at the dirt, as if he could see 'em, the men who got buried."

After Mrs Burton had spoken these words, there seemed nothing left to say. Some moments crawled past as the silence grew deeper, and Max rose slowly, and Martha took his cue, standing also. Mrs Burton was still seated, staring at the floor, a vacant, distant expression in her eyes. "He never really came back, did he?" she said to nobody. "Not properly."

"None of us did," Max said.

He bent over, reached out his hand and took Mrs Burton's, slipping her some folded paper.

When she unfolded it, she was holding a twenty-pound note. She shook her head, held it out. "I don't want no charity, thank you."

"It isn't charity. I owed him this. Last time I saw him, he lent me twenty pounds. I never got the chance to pay him back, though I always meant to."

Mrs Burton stared at the banknote. "I don't believe you, sir. Dan would never have had twenty quid to give to no one."

"Then, if you won't accept it for yourself, take it for your sons."

Max and Martha walked out of the house, leaving Mrs Burton with a little money and a lifetime of grief.

Chapter Thirty-One

They were eating – or, more precisely, not eating – dinner in the hotel restaurant. Max picked at his roast beef and vegetables while Martha poked her plaice.

There was a background hum of clinking cutlery on china and quiet talk. The windows pattered with the sound of rain and rattled with the strong gusts of wind.

Max was wearing a grey herringbone suit and a simple silk paisley tie. He'd slipped the jacket over the back of the chair and had undone his top button, loosening the tie so that it didn't really serve any purpose at all, except to indicate to people that he didn't care much for the etiquette of fine dining, which he didn't.

Martha was wearing a pale blue dress, simple and stylish and effortlessly elegant, as were all the clothes she wore.

Each thought their own thoughts, recalling the grief and anger in that small house, analysing the words used, the emotions felt. There was a difference in their musings, though. Whereas Max couldn't shift from his mind the image of Dan Burton staring into the mud, as Max had often found himself doing, Martha was thinking more of her husband.

Presently, abandoning the semblance of eating dinner, she dropped the knife and fork and pushed the plate away. She gazed at Max, who gazed at his food, or, rather, at a space approximately where his food was.

"That was the first time I ever heard you speak at length about your childhood," Martha said finally.

Max looked up at her. "I know," he said.

"Why is that, Max?"

"I don't know. I mean, I don't know why I've never said much before. I know why I did today."

"Why?"

He rested his knife and fork on the plate. "I think because I knew her, Lilly. Or, rather, I knew her life. I saw my mother in her eyes, in the lines on her face, years before they should've been there, and in her calloused hands. I know what it's like. Even the house was the same. We had a two-up two-down in Bethnal Green, those wrought iron railings in the front, the red tile polish on the front step, the scullery at the back leading to the small yard where the privy was. And that parlour. It was almost exactly as I remember my parents' one – the kind of room that the working class thought made them look middle class. When they'd finally managed to live in a house, away from their parents, they seized the opportunity to dedicate one of those rooms as a shrine to their good taste and middle-class behaviour. It was there that they drank from teacups and viewed their Constable prints and received special guests."

"You sound bitter."

"Do I? Maybe I am."

"Tell me about it."

Max took up his knife and fork again, and continued eating, though with little enthusiasm. "There isn't much to tell. My dad was a railway man. He died in an accident. Someone hadn't fastened the rolling stock, and he was crushed by a coal wagon. But you knew that. Afterwards, my mum tried but she couldn't cope. She spent all her money on gin. I don't know what happened to her."

"And that's when you were adopted."

"Yes. I was adopted. They were nice, taught me how to speak properly, how to behave in company, that sort of thing. But they were quite old and died too."

"I'm sorry."

Max shrugged. "It was a long time ago. I don't remember it that much."

Martha pulled her plate closer and made another attempt to eat her fish. "What are we going to do now?" she said.

"I've been thinking," Max said. "About what Lilly said – that Dan left on Thursday, and not Friday, when he arrived in London. And that he went from Peterborough, not Wisbech."

Martha had finally conceded defeat to her fish. She pushed the plate away. "Yes?" she said.

"Well, suppose he had something to do before he went to London. Something in or near Peterborough. That would explain it."

"Something to do," Martha said, "or someone to meet."

Max's fork stopped on the way to his mouth. He lowered it and looked at Martha thoughtfully. "Yes. Someone to meet. Yes, of course. That would make sense."

He thought about this for a moment. "Hmm," he said. "I wonder."

"Well?" Martha said impatiently. "What do you wonder?"

"If Burton took the train from Peterborough, it might be the case that he met someone here, on Thursday. Then, Friday, he goes straight to London."

Martha rolled her eyes and sighed dramatically. "For God's sake, Max. Tell me what you're thinking."

Max smiled at his wife and said, "If you had taken the train from Wisbech on Thursday morning, and arrived here, at Peterborough, and you were planning to meet someone before taking the train to London the next day, where would you arrange to meet them?"

"I… uh…"

"What about in a large hotel near to the railway station?"

"You mean *here*?"

"It's likely, I'd say."

"No. Lilly said they were hard up. He couldn't afford to stay here."

"He could, if Rice had arranged it. And I think that's what he did. After all, he went over to Burton's house on the Wednesday."

Martha stood up abruptly. "Well, what are we waiting for?"

"I haven't finished my dinner."

Martha made that noise again, the one that was partly a growl of frustration, partly a scream and partly a sigh of despair. It sounded something like this: "Grrraaaaaghhh."

With that, she marched out.

Several people were staring at Max and, of those, the women were looking at him with particular disdain. Martha's cry of disapprobation was a familiar call of distress, immediately signalling that the male had done something especially annoying. Or, at least, that was how it seemed to Max.

He dropped his knife and fork, wiped his mouth on the napkin and followed his wife.

The receptionist – who was now a middle-aged lady in a flowery dress – was apparently perfectly willing and able to give out any information about her guests, past, present and future. She left the desk to go and collect the register from a back office.

"I think we need to go and see Major Rice's wife," Max said. "We should ask the receptionist if she has Rice's home address."

"Are you sure that's a good idea? After all, she probably knows by now that Scotland Yard questioned you, and that you're probably the man who murdered her husband."

Just then, the receptionist returned. She said, "Hello, Mr Tomlinson."

Max and Martha turned to see a small elderly man with a moustache and a rather frightened expression. He tipped his hat at Max and Martha, apologised for interrupting, received his key from the receptionist and said, "I didn't hear anything. Not at all. I don't know anything about anyone getting murdered."

With that, he turned and left for the bar.

"I wonder what's wrong with old Mr Tomlinson," the receptionist said. "He looked very pale. He has heart problems, you see."

She looked back through the register and said, "Ah, yes. I thought I remembered him. Major Rice arrived here on Wednesday afternoon."

Max smiled at Martha. "I wonder if we could have his home address?"

"Oh. I don't believe he left it."

"Was he alone?" Martha said.

"Yes, no," said the receptionist. "I mean, he arrived by himself, and booked a couple of rooms under his name."

"That'll be one for him and one for Burton," Max said to Martha.

"No," the receptionist said. "I mean, he'd already booked his room on Wednesday. He'd telephoned, you see."

"I don't understand," Max said. "He booked one on Wednesday and another when he arrived?"

"No. He booked two more when he arrived."

"Two? Are you sure?"

"Oh, yes. One, as you said, for a Mr Daniel Burton, and one for a Mr John Crawford."

Chapter Thirty-Two

"Crawford," Max said. "John Crawford."

They were sitting at a table in the small, cosy bar of the hotel. Martha had a Martini before her, Max had a beer. They were both smoking and they were both looking confused.

Around them, the air was thick with smoke and chatter, a convivial atmosphere having developed as the patrons had decided to supplement their dinners with considerable alcohol and cigarettes, pipes and cigars.

"And you're sure you've never known anyone called Crawford?" Martha said.

"Very sure. When Inspector Longford told me that the dead man in London was called Crawford, I was bewildered. And after I realised it was Burton, I forgot the name Crawford. Forgot, actually, that Burton had had the man's identification on him."

"It's a stumper."

"Yes."

"Well, look, let's assume that Rice and Burton knew Crawford, and that they all met here. After all, they had rooms booked, didn't they?"

"Yes? Go on."

"Um…"

Max rolled his eyes. "The great sleuth."

"I'm struggling to keep things in order," Martha said. "It's like a murder mystery and we've only read half of it."

Max sipped some of his beer and crushed his cigarette, immediately lighting another. He said, "We need to be logical."

"You be logical. I'll be confused."

"It's well known that women's minds are not as competently logical as men's. You think emotionally, not rationally."

"Agatha Christie is a woman. And Dorothy L. Sayers. Besides, it's equally well known that a man's mind is incapable of performing multiple tasks simultaneously."

"Nonsense. I've been ignoring you and your mother simultaneously for years."

"Well, that's true. Now, how are we going to sort out these murders?"

Martha then happened to glance at the next table, and she saw old Mr Tomlinson, the man they'd met at reception an hour earlier. For some reason, he was staring at her and Max with a look of terror on his worn face.

"I beg your pardon," he said. He stood unsteadily, took his coat from the back of his chair and backed away a few steps before turning and walking quickly.

Martha and Max watched him go. Then Martha turned to her husband and said, "I'm still confused."

"I've just remembered something," Max said. "When Inspector Longford told me Rice was missing, he said that Rice's wife had given the police in Lincoln a detailed description."

"We should be able to find his wife, then."

"So Rice came down from Lincoln on Wednesday and booked into a hotel in Peterborough. This hotel. And then he booked two other rooms, for the following day – one for Burton and one for someone called Crawford. Next, on Wednesday evening, he goes off to see Burton. We don't know what they talked about, but Rice returned here later Wednesday evening. On Thursday morning, Burton leaves his home in Wisbech. It would seem that Burton came here on Thursday and then, on Friday, he and Rice left for London, arriving at King's Cross, where Burton buys a late edition of the *Standard*. Then they book into a hotel not far from where we live."

"That makes sense, but it doesn't tell us much."

"No, it doesn't. I think we have to make some assumptions. First, Burton urgently sought me out, and was killed. Rice may have been killed after that or while Burton was on his way to meet me, but not before."

"Why not?"

"Because if Burton had known of Rice's death, I think he'd have called the police. So, it's logical, I think, to assume he didn't know of Rice's death. And, most probably, Rice didn't know of Burton's."

"Right. I understand that. Except…"

"Except what?"

"Well, what if Burton killed Rice?"

Max downed some more of his pint and lit another cigarette from the dog-end of the one he was smoking, which he dropped into the ashtray. "I suppose that's possible, but I don't think so. No, they must've trusted each other enough to do whatever it was they were doing."

He took a drag of his cigarette and blew the smoke out slowly, watching it dissipate, as if his thoughts were dissipating too. "Second, Burton hadn't been expecting Rice to call on him, so the affair – whatever it is – was unknown to Burton until then, but not to Rice. Which leads on to point three: Rice must've been acting urgently, and thus on information he himself had only just learned and which he told to Burton that night."

"Why?"

"Because of what Lilly said about the night Rice arrived. Burton hadn't been expecting him, didn't introduce him. And Rice apologised for interrupting their evening."

"'I'm sorry to inconvenience you, Mrs Burton.' That's what he said."

"Exactly. So it wasn't a pre-planned meeting. So, Rice's actions were urgent. Next: after Rice went to see Burton on Wednesday, he must've told him to meet him here, at this hotel, the next day. Why else would Rice have booked the room for him?"

Martha then became excited, tapping Max on the arm. "And what about those men who were trying to break into our flat? They're involved in it. They must be."

"True. And one had a flick knife. He might've killed Burton. And Rice. But, then, why were they at our place? What were they after?"

Martha shrugged. She was becoming confused again. "Tell me about Rice," she said. "You've told me about Burton, but I don't know much about Rice."

"Well, he was a company CO, but not my company, so I didn't know him too well, but I knew him enough. He was an old regular – meaning he'd been a professional soldier before the war started. I think he'd fought the Boers as a young subaltern, and the Mahdi's dervishes."

"The what?"

"Sudan. A man they called the Mahdi established a caliphate and kicked the British out – you've heard of Gordon and Khartoum. Well, Kitchener led a force to retake Sudan in '98. Tough campaign."

"What sort of man was Rice?"

"He was one of those even-tempered men," Max said, before adding, a little acidly, "the kind that England breeds to lead the rest of us."

"Max."

"Sorry. Well, let's see. Like I said, I didn't know him that well, but he always seemed calm under pressure, experienced, I suppose. He won the Military Cross, but I forget when. He was dull, really. A company man, so to speak."

"Logical? A good administrator?"

"Exactly."

"And he was friends with Captain Palgrave."

"Yes. They'd known each other for years, were regulars together. Palgrave was younger, so he might not have been as experienced."

"Is that why Palgrave wasn't as calm as Rice? Is that why he panicked in the shell hole?"

Max thought about that. "We all have our breaking point. That was Palgrave's. The gas, I suppose. It could've been Burton or me just as much as Captain Palgrave."

He stood up, drank the rest of his beer and said, "I'm going to get a whisky. Would you like another Martini?"

"Yes. A large one. Actually, make it two large ones."

"I'll buy a bottle of gin and put an olive in it."

While he was gone, Martha tried to follow some of Max's reasoning regarding Burton and Rice. Instead, she found her mind wandering back to their meeting with Lilly Burton.

Max returned and put their drinks down – a large whisky for himself, and two large Martinis for Martha. "Since we're making assumptions," she said, "and since I'm clearly not up to logical ones, I'll make an emotional one: whatever Burton and Rice were doing, it must've been terribly important. But I don't think Burton realised it would be, or, perhaps, he didn't expect to be as involved as he became."

"Why would you think that?"

"When you told Lilly that the man who came to visit them that night was Major Rice, she was upset."

"Her husband was dead. Of course she was upset."

"No. That's grief. This was something else. She was upset that her husband hadn't introduced Rice to her. She'd heard of him, after all. And he'd been an important figure in her husband's life. And, from the way she spoke of him, I think theirs was an open and honest marriage. Otherwise, she wouldn't have been upset by the omission. She would've been used to it."

Max thought about that. Then, nodding slowly, he said, "Okay. But that doesn't tell us anything. He clearly had other things on his mind."

There's something else – and this is where my poor logic takes over – it was the way that Lilly told us of Burton's leaving. He kissed her in the morning, as he always did. And he told her he'd be back first thing. However urgent the affair, I don't think he'd have left her worrying about him for a couple of days. Not informing his boss is one thing, but not telling Lilly? I don't think he'd have done that. Ergo, he expected to be back quickly. Ergo, he probably didn't expect to go to London. Ergo, something happened between his leaving his home and his arriving in London – something that he, and probably Rice, hadn't foreseen. And that, my darling logical husband, might explain why he was desperately trying to find you on Friday night."

Max thought about this for a long time. He'd forgotten his cigarette, which was smouldering away in the ashtray. Finally, he remembered his cigarette and mashed it out. Then he remembered his whisky and drank it. Then he remembered his wife, and said, "I wonder."

"What?" Martha said, sipping the first of her Martinis.

In reply, Max stood abruptly and said, "Come with me."

He walked out of the bar. Martha made that peculiar growling noise again and abandoned her Martinis.

By the time she caught up with him, Max was at the receptionist's desk, speaking to the lady in the flowery dress. Martha heard her say, "Hello, sir. Is there anything—"

Max said, "You said that Rice booked a room for someone called John Crawford. Can you tell us anything about him?"

"About Mr Crawford? No, sir. I can't tell you anything. He didn't arrive, you see."

Max turned to Martha. "I think you're right. I think something did go wrong – Crawford didn't show. That's why Burton didn't go back home the next day. That's why he went to London."

"So, what do we do now?"

"We go and meet Mrs Rice. We go to Lincoln."

Chapter Thirty-Three

Mrs Rice poured the tea from a Georgian silver teapot into the three bone-china Worcester teacups, all hand-painted with scenes of the Scottish Highlands, lots of Angus cattle and heather. The tea leaves mostly gathered in the metal strainer, with a few floating in the tea.

"I have a mote spoon," Mrs Rice said. "But I don't think we'll worry about that. I don't mind a few leaves if you two don't."

Neither Max nor Martha had any idea what she was talking about, and both chose to say nothing, just in case Mrs Rice should want to explain.

They'd checked into a hotel shortly after arriving, in the late morning of Tuesday. This hotel was close to the cathedral, for which Max had a particular affection. He spent some time on the train journey explaining to Martha the importance of Lincoln Cathedral, and telling her that it housed one of the few original copies of the Magna Carta.

"You have heard of the Magna Carta," he said, following an extended silence.

"Of course I have. Something to do with revolting peasants."

"Hmm."

After booking into the hotel, they freshened up and set out again.

Martha had changed her shoes and was now wearing a pair of lace-up flat-soled brogues. She'd had enough of walking in heels, which were especially unforgiving on the Lincoln cobbles.

They viewed the cathedral from a short distance and walked to the address Max had attained from the directory enquiry bureau. There was only one Major Frederick Rice listed in all of Lincolnshire, and he'd been located close to the cathedral, in a Georgian house near a place called the Eastgate, which, as Max explained at length, was an old Roman ruin.

"Before we meet Mrs Rice," Max had said, "we have to remember that she wouldn't know her husband's dead."

"Oh, God," Martha said. "You're right. I hadn't thought about that."

"She's reported him missing, but only we know he's dead. So, don't let it slip out, otherwise she'll wonder how we know what the police don't."

Mrs Rice sat and offered Max and Martha some small, delicate cucumber and smoked salmon sandwiches. Max took one to be polite.

Mrs Rice was a short, buxom woman somewhere at the beginning of her sixties, elegant in appearance and manner. She was wearing a plain grey dress with a white collar and a jet brooch, carved into the shape of a tied ribbon bow.

At first, she hadn't seemed to know what to make of Max and Martha turning up on her doorstep, asking whether they could speak to her. "I've already spoken to the police."

"We're not with the police," Max said. "I knew your husband. I served with him. My name's Max Dalton."

There was a look of confusion on Mrs Rice's face. She said, "I… uh… Dalton? I don't understand."

"We're very sorry," Martha said. "But it is important. We know your husband's missing. We…"

"We need your help," Max said.

Mrs Rice seemed stumped by the intercourse, and could only stammer for a moment, before finally saying, "Have you seen him?"

Max hesitated for a fraction of a second. "I'm afraid not," he said. "But I… I've spoken to the police in London. We might be able to help."

Still apparently baffled, Mrs Rice eventually invited Max and Martha in and then insisted on going off to make them some sandwiches and a cup of tea, which they were now pretending to enjoy.

The room was pleasant in a Victorian fashion – lots of overdone decorations, bright flowery wallpaper, paintings and prints of the Scottish Highlands, more purple heathlands and cattle and misty castles. It was cosy and stuffy and was making Max feel claustrophobic. It was… very pleasant.

Major Rice's presence was there, too. A couple of bookshelves were full of neat leather-bound volumes, mostly of military history, all immaculate. On the wall was a framed collection of medals pinned against a white silk backing with Rice's MC on the left. Next to that was a mounted silver-topped swagger stick.

"We know that your husband booked into a hotel in Peterborough on Wednesday," Max said to Mrs Rice, "and that he booked a further two rooms – one for a man called Daniel Burton, who served in my platoon during the war, and one for a man called John Crawford, who failed to arrive. Is there anything you can tell us about that? About why your husband was in contact with Mr Burton? And who Crawford is?"

"I'm… uh… I don't think I know anyone called Burton. Or Crawford. I don't know what you want me to tell you."

"Anything that can explain why your husband went to Peterborough."

"I didn't know that he did. All I know is that he left here on Wednesday and—"

"And?"

"And I haven't seen him since."

"So—"

"Can I get you some more tea?" Mrs Rice said.

She didn't wait for an answer but stood and lifted the tea tray, cups and teapot included, and walked off with them.

It was at that point that Max and Martha both began to think something was wrong with her, and their exchanged glances conveyed as much. Mrs Rice wasn't behaving as they thought she might. She seemed lost, bewildered, even. Surely she'd want any help possible to find her husband?

Max took the opportunity to wander around the room, glancing at the photographs and at the books on the shelves.

There were plenty of photographs dotted around, many of them depicting Rice in service. Some were formal portraits of him in dress uniform, but many were of him on active service, standing erect alongside comrades or before a foreign field. Max saw one with Rice and Palgrave together, both young subalterns, tanned, confident. They were standing next to a pale mud hut in what Max assumed was Sudan, or somewhere near. In Palgrave's hand was a brutal-looking sword – a kaskara.

Then Max saw a book lying on the sideboard. Its spine had been cracked to keep the book open. Max had a closer look, and saw that one page had been dog-eared. He lifted the book and read the lettering on the spine.

With shaking hands, Max read the dog-eared page. There was a single word written in the margin and, in that word, Max's greatest fear became confirmed.

Max replaced the book and went back to his seat. In a quiet voice, he said, "I think I'm in trouble."

"What?"

"Rice has a book. It's over there. It's a history of the Guards in the war. There's an account of my Military Cross, and Palgrave's death, and one word written in the margin.

"Which word?"

Max took a breath and said, "Lies."

"Oh, Max."

"I think Inspector Longford was right. I think Rice was investigating my account of Palgrave's death, and I think he might have something to prove the truth."

Just as Martha was about to reply, Mrs Rice came back with more tea, and some biscuits. "Help yourselves," she said.

"Mrs Rice," Max said, "can you tell us anything at all about why your husband was in Peterborough or—"

He almost said 'or London', and realised just in time that if he admitted to knowing that, she'd wonder why. He said, "—or whether he'd had any business recently with old army colleagues?"

"Old army colleagues? My husband retired a long time ago, young man. He occasionally sees General Monroe; they were friends, you know. But nobody else, I believe. He lost his other friends."

Max sighed and nodded. This was proving more difficult than he'd expected. Either Rice had told his wife nothing, or she simply wasn't prepared to tell a stranger.

After her third cup of tea, Martha had to excuse herself for a few minutes.

"Upstairs," Mrs Rice said. "Last door on the right."

With Martha gone, Max found that Mrs Rice became more introverted, not even looking at him as she nibbled on biscuits.

Max was trying to shape a question that might not seem too onerous or perplexing for Mrs Rice. He was still framing the question when a doorbell sounded.

"I wonder who that could be," Mrs Rice said.

She left the room. Max heard her open the door and mutter to someone. He heard a man's voice mutter back. Then the door closed.

When Max looked up, Mrs Rice entered the room, a grim expression on her face. Max was about to ask her whether anything was wrong, but he didn't need to. Behind

Mrs Rice were two police constables, and they didn't look like they'd been invited for tea.

"I know who you are, Mr Dalton," Mrs Rice said. "And I know you killed my husband."

Max jumped up, but there was nowhere to go. The two constables rushed forward, each grabbing and holding one of his arms.

Then Martha came out of the kitchen and walked into the sitting room. "I hope you don't mind..." she said, stopping suddenly when she saw the policemen.

"Martha," Max said, "run."

"What?"

One of the coppers had turned now and had seen Martha.

"She's part of it," Mrs Rice said, stretching an accusing arm and finger towards Martha.

"She's a killer."

Chapter Thirty-Four

Martha burst out of the house and past the police car parked outside. She ran along the cobbled street for two minutes, before half-collapsing against the side of a tall flint wall.

She felt faint, her heart hammering in her chest. She was hot from the run, and yet the air was cold, reaching into her skin and freezing her throat. She'd left her handbag in the hotel, and her coat at Mrs Rice's.

She had to think. She was scared.

She looked back to see if she was being followed, but there was nothing that way except the street and houses, and an old man on a bicycle, slowly cycling away from her.

She needed to recover her breath, to calm down. And *think*.

When she looked around her, she realised she was next to the cathedral. She gathered herself, walked calmly towards it and, entering, took a seat at the back of the nave.

She went into herself, leaned forward in her seat.

Some of the people in the cathedral had noticed her, but to them she was simply a young woman praying ardently, perhaps for a husband who'd been posted to a far-flung part of the empire, perhaps for her child, sick with some life-threatening illness.

In fact, she was trying desperately to think through the course of events that had led to her fleeing to this sanctuary, and which had deposited her on a seat in Lincoln Cathedral with her hands clutching each other while her brain fought her panic.

Mrs Rice came into her mind. They'd been right to suspect something was wrong. So, she'd known of Major Rice's death before they'd arrived. That meant the police in London now knew, and most likely suspected Max, and Martha, of involvement. Well, that would make sense; there were witnesses who could place them in the hotel.

"Damnation," Martha said, a little too loudly, causing one young cleric to glance at her sternly.

She sat up, opened her eyes. "Of course," she said to herself.

She was thinking about Mrs Rice's appearance, and how incongruous it seemed with the idea that she'd just learned of her husband's death. But if she'd found out only today or the day before, then she might not have prepared a black dress. That piece of Whitby jet jewellery, though, was an indicator. It was a mourning brooch, and Martha had seen it and hadn't made the connection, and now Max was in police custody as a result.

"I'm an idiot," she said aloud.

She was starting to think clearly now. She had to get back to London, speak to her parents, and to Mr Pork. First, she needed to get back to the hotel, change into something more practical and collect their bags. She'd settle the bill and make her way to the station. She'd get the first train to London.

Everything would be all right. They hadn't done anything wrong, after all. And innocent people didn't have anything to fear, did they?

She felt a terrible sickening feeling inside, in her stomach and her heart.

A couple of hours later, she was sitting in the station tea room, smoking a cigarette and forgetting the tea, which was getting cold on the table in front of her. She hadn't wanted a drink, but she had to have something to make her appear normal. She didn't think she'd ever want tea again after that experience with Mrs Rice who, clearly, had delayed them for as long as possible, awaiting the arrival of the police.

Then, as Martha was sitting, gazing vaguely at the people coming and going and coming again, she saw two things that changed the whole situation. The first thing she saw was a man called Ronald Kirby, a plumber's mate, who was seated on a wooden bench, reading a newspaper.

Chapter Thirty-Five

Max was feeling the cold in his bones. The cell was concrete-grey and damp, with a single bare light bulb hanging eight feet above him and a wooden bench along one side. There was a heavy iron door, painted to match the concrete-grey of the walls, ceiling and floor. In this door was a small glazed eyehole. It was a holding cell; no windows and no sink.

After the policemen had taken him into the station, a desk sergeant had noted his name, date of birth and home address and then, leaving for a moment to confer with another, presumably more senior colleague, had returned and said to the accompanying officers, "Right, put him in three."

So, here, in cell number three, Max had sat and waited and shivered with cold and fear while the greyness around him crept into his bones and made him shiver more.

After a couple of hours, the door creaked open and Max looked up to see the imposing figure of Inspector Longford standing behind the duty sergeant. Longford was wearing a dark overcoat and a trilby hat. The fact that he didn't remove them told Max what was going to happen.

"I'm afraid your solicitor won't be able to rescue you this time," Longford said. "If he even knows where you are, it'll take him a few hours to get here."

"Why am I here?" Max said, his voice trembling more than he would've wished. "You haven't arrested me."

"You've been arrested, sir, by the Lincolnshire Constabulary. I asked them to do that on my behalf. You'll be formally charged when we get back to Scotland Yard."

With that, Inspector Longford reached into his coat pocket and removed a pair of handcuffs. He unlocked them using a small key, which he kept on the end of his fob chain. He locked one half of the handcuffs over his own right wrist and secured the other half over Max's left wrist.

"There's a car outside. It'll take us to the station. Do you need anything before we go?"

Max shook his head.

"All right, then," Inspector Longford said as he followed the sergeant out of the cell with Max unable to do anything except trail behind.

The journey to the station went past in a blur. Max felt as though he were caught in some invisible trap, condemned by unknown forces. Longford's silence made the situation worse. Although Max preferred silence to anything else at that moment, he assumed that Longford's silence meant he must've been feeling confident of his suspicions. But perhaps this was another of Longford's tactics.

The two men received the occasional second glance from commuters at the station who'd spied the handcuffs, but, to Longford's credit, he walked closely by Max's side, keeping his hand low and maintaining discretion. Indeed, the two men, both well dressed, both tall and broad-shouldered, seemed more like colleagues than policeman and prisoner.

Longford had already purchased a ticket for Max, and, once aboard the train, they moved along the narrow corridor until they found an empty smoking compartment. Longford closed the door behind them, and they sat.

Longford removed his hat, which he put on the seat opposite, then took his pipe and a packet of tobacco from his coat pocket. When he'd lit the pipe, Max took out a cigarette. Longford struck a match for him.

"Thanks," Max said, blowing the smoke at the door.

The whistle sounded and the train jerked a couple of times, then moved off slowly, lurching and gradually picking up speed.

There was a smell of soot and stale smoke in the compartment. It was cold, and the windows were coated in nicotine, making it dim inside, hardly more than an extension of the prison cell.

Longford had finished smoking and now removed a brown paper bag from his coat pocket. He unwrapped a ham and mustard sandwich, offering half to Max, who declined.

"This goes all the way through to London," Longford said. "So if you want to get some sleep, sir, you could rest against the window."

"I'm all right."

They moved through the centre of Lincoln, and then into the suburbs, rows of houses and gardens passing quietly, as if asleep. Then into the working part of town, industry and dirt. They passed factories and warehouses, some abandoned because of the lack of trade. They passed men in flat caps and hobnail boots, lifting and loading and pushing.

Finally, they left all that behind and entered the countryside.

Max watched the flat, bleak land speed by. He liked train journeys. He liked to watch the world go by as the soporific rhythm of the wheels on the track lulled him. Now, though, that rhythm merely signalled his destination.

In spite of himself, Max did begin to doze and was only half-conscious of the stops and starts as the train pulled into stations like Essendine and Little Bytham, small bleak places where the sky and fields were different shades of grey and the grass was greyer than both and the wind blew across the flat landscape, blasting the people on the platforms with icy gloom. The train would grind to a halt and pick up a handful of travellers before rolling off again to the station master's whistle.

Max opened his eyes and looked around him, taking a moment to slide out of the waking-dream state. When he saw Longford, emptiness opened up inside.

"We've just passed through Peterborough," Longford said. "You've been asleep an hour or so."

"Have I?"

Max lit a cigarette and sat up in his seat. He looked out of the window, but now the view didn't seem so peaceful, and his destination was too close. After a while, he turned to Longford and said, "Do you really think I'm a murderer?"

Longford looked at the bowl of his pipe, then tapped it out on the bottom of his heel. He started to refill the pipe with tobacco. "I just follow the evidence, sir," he said. "And I think you're lying about something."

"That doesn't make me a murderer."

"No, but until I can eliminate you from the inquiry, I have to follow what I have. Besides, more has come to light since we last spoke, and it doesn't help your cause any."

"What more?"

Longford put a match to his pipe, sucked in several times and finally exhaled the blue-grey smoke. He looked at Max. "When we reported to you that the deceased was called Crawford, you claimed not to know of him."

"And I didn't."

"I might've believed you except that we've since discovered you went to a hotel called the Alderney, on Ebury Street. We have two eyewitnesses who describe a couple, whom we believe to be you and your wife. At this hotel, you gained access to a room occupied by a Daniel Burton. We now know that Crawford was, in fact, Daniel Burton. He's been positively identified. So, my question to you is how would you know where to look for Burton if you didn't know he was Crawford?"

"I didn't know. I suspected, but only towards the end of my interview with you. After that, I thought about it and decided that it was possibly Burton who'd been killed."

"I see. In that case, why you didn't correspond these suspicions to the police?"

"Well, I wasn't sure, you see. I thought I'd see whether I could find Burton and then I'd know for sure whether it was him. If it was, I'd have contacted you, naturally."

"I see. So, at this point you still thought it might have been the case that your friend was alive and well?"

"Yes. Precisely."

"In that case, may I ask you why you didn't ask the receptionist at the hotel to call Mr Burton's room? Or why you didn't go up and knock on his door?"

"I…"

"Because, sir, it looks suspicious that you didn't do either of these things, if you suspected he might be alive. In fact, one of our eyewitnesses states that you claimed to be Burton, and it therefore looks more suspicious that you went up with the sole intention of entering the room. After all, if he'd been alive, you might have burst in upon him. That's not how you behave with your friends, is it, sir?"

Max didn't have an answer for that. Of course, Longford was right. He'd been stupid to try to get access to Burton's hotel room, and then even more stupid to gain access fraudulently.

"There is another point to make, sir," Longford said, hardly allowing Max the chance to consider a plausible excuse for the hotel incident. "If you knew Mr Burton was staying at the hotel, and you suspected he might be the deceased, why didn't you mention him to us when we questioned you the second time?"

"Well, I didn't think—"

"Because, again, it does look suspicious, doesn't it? I mean, we did ask you to give us an account of your whereabouts on Friday night, and we asked for the names of anyone who could collaborate your story, and yet you didn't once mention Daniel Burton. Why was that?"

"I'm not sure. I didn't remember that night too well."

"But your memory returned."

"No. I mean, yes."

"That's convenient, sir."

Max clenched his jaw. He wasn't helping his cause. But Longford wasn't finished. He said, "Apparently, nobody had been in the room for a few days. There was a 'Do Not Disturb' sign on the door, so the maid left it. After your visit, the receptionist became suspicious and informed his manager. Only then was the door opened. What do you think they found, sir?"

Max knew, of course, and his blood ran cold with the knowledge, and with the fear of his position. Longford didn't wait for an answer. He said, "They found the body of a man, sir. And they called the police, and that's when we discovered that the dead man was Major Frederick Rice."

"That doesn't mean I killed him. He was dead already."

"If you'd found him dead, sir, why didn't you contact the police yourself? You see, at the very least you're guilty of failing to inform the police of a crime."

Longford took a handkerchief from his coat pocket and blew his nose. He took his time doing it. When he'd put the handkerchief back in his pocket, he said, "Then there's that strange comment from General Monroe. Now, you admit that he was your battalion commander during the war, and Rice was a company commander in the same battalion, and you were a lieutenant in another company of the same battalion."

"Yes, I admit all those things."

"Then why would General Monroe tell us that Rice had nobody to fear except you? After all, sir, we couldn't have a more unimpeachable character witness than General Monroe – Chief of the Imperial General Staff."

"Why don't you ask him?"

"We did. But I'd like to hear you explain it to me."

Max was quiet for a while, considering how much he should reveal. He knew he should wait for Mr Bacon, or some other lawyer. But he also knew he was in a lot of trouble, and Longford's suspicions were increasing. Indeed, they were becoming certainties.

Max said, "In war, people do things that otherwise would seem wrong. That was a bad war, and lots of men did things that they'd be ashamed of in other circumstances."

The inspector considered what Max had said and, in a soft, measured tone, said, "I'm a civilian policeman. Anything that happened in the war would be out of my jurisdiction, even if I could prove it."

"Monroe was friends with a couple of the company commanders. Something happened once, and I think he suspects me of… killing one of them."

"And Major Rice?"

"He was another of the man's friends. They were old campaigners, and they'd known each other for years."

"And, of course, they were officers."

"Yes."

"And upper-class, one would imagine."

"Does that have any bearing?"

Longford didn't answer that question. Instead, he sat and sucked on his pipe for a while. Then he said, "I admire your honesty, Mr Dalton. Although…"

"Although what?"

Longford looked at his pipe and tapped the embers down with his matchbox, which brought Max's handcuffed hand up. "Well, as I said, I'm a civilian policeman. What happened in the war isn't my concern, unless it relates to something in the civilian world. Unfortunately, sir, you've just given me a reason why you'd want to kill Mr Burton and Mr Rice. You've given me a motive."

"What do you mean? What motive?"

Longford cleared his throat and said, "For instance, blackmail."

"What? That's insane."

"Not at all. Suppose Major Rice had some financial problems. He might hit upon the idea that he could blackmail you, the husband of a wealthy woman, and a man with a solid reputation to maintain. He might realise that he and Burton together would be able to provide enough evidence against you, and that you would be forced to pay them. Then, having understood their plans, you might have realised that your only course of action would be to kill them. All the evidence fits such a hypothesis. And you yourself have admitted that Rice, and, indeed, General Monroe, suspect you of murder."

"You can't be serious."

Longford was just about to explain that he was serious when the compartment door opened. Both men looked up and saw a young woman standing in the doorway. She was wearing a grey trouser suit and carrying something large in her hands.

"Martha?" Max said.

"Mrs Dalton," the inspector said.

Martha took a step, raised a large cast iron wrench and dropped it on Inspector Longford's head.

"Ouch," he said, furiously rubbing his head.

"Sorry," Martha said, hitting him again.

"Ouch. Madam… Mrs Dalton, will you *please* stop doing that."

"I have to," she said.

"Martha—" Max said.

"I'm going to have to arrest you for striking—"

Martha swung the wrench again, but Longford dodged it. The wrench slipped from Martha's grip and landed on Longford's foot.

"Ow, my bloody foot," he said, followed by another exclamation that was less constrained, and more anatomical.

"I'm really sorry," Martha said.

Longford's face was red with fury.

Then Martha kicked him in the shin.

He jumped up out of his seat, slammed his head in the luggage rack, and fell, unmoving, to the floor, pulling Max down with him.

Martha stared, her hand over her mouth, her eyes wide. "Oh, my God, I've killed him. I've killed him."

"Calm down, Martha."

"We're all going to hang. Quick, we have to run for it. Come on, Max. Max."

"I'm handcuffed to him. I can't run."

"What are we going to do? Max, what are we going to do? He's dead. He's *dead*."

Just then, the door slid open. Martha looked over and was surprised to see old Mr Tomlinson who, ashen-faced, was staring at the scene before him and clutching his chest. He staggered away. "Ooh, that was dear old Mr Tomlinson," Martha said.

"What? Who?"

"Oh, no. He's going to get the guards. He's going to squeal, he's going to dob us in, Max."

"You're talking gibberish."

"We're going to be caught. We have to go. Now. Max. Max!"

"I have to get out of these handcuffs."

"Cut his arm off," Martha said desperately.

"You're panicking."

"I'm not panicking," Martha screamed. "Cut his arm off. Cut all his arms off."

"The keys are attached to his fob."

Martha scrambled to find the inspector's watch and followed the fob chain, finding the keys attached to the end, in his waistcoat pocket. Her hands were shaking as she tugged at the chain.

"Calmly, Martha."

"Yes. Nora Charles."

"What?"

"*The Thin Man*, remember?"

"Get a grip, for God's sake."

Calmly, Martha stretched the chain over to Max's wrist and unlocked the cuffs.

"Actually," Max said, rubbing his wrist, "I think it's more like *The Thirty-Nine Steps* now. That makes me Robert Donat."

"You remind me of Robert Donat. Who am I, by the way?"

"Madeleine Carroll. Now, let's get out of here."

"I don't feel very well."

"You're in shock. Take a deep breath."

Having released his wrist from the handcuffs, Max attached the empty cuff to the metal leg of the seat, which was securely screwed into the train floor. He then pulled down the window and threw the key out. "Right," he said. "What now?"

"What would Robert Donat do?"

"Robert Donat can't help us now."

"I mean, what did he do in *The Thirty-Nine Steps*?"

"Uh, they stopped the train on the Forth Bridge, and Robert Donat escaped."

"A bridge, Max," she cried. "We need a Forth Bridge. Where is it?"

Max grabbed Martha by the shoulders and turned her to face him. "You're hysterical. Will you for God's sake calm down."

Martha, breathing hard, looked directly, and with some anger, at Max. "If you slap me, I'll turn you in myself."

"I'm not going to slap you. Are you calm?"

"I think I'm going to faint."

"You're not going to faint. Now, hold on to something."

He went into the corridor, grabbed the communications cord and yanked it down.

The train screeched and juddered to a stop. Further along the corridor, there were angry shouts, a woman screamed, things crashed to the floor.

Max opened the door and jumped from the train on to the side of the tracks, then lifted Martha down.

They were at the edge of a grass field. Max helped Martha over the wooden fence, and they started to walk quickly towards a road in the distance.

"I bet you're glad I brought my trouser suit now," Martha said.

Along the train, people were opening windows and peering out, pointing at the two fugitives. Martha turned briefly and caught sight of an elderly man, his head out of the window, breathing heavily as though in some physical distress.

"Oh, look," Martha said, "it's old Mr Tomlinson."

Old Mr Tomlinson happened then to see Martha and Max.

"It's all right," Martha shouted to him, "we didn't cut his arms off."

Chapter Thirty-Six

Once at the road they walked south and managed to flag down a small flatbed truck carrying engine parts. The driver was a grizzled fellow with unkempt dark hair and a face of thick stubble. He emanated an odour most commonly associated with livestock. Martha, however, didn't seem to notice.

In fact, she was very quiet over the course of the journey, shivering now and then, either from the cold or from delayed shock. Max put his arm around her shoulders and held her close.

The driver dropped them in the centre of Huntingdon before continuing his journey, taking his excessive craniofacial hair and strange anatomical smell with him.

Now Martha and Max were in the far corner of a small tea house in Huntingdon, along a quiet street just off the market square.

"He was very nice," Martha said, "that driver."

"He wasn't nice, Martha."

"He brought us here. He could've dropped us anywhere."

"He brought us here because the three of us were squashed in the cabin, and you were sitting next to him."

"Oh."

They shared a cheese sandwich and a pot of tea. Money was becoming an issue and, since they'd had to abandon all their luggage, they were ill prepared for flight.

"What are we going to do, Max?"

"I don't know."

Martha hugged herself. "Well, I suppose it could be worse," she said. "We're together, at least. And you're not in prison."

"How did you find me, anyway?"

"I decided I had to get back to London, speak to Mr Ham. So, I checked out of the hotel in Lincoln, went to the station and sat in the tea room while I waited for the train. And I saw you and the inspector."

"I see. And that weapon you used? The wrench?"

"There was a man there, on the station concourse. And he had a bag of tools, and the wrench was poking out of the top. When I saw you, I got up to follow, but then I thought that Inspector Longford might have you handcuffed. So, I bought the wrench from this fellow. And... well, here we are."

Max smiled, leaned forward and kissed her. "We can't go back to London," he said, "not without knowing what we're going to do. The police will be looking for us."

"Can we call Mr Bacon?"

"Maybe, but if the police asked him anything, he'd be obliged to tell them. He's an honest man."

"But he's your solicitor. He can't divulge information to the police."

"He can if that information obstructs an ongoing investigation."

Martha sighed. "We can't stay here, and we can't go anywhere else. What are we going to *do*?"

"We need to figure it out."

"Can we?"

"I don't know."

"I'm scared."

"So am I."

They were both quiet for a long time. They could hear a tinny radio, far off in the kitchen. It was playing music from one of the big bands, but it was too faint and distorted to make out. After a while, Max lit a cigarette. Then he looked at Martha and said, "Thank you, by the way."

"For what?"

"For rescuing me."

"Any wife would do the same."

"I don't think that's true."

He watched the smoke curl and became lost in the beauty of it. "I remember when I first fell in love with you," he said quietly, dreamily. "It was at a party. I can't recall whose, someone rich in St John's Wood. It was the second time I'd seen you. You moved like the flame of a candle in still air, and as the men fluttered around you, I felt such a sadness, the grief of loss. I watched as you walked past me and then I looked down at my drink. I was smart enough to know how stupid I'd have looked if I approached you. And stupid enough to think I was smart. I've never told you that, have I?"

"You've told me lots of times, Max, but always when you're drunk. And I never quite understand it all. You fell in love with me because I looked like a candle." She smiled.

"That wasn't why," Max said. "That's what attracted me to you, certainly – your calm beauty. But that wasn't why I fell in love with you."

"Oh? What was it?"

"On this night, at this rich person's party, a small boy came into one of the rooms. It was the child of the hosts, and he'd woken up and come searching for his mother or father, and he couldn't find them and was crying. You went over to him and crouched down and spoke to him. Then you took him by the hand and left the room. Half an hour later, I wondered where you were so I walked around the place, went from room to room. And I couldn't find you. Then I went upstairs and I saw a door ajar and I looked in and you were sitting on the end of this boy's bed, reading to him. And he was fast asleep, but you still kept on reading."

He was looking at Martha now and it seemed to her that Max was that boy, lost and alone.

"I never told anyone that before," he said. "No one has ever known. You see, everyone thinks I married you because you're beautiful or rich or elegant, or because you know everyone, or because you're smart and witty. But I didn't. I married you because I loved you, and I loved you because you feel pain when you see others hurt, even if you pretend you don't really care about anything."

"I didn't know whose party it was," Martha said. "So I couldn't take him to his parents because I didn't know who they were and I couldn't very well ask anyone whose party it was. That would've been rude."

A police constable entered the tea shop and approached the counter, desperately in need of a strong cuppa. As was his habit upon entering a public place, the bobby scanned the customers, just in case there were fugitive killers among them. He saw the young couple in the corner, and smiled wistfully as he watched them, their foreheads touching each other, the man's hand on the woman's cheek. The policeman slid a threepenny bit over to the girl behind the counter and took his tea to a table, far away from the young lovers.

"It's my fault you're involved in this," Max said.

"There's nowhere I'd rather be."

Chapter Thirty-Seven

It was getting dark, and they still didn't know what to do. They were wandering slowly, arm in arm, along the bank of the Great Ouse, the ancient stone bridge at their backs.

Max had called Sheridan Lyle, but he'd had nothing new to tell them.

"It's all gone quiet," Lyle had said. "Which scares the hell out of me. The old man has disappeared somewhere, but he left orders to leave the story."

"So, they're keeping out of it," Max explained to Martha. "Even my own paper thinks I'm guilty."

They passed a huddled figure wrapped in a blanket, a fishing rod reaching out to the dark, oily, slow-moving water.

"I keep thinking about those men who tried to break into the flat," Max said. "Why? What were they after?"

"They must've thought you had something."

"Yes, but why?"

"Well, surely they thought Burton gave you something, and they wanted it."

Max thought about that. "Perhaps he intended to, but didn't have the opportunity. Then there's Crawford, whoever he is."

They continued in silence for a while.

"There's something that connects everything," Max said. "That's what we need to find. So far, I'm the only link."

"Not just you, darling. The past – that's a link."

"Yes. And that scares me. Come on, let's get a drink."

"We'd better find somewhere to stay the night."

"Sure, somewhere with a bar."

The place they found was an hotel situated alongside the bridge. It was a cosy place with a small pub-like lounge and bar, and those low beams that Martha thought were quaint, but which annoyed Max because he had to keep ducking under them.

They picked a table in the corner, from which Max could survey everyone who came into the place. They ordered a small meal, neither being in a hungry mood. Afterwards, they sat and smoked and sipped wine, which the young barman was eager to replenish.

"Let's go through it again," Max said. "One thing at a time, everything we know for certain, only now we'll start way back. We're going to start with the war. So, first, Burton and I were in the same company, and Rice was in the same battalion. We fought together at a number of battles. I was friends with Burton, but not Rice. I haven't seen or heard from either of them since the end of the war. Now, for some reason, Rice meets up with Burton, and the two of them go to Peterborough, where they're supposed to meet a third man, called Crawford, who doesn't arrive."

He considered what he'd just said and sighed. "This is like a labyrinth. The further in we go, the more we get lost."

"We need a new approach," Martha said. "We need to think about things logically. I'm sure we have the information, it's just that we don't know how to use it. We need to be like Nick and Nora Charles, remember? Let's *think*, Max."

Max took a deep breath. "If I'm going to have to think, I'll need a pint of best."

He slid his wine over to Martha and ordered a beer. When it came, he lit a cigarette, leaned back and said, "I think we can assume that Rice went to see Burton with the express purpose of bringing him to Peterborough to meet Crawford. That explains Rice's visit to Burton's house and also why Burton intended to be away for only one day. Furthermore, we know it must've been an important meeting because Burton wore his silver cufflinks and best suit, and because he didn't introduce Rice to his wife."

"I don't follow."

"The idea of introducing Major Rice to Lilly clearly didn't enter Burton's head. Thus, the nature of the meeting must've been such that something that he would otherwise not fail to do became merely a triviality, which wasn't at the forefront of his mind."

"All right," Martha said. "But, why Peterborough?"

"Well, we know it's close to Burton and en route to London for Rice."

"So why didn't Burton and Rice meet at King's Cross or at the hotel, or wherever? That would've been logical for both men."

"Um… well…"

As Max was considering this question, Martha's face lit up. She said, "Suppose it was Crawford?"

"What?"

"We're thinking about Rice and Burton. But we've neglected Crawford. He was supposed to be at Peterborough. So what if it was more convenient, or even safer, for Crawford to meet there? And that would explain why they chose the station hotel. To make it as easy as possible for Crawford."

"Yes, that makes sense. We know from Rice's actions that there was urgency about the meeting, otherwise he wouldn't have gone to Wisbech – he'd have simply wired Burton to meet him at Peterborough."

"And Rice booked the hotel rooms," Martha said, "so he must've had a reason for choosing Peterborough."

She paused for a moment, her brow scrunched up in concentration. "You said that Rice was logical, even-tempered."

"I said he was dull too. But, yes. He was the kind who could've formed square and turned it on a pinwheel while screaming Beja hurtled towards them."

"I have no idea what you're talking about."

"He was logical and calm under pressure."

"Good. That means if he booked the hotel in Peterborough for a reason, it was probably a logistical one."

"Maybe. So what?"

"If we use Peterborough as the centre of a circle, and Lincoln as the end of the radius, we can draw an area approximately where Crawford might have been. If Rice was dull and logical like you say, isn't that the sort of thing he'd do?"

"Yes."

Martha's eyes were sparkling fire. Her cheeks were flushed. She said, "Let me have a map, Max."

Max went to find the hotel receptionist and returned with a tourist map of England with pictures of castles and cathedrals and that sort of thing. "It's to scale," he said, "so it'll do."

They cleared the table and unfolded the map. Martha took a pin from the scarf she was wearing around her neck. She untied her shoe and removed a shoelace. Then, holding the end of the shoelace so that it touched the map at the point of Lincoln, she put the pin into the map at the point where it indicated Peterborough. She then moved the shoelace in a circle, scoring the circumference with her fingernail. "There," she said proudly.

Max looked at the circle, "It's too big, Martha. Look at all the places the circle includes: Leicester, Coventry, north London, Cambridge. Half of it's in the North Sea."

"We don't want what it includes, fool. We only want to know the places on the circumference. It's the distance to the middle of the circle that matters. If Peterborough was central for Rice, Burton and Crawford, then Crawford's location must be somewhere around this circumference."

She scrutinised the map for a moment, looking at all the places on her circumference, and said, "I admit, this probably doesn't help us much."

"Maybe we're making too many assumptions."

"No, we're not. We're making logical deductions."

"I stand corrected. I apologise for my earlier comment regarding the female mind. I now see that it's extraordinarily logical, and brilliant."

"Thank you."

Now that Martha had again invoked the characters of Burton and Rice to aid deduction, Max was beginning to appreciate that her mind worked, in many ways, much better than his. Yes, perhaps it was true that a man's mind was better at logic, but if it was equally true that a woman's mind was more emotionally attuned, it stood to reason that Martha would be able to understand a person's actions better and, as such, she'd be better able to infer certain facts.

For some reason, Max now found his mind revisiting Rice's house. And something was nagging him about it. Something to do with this emotional logic of Martha's. But the scene was nebulous and refused to cohere.

"You know," Martha said, "I've been thinking about their clothes."

"Huh?"

"Pay attention, Max. Burton didn't take a change of clothes to Peterborough, and he told his wife he'd see her first thing. To me, that means first thing tomorrow."

"You think he only intended to stay one night."

"I'm sure of it. Then there's his attire. He wore his best suit and Guards cufflinks. That bothers me."

"What? Wearing his Sunday suit?"

"Yes, and the cufflinks."

"He probably wanted to impress Rice. After all, Rice was a battalion CO."

"No, it's more than that. Look, when a woman goes out, she likes to dress well, but she'd only ever wear her best dress or a priceless diamond brooch if she were trying to impress someone. A Sunday suit and his silver-plated cufflinks were Burton's equivalent of a beautiful gown and that diamond brooch. But why would he be trying to impress Rice?"

"Um."

"What if it wasn't Rice he was trying to impress? Who else was he supposed to meet?"

"You mean Crawford?"

"Yes. That's significant."

"I see what you mean. It's like Rice summoned him to meet Crawford, and Burton took it so seriously that he wore his top clobber. That means Crawford is someone important. And Rice wanted Burton to meet him. And then Burton was to return home the next day."

They were both quiet for a while, soaking in the information, trying to make sense of it.

"You have a Guards tie, don't you?" Martha said.

"Yes. And a tie pin."

"Well, when would you wear those?"

"To a ceremony of some sort, I suppose, or a Guards reunion."

"Obviously, neither of those is the case here."

"You know," Max said, "about ten years ago I was trying to make my living as a writer, and it wasn't paying enough. So I decided I'd better get a job of some sort. I looked in the paper and saw a position for a bank clerk. I went into the branch and met the manager and applied for the position, and I got a formal interview. The manager was a stuffy sort, all whiskers and popping veins, but I was determined to impress him. That was the last time I wore my Guards tie and pin."

"I didn't know you worked in a bank."

"I didn't. It turned out the manager was an old navy man, hated the army."

"An interview," Martha said thoughtfully. "So, why book a room for the night?"

"They must've expected the meeting to take some time."

Martha said, "It sounds like they didn't know what they were looking for."

"Yes," Max said decisively. "That's exactly what it seems like. So, an interview, perhaps, with Crawford, but one in which Crawford wasn't sure what he was looking for."

"That would fit the facts perfectly."

"Doesn't help us, though. I mean, why would Burton have an interview with this Crawford chap?"

"I thought you were supposed to be some kind of journalist."

"I am some kind of journalist. I mean, I *am* a journalist."

"Well, then, don't journalists interview people who were present at an event?"

Max frowned and said, "You think Crawford's a journalist?"

Martha rolled her eyes. She said, "Often, I think you have the greatest mind of anyone I've ever known. And then you say something stupid like that. The point is that both Burton and Rice were present at the same place and the same time, during the war. Now, for what reason would someone want to interrogate those two men, together?"

"I've already given you a reason – Palgrave's death."

"*Other* than that," Martha said sternly. "Is there something we can do to try to find out?"

"Well, I suppose we could find other men in my old company. See if they can help us."

"Yes, of course. Oh, we're stupid, Max. We should've thought of that ages ago. Now, how do we go about finding them?"

"I've no idea."

Martha made that throaty growling noise, and Max realised he was close to being in trouble. So he said, "But I know someone who would: Mr Bacon. In which case, we need to get to London."

"Can't we telephone him?"

"They might be monitoring his calls."

"Is that legal?"

"I don't know. It's what they do in the pictures, though. They'd probably be monitoring our home, too."

"What about Alwyn?"

"Alwyn Frost? That stuffed shirt would turn me in quicker than he could sing the national anthem."

"Lindsey? No, he's no good. Um, my father. He'd help. I know he would."

"I think he would, but I don't think we can involve him. He's too old. Besides, your mother would find out and she'd turn me in faster than Frost would."

"You'd be surprised what my mother would do. But, yes, we can't involve them. What about telephoning Mr Hart?" Martha said.

"Who?"

"The chap at the dinner party. He likes you, even wants to talk about your books. He gave you his card, remember?"

"Yes. But, no. If he's a friend of Frost's he'll be one of those upright blokes, might turn us in."

"What about Flora?"

"No. They might have her under watch."

"What about Eric?"

"Flora's Eric?"

"Yes, he'd help. And he has access to a vehicle – his butcher's van."

Max considered this for a moment. Then he said, "Brilliant."

So Martha went off to find a telephone box from where she called Mr Stone's butcher shop. Of course, the butcher shop would be shut, but Mr Stone lived in the flat above.

While she was gone, Max tried to apply his reason to the situation, but, oddly, it didn't work for him alone as it did when he was with Martha, which, for a moment, amused him. Then the humour faded and was replaced by a warm feeling, and he wanted Martha to hurry back.

She did hurry back, and looked sheepish.

"Did you get through to Eric?" Max said.

"Yes."

"And will he come to pick us up?"

"Yes. Straight away. In Mr Stone's van."

"That's wonderful."

"It is, but… er…"

"What is it, Martha?"

"I had to buy some meat from Mr Stone, otherwise he said it wouldn't be economical."

"How much did you buy?"

CHAPTER THIRTY-SEVEN

"Well, all of it. Everything in the van. A lamb…"

"Oh, well."

"…and a pig. And half a cow."

"What?"

"It'll be delivered to any address we choose. So, I thought it best if Eric takes us to my parents'. I've telephoned my mother to tell her we would have to hide out there for a while."

Max sighed and said, "Oh, God. What did she say?"

"She wasn't very happy about it. She kept saying she didn't want a murdering fugitive in the house."

"I know we don't get on," Max said, "but that's a bit of an over-reaction, isn't it?"

"I told her you were innocent."

"That's a relief."

"Plus, I bribed her. The meat is hers."

Chapter Thirty-Eight

Mr Stone had told Martha that Eric would be a couple of hours, so Max and Martha moved into the hotel lounge, taking their map with them.

"You know," Martha said after a while, "when we were considering what Burton was wearing in Peterborough, we neglected something."

"Oh?"

"He was wearing the same clothes in London."

"So? He didn't go home, we know that. And if he hadn't brought a change of clothes, he would've had to wear the same things in London."

"You're missing the point. It's the urgency of it that's so puzzling. Crawford didn't turn up in Peterborough and instead of going home to collect some more things, Burton went straight to London, with Rice."

"I see what you mean. How does that help us?"

Martha shrugged and lit a cigarette. "And what about those two horrible men who tried to break into our flat?" Martha said. "We still don't know what they were up to."

"We have to assume they killed Rice and Burton, or were involved in it. If so, they would've searched the hotel room after they murdered Rice, and they must've searched Burton's body after killing him, and still they couldn't find what they wanted, so they came to our flat because they saw Burton talking to me."

"They don't know your relationship to Burton," Martha said. "Otherwise they'd be trying to question you. Or kill you."

"My head hurts."

After they'd gone over everything again, so that they felt thoroughly defeated, Max looked up and saw a young man in a woollen suit walking towards him. "There's Eric," Max said.

Then he spotted a young woman straggling in his wake. "Oh, no."

"Flora?" Martha said. "What are you doing here?"

"Eric called me up, ma'am. He told me what he was gonna do and I wanted to come along. I know you ain't killed no one, sir. I'm here to help."

"That wasn't a good idea," Max said.

"Plus," Flora was saying, "Eric refused to leave me behind. Said that he couldn't trust I wouldn't get snatched while he was gone."

"Flora told me what happened, sir," Eric said. "I know you didn't do it. I know it was them men, the ones who tried to take Flora."

Max was about to point out that nobody had tried to take Flora, but Martha squeezed his arm, which, as Max well knew, meant 'shut up'.

Max sighed and said, "Well, come on, let's go."

"Van's outside, sir," Eric said.

They traipsed out and saw the vehicle, painted dark green with the words 'Stone's Butchers, Lupus Street, Pimlico' followed by the telephone number. It was a very nice van, a Bedford, and only a few years old. However, there did seem to be one problem, which Martha expressed by stopping short and saying, "What on earth is that thing?"

Only at this point did Eric and Flora realise they'd made an error. The van was certainly very nice, and certainly very small. There was room in the cabin for two people, or three at a squeeze, but hardly four.

"We'll have to travel in the back," Max said.

"Ah," Eric said. "Um…"

Max opened the back doors, stared at the contents and said, "What the hell is that?"

"Well, sir," Eric said, "it's a whole lamb, whole pig and 'alf a cow."

"What?"

"Your meat, sir. All butchered, like Mrs Dalton wanted."

"You weren't supposed to bring it with you," Max said. "We only wanted the van."

Eric was quiet for a few seconds before saying, "Oh."

"Right," Max said, "we'll have to dump it."

"We'll do no such thing," Martha said. "Do you know how much that cost?"

Max felt they were all going mad. He said, "We're on the run from the police. I'm suspected of two murders, you've assaulted a Scotland Yard inspector and there are killers out there who probably want to do us harm. And you're worrying about the cost of a load of meat?"

"Well, it *is* my mother's. Are you going to tell her you threw it away?"

So, after much experimentation, it was decided that Max, as the tallest, should sit by himself, which necessitated that he drove the van. Then Martha squeezed next to him on the seat, with Flora wedged tightly between her and the door. Poor Eric had to content himself with curling up on the floor, his face squashed against Martha's legs. Flora glanced down at him now and then, to make sure he was okay, and was dismayed to see that he seemed perfectly content.

Finally, they pulled out, Max steering the van through Huntingdon and towards Godmanchester and ultimately the Great North Road, which would quickly take them back to London.

The Bedford was designed for light delivery work, and the total weight of four humans, a sheep, a pig and half a cow was testing it to the extent that the suspension was almost non-existent, which meant that every bump in the road shook their skeletons. Eric was especially suffering, and the appeal of lying close to Martha's legs had soon been superseded by the dismay of knowing there were sixty-odd miles of this bone-jarring journey left.

It was fully dark now, and there were heavy, thunderous clouds, blotting out any moonlight. The way to Godmanchester was narrow, the odd dim streetlamp and pale light from roadside cottages just enough to aid driving. A flurry of snow floated in the air and dotted the windscreen.

Once through Godmanchester, the road became twisting, and the high hedges on either side made it seem narrower still.

They made slow progress; each turn had to be contended with from a distance, otherwise, Max felt, the whole van was liable to tip over. So he went as fast as he could along the straights and slowed down when the headlights revealed a bend.

Then the road suddenly lit up as a car approached them fast from behind. Max said, "What the hell?"

He glanced in the wing mirror, and saw the car weaving left and right behind them, trying to find a gap through. Just as he was cursing the driver, he saw a flash and heard the crack of gunfire.

"Max?" Martha said.

Then Max saw a figure lean out of the open window of the car. He was a heavy-set man with a face that seemed spectrally pale. The man manoeuvred his shoulder and arm through the window and held out a pistol.

The shot was wide, but they all heard it smack into the bodywork.

"It's them," Max said.

"What?" Martha said. "How?"

"Must've followed Flora from the flat."

He glanced at Flora, who was staring resolutely straight ahead.

"They're going to kill us all," Martha said.

"No, they aren't. They're trying to shoot the tyres out."

"They're after Flora," said a muffled voice from the floor.

Flora let out a yelp.

Max said, "They are not after – oh, never mind."

Eric said, "They won't get her."

Max watched the car's headlights in his wing mirror. It was a big car, and powerful, something like a Ford V8.

"I can't outrun it."

The road was narrow, and Max was able to swerve, albeit slowly, from left to right.

Martha said, "Quick, Max. Go faster."

"I'm going as fast as I can."

"There," Martha said, pointing to something dark on the offside of the van.

"What?"

"A road. Too late."

Max was swinging the van more fervently now, which sent everyone squishing first left, then right, then left again. Flora, at the left of the seat, was periodically being squeezed senseless between Martha and the door.

"Ow, you bleedin'... ooof... bastar... uurgh..."

All everyone heard from her for a full minute were sounds approximating words of dubious content. Finally, Max swung the van around a corner so violently that Flora, Eric and Martha crashed as one heap into the side door.

After he straightened up, there was a sound like this: "Gefffoooomooooooffff."

"What was that?" Flora said.

"I think your foot is in Eric's mouth," Martha said.

Max, sweat now beading on his forehead, tried desperately to work out an escape. Sooner or later, they'd be forced off the road and the men in that car would have the time and means to do whatever they wanted.

"Look for a house or something," he said. "They won't kill us in front of witnesses, that's why they've waited until now."

"What if they kill the witnesses?" Martha said.

"A farm," Flora said. "They'd have guns."

"Yes," Max said. "Look for a—"

"There," Martha said, pointing at something to Max's right. "That was a farm."

"I didn't see it in time."

"I pointed it out to you."

"Darling," Max said between gritted teeth, "I can drive forwards and I can drive backwards, but I can't drive sideways."

There was a crunch and the van lurched forward, which made Martha say 'oof', while Eric let out a cry of pain and Flora said something unpleasant.

Then the high hedgerows disappeared, and the van entered the flat open countryside of the Fens. The road was straighter now, with only the occasional thin tree scattered along the sides.

"Damn," Max said.

"That was a road sign," Flora called out. "Offord Cluny, two miles."

"I can't hold them off for another two miles. They'll be able to overtake us now. We've had it."

"Yuuddarainitch," Eric said.

Max said, "What?"

"He said, 'use the drainage ditch'," Flora said.

"The drainage—?"

Max slammed on the brakes, sending all four of them crashing into the front of the cabin, hurling them into dashboard, steering wheel, glass and metal. Immediately, Max saw the lights of the chasing car swerve left as they tried to avoid piling into the van. Max put the van back into gear and pulled off as quickly as he could, which was very slowly.

After a hundred yards, he said, "Flora, look out of the window."

Flora wound the window down, stuck her head out and said, "They're in the ditch."

"Well done, Eric," Max said.

"Flwiedlehfle," Eric said.

Chapter Thirty-Nine

Seymour entered the sitting room pushing a trolley of tea and biscuits. He then walked out, leaving Mrs Webster to roll her eyes and serve everyone, including Eric and Flora, a task that didn't come easily to her. Furthermore, Seymour had forgotten to make the sandwiches, but Mrs Webster decided to overlook that fact; *she* certainly wasn't going to make them.

Eric dunked his biscuits, which elicited a nudge from Flora.

Mr Webster came into the room and said, "I telephoned Mr Bacon. He seemed upset at having his supper interrupted, but when I told him what the matter concerned, he said he'd get right to it. He should be here in half an hour or so."

"Thank you, Donald," Max said.

"I don't understand why the police let you go, Max," Mrs Webster said, pouring the tea.

"They didn't," Martha said. "I… uh…"

"Martha rescued me," Max said.

"You lammed it?" Mr Webster said, falling back into his fireside chair and raising his newspaper, the crossword of which he was still trying to do.

"Donald, I do wish you wouldn't use those crude terms."

"Nevertheless," Max said, "Donald's right."

"And how exactly were you able to rescue Max, darling?" Mrs Webster said.

"Uh, well, I walloped Inspector Longford."

"Walloped him?"

"On the head."

The tea had stopped flowing, and Max suspected, correctly, that Mrs Webster was going to have to sit down.

"With a wrench or spanner or whatever it's called."

"You hit a Scotland Yard inspector?"

"Yes. Like I said, on his head, and foot. I had to. And then we ran."

"She was magnificent."

Mrs Webster seemed to be on the point of fainting and had to put her cup and saucer on the small table to her side. "This is terrible, Martha. What will Mrs Dunaway think?"

"Hell with that old bat," Donald said.

"Donald, really."

"Well, I think it shows fine mettle. Moxie."

"Donald!"

"Thank you, Daddy."

Eric and Flora, sitting quietly and not daring to speak, were becoming bewildered by the chatter, and consequently had slurped more tea and crunched more biscuits than propriety would allow. Eric, in particular, was over-indulging in the biscuit area and had a coughing fit when he forgot that he wasn't dunking them, and had tried to swallow a large piece of shortbread without sufficient lubrication.

Fortunately, this episode, involving some hitting of the back and much conflicting advice, was forgotten with the arrival of Mr Bacon, who was also treated to tea and biscuits.

Max then explained to Mr Bacon that he wanted him to investigate the whereabouts of the men in his former company. "Obviously, I can't ask the police to help," he said.

"They're on the lam," Mr Webster said.

"Lamb, Bacon," Mrs Webster said. "It's very confusing."

Eric, now recovered from his biscuit incident, secretly agreed with the old lady.

Mr Bacon was about to point out that he wasn't a private investigator and wouldn't know how to go about it, but upon seeing the hopeful expression on Martha's face, said, "Of course, I'd love to help her – I mean help Mrs Shearer – I mean, yes, of course."

He took as many details as Max could provide and said, "I think you should all stay here for tonight. If the police ask me where you are, I'll be obliged to tell them, but they can only do that if they find me, and I'll make that awkward."

"Thank you," Max said.

"I'll contact you tomorrow."

Mr Bacon left, and Mr and Mrs Webster retired for the night. Eric took Flora to her parents' house, after which he returned the van to Mr Stone and returned the meat, which Martha had decided to pay for, thus compensating for the damage to Mr Stone's van.

"They're what?" Mr Stone said when Eric explained.

"Bullet holes. They tried to take Flora."

Chapter Forty

Max and Martha slept late the following morning. Max spent most of the afternoon pacing the library while he attempted to work out what was happening. Martha spent most of the afternoon trying to convince her mother not to turn him in.

Mr Bacon returned to the house at half past six that evening and met Max and Martha in the library.

"Have you discovered anything?" Martha asked Mr Bacon eagerly, taking his hat and coat.

"Yes."

They all sat. Martha and Max prepared themselves. Mr Bacon opened his briefcase and reached in. "Of the men in your company, sir, I've only been able to find out about fourteen. Unfortunately, I didn't have time to do any more, but I could continue tomorrow."

Max frowned. "Well, it's quite urgent," he said.

But Mr Bacon hadn't heard him. He was scanning the documents in his hands. "Beginning, then, with your platoon: David Beatty is a teacher in Aberdeen. He was a lance-corporal, I believe, at the end of the war. Ernest Russell is currently living in the United States of America. In somewhere called Greensboro, which is in North Carolina.

Third, there's Joshua McLaughlin, who is a carpenter in Hastings—"

"Mr Bacon," Max said sharply, "you don't need to tell us the details of those who are alive."

Mr Bacon nodded solemnly, cleared his throat and said, "This is where the information might become distressing to you, sir: William Halford, formerly a private, died in February this year of a heart attack."

"Halford?" Max said.

"Yes, sir," Mr Bacon said, looking up from his papers. "He was forty-four. He smoked and drank heavily, I believe."

"He did, yes. Damn. I didn't know he was gone."

"The family had a small service in Swindon. There was another death, sir," Mr Bacon said, running his finger down the page. "Clive Ward from Salisbury. He crashed his motorcycle two years ago. It seems that no other vehicles were involved. Finally, there's Alan Kent. He died in November of last year. There was an inquest in that case, and the coroner ruled it a suicide. It seems he had lingering shell shock, and his death followed shortly the death of his wife."

"Kent too?" Max said. "God."

Martha moved closer to her husband and put his hand into hers. "Three out of fourteen dead," she said. "Isn't that rather extraordinary, Mr Bacon?"

"I think it's uncommon."

"And two of the deaths were violent," Max said.

Mr Bacon replaced the documents in his briefcase, which he put under his arm. He removed his glasses and wiped them with a handkerchief. "That is more unusual, sir. Especially when you consider the recent death of Mr Burton. That makes four from your company, Mr Dalton, that we know of."

"Is it enough to go to Longford with?" Martha said.

"In itself, no. But we have been investigating the events of Friday night ourselves. Just an hour ago, I received a telegram in answer to one I despatched yesterday. It was from a tobacconist called Barnes who has a stand along Surrey Street. You're a regular customer, I believe, sir?"

"I know Mr Barnes. I often buy smokes there when I'm going past."

"Well, he clearly remembers you, sir. You bought a packet of cigarettes from him just a few minutes after Mr Burton left The Lion public house."

"How does that help us?" Max said. "It's not an alibi. I could've killed Burton and then gone for cigarettes."

"It's not an alibi, sir, no. It's his description of you that helps us."

"And what's that?" Martha said.

"I won't use his words, Mrs Shearer, if you don't mind. To paraphrase, he said Mr Dalton was so intoxicated that he could hardly stand. In fact, sir, he remembers you walking into a lamp post."

"I thought I felt a bump on my head."

Mr Bacon was frowning. He said, "I think we have enough to go and see Inspector Longford. I suggest nine o'clock tomorrow morning. Shall I meet you outside Scotland Yard at ten to?"

Max nodded, but wasn't paying much attention. "Mr Bacon," he said, "would you tell me again the names of the men from my company who had died?"

"Certainly, sir. William Halford, Clive Ward and Alan Kent."

"And Burton makes four."

"Yes, sir."

"And they were in your company?" Martha said.

"More than that, they were all in my platoon."

"How many men are in a platoon, sir?" Mr Bacon said quickly.

"It depends. But, on the whole, between thirty and forty, each commanded by a subaltern like me."

"So, if we consider that, perhaps, three-quarters of your platoon survived the war, that leaves, at most, thirty men."

"Thirty men," Max said. "And four of them dead in the last two years."

"And the ways they died," Martha said. "All suddenly: heart attack, suicide, motorcycle crash and murder."

Mr Bacon looked from Martha to Max, his expression sombre. "Now, that does seem extraordinary."

After Martha had thanked Mr Bacon and shown him out, she turned and looked at Max with dread in her heart. "Max?" she said. "Those men in your platoon. It's too much to be a coincidence, isn't it? And Burton too?"

"Yes."

"So why are you still alive, Max? Why you and not those men? There must be a reason. After all, if you had been a target, they could've killed you at any time. My God, they could've got you when they got Burton."

"Yes."

Max stared into empty space. This upset Martha, who knew it was that sadness again, washing over him, travelling from a deep part of the sea or, perhaps, from far back in the past.

"Perhaps it's not by accident," Martha said. "Perhaps you weren't on the list."

"What list?" Max said, only now looking at Martha.

"Well, the death list."

Chapter Forty-One

Inspector Longford had a bandage wrapped around his head when Max, Martha and Harold Bacon were admitted to his office.

Once Mr Bacon had presented his evidence, Longford agreed to release Max, for the time being, at least. "Don't leave London again," he said. "And tell me first if you find anything else."

He was more reluctant to drop the aggravated battery charge against Martha, but she told a story of how a wife had to believe in her husband's honour, and how she had a duty to defend that honour, no matter what. Then she appealed to the inspector's innate duty to defend an emotionally upset and vulnerable woman. Then she cried.

Logically, Martha's argument had holes, and nobody could have called her vulnerable, but her delivery was such that every man in the room melted with a desire to protect her.

The consequence of this was that Max and Martha were able to return to their flat. The inspector even laid on a car for them.

As soon as they got back to the flat, Eric and Flora arrived. Eric, determined that he wouldn't leave Flora unprotected, had brought her from her parents' house and had walked her up to the flat. He'd then stayed for a cup of tea and a few biscuits.

There was another knock on the door. Max and Martha looked at each other, each thinking the same thing: here's Longford again.

Max waved Flora to sit back down.

But it wasn't Longford. Not this time. It was Mr Hart, Alwyn Frost's friend from the dinner party. Then Max remembered that Hart had wanted to pop by some time, to discuss Napoleon or something. Max sighed with relief, and started to tell Hart that this wasn't a good time.

Instead, Hart pushed past him and, immediately upon doing so, removed a gun from his pocket and levelled it at Max. "I am sorry about this, Mr Dalton," Hart said, not looking at all sorry.

Two men followed him through the door. One was tall and thin, with a dangerous angular look to his face. The second man, also holding a pistol, was thickset with pale hair and a paler face. Eric looked at them and knew immediately who they were.

"They've come to take Flora," he cried, jumping up.

The fat man knocked Eric back with a backhanded swipe that cut Eric's lip.

Hart glanced at Eric, then at Flora and Martha, finally resting back on Max. "I had hoped that I would be able to explain the situation to you and get your cooperation but, after dining here, I saw that your views wouldn't allow you to… uh… reason with me."

"Reason with you?" Martha said. "What are you talking about? Who are you? And these… these hooligans, who are they?"

Max had moved backwards and was now standing next to Martha. He put a hand on her arm and said to Hart, "So that was the reason you invited yourself to our dinner?"

"What's happening, Max?" Martha said.

"It seems that Mr Hart here is in league with these two men who, I assume, are the ones who tried to break in a few days ago. Right, Eric?"

"That's 'em," Eric said, his face red and fierce.

"And Frost," Max said to Hart, "is he a part of this?"

"Frost's a fool," Hart said. "Most of the British government are fools. I learned, of course, that Frost knew you and your wife. Once we'd identified a suitable liaison, it was only a matter of gaining his confidence and infiltrating your little party. I simply met him in his club and started talking with him. As soon as I mentioned my interest in the history of the Napoleonic wars, he mentioned you."

"You met him in his club?" Martha said, incredulously.

"Yes. We have influential friends in England. It wasn't difficult to get into one of your gentleman's clubs. Of course, that alone meant that Frost would trust me. You are blind, you people. We are fighting a war and you are playing cricket and drinking tea."

"I think I can guess who you are, Mr Hart."

"Really?" Hart said, a small patronising smile on his small patronising face. "I'd be most impressed if you could. After all, none of your… authorities have identified me."

"You're Gestapo," Max said, "or some sort of ridiculous equivalent."

Hart's patronising smile fell away. In its place was the truth of the man. His eyelids lowered, his mouth spread wide and his lips thinned into a kind of snarl. "What makes you say that?" he said.

"It was what you said at the dinner party. And how you behaved. I hadn't thought anything of it until this moment, but now they fall into place. All that stuff about race and how our ancestry makes us what we are."

"Many people have the same feelings. Mrs Dunaway, as I recall, in particular."

"Mrs Dunaway's an idiot. Besides, she was plastered and only spewed generalities. You were specific – how important the Anglo-Saxon stock is – and, what's more, you actually seemed to ardently believe it all."

"Of course."

"Next," Max said pointedly, "you didn't know anything about leg theory. Only a European or someone from the Americas would've failed to know about that. But you spoke with an English accent, so I have to wonder where you could've been in '33 to have missed the controversy. Certainly not in an empire country. Thirty-three was the year Hitler assumed complete power, wasn't it? Then there was that joke Lindsey cracked about the SS uniforms. Mrs Dunaway thought it amusing, even Frost smiled, and he has absolutely no sense of humour. But you seemed... uncomfortable."

Hart was quiet for a moment. He glanced at the thin man and at the stocky man, and Max realised he'd made a terrible mistake. Hart nodded to the thin man, who removed coils of rope from his jacket pocket. "I'm afraid we're going to have to tie you all up," Hart said. "Anyone resisting will be shot."

Nobody moved, nobody uttered a sound. What had been a frightening situation had become, now, terrifying. Max was making quick mental calculations, but Hart and the fat man with the gun were too far away to jump. They'd get one or two shots away, and Max couldn't risk that. He glanced at Eric and saw that he was thinking the same thing. If they could coordinate a move…

"My friend here is a dead shot," Hart said, knowing what the men would be thinking.

Meanwhile, the thin man had left the room and returned with two dining chairs. He hoisted Eric first, pushed him down and, with swift and efficient moves, tied his wrists together, behind his back, securing the binding to the slats at the back of the chair.

When all four of them were tied, Hart put his gun back into his jacket pocket.

"What now?" Martha said. "Are you going to rob us?"

"No," Hart said. Turning to Max, he added, "I want to know what your friend Burton told you, Mr Dalton, and what he gave you."

The implications of this scenario were only now becoming evident to Max, and he felt a cold panic begin to move through his blood and bones.

Hart tilted his head at the tall, gaunt man. "This is Wilhelm," he said. "He works for me. He likes his work, and he's very good at it, but he doesn't understand English too well. So, if you don't tell me what I want to know, I'll tell him to cut off someone's fingers, then their toes, and he won't stop until I tell him to."

Max muttered something. Hart said, "What did you say?"

Max muttered something again, and when Hart went in close to hear, Max moved his head back and, with all his force, butted Hart on the nose.

Hart fell back with a shriek, holding his nose with both hands while blood poured out.

Wilhelm made a move towards Max, but Hart held up one bloody hand. "*Nein!*"

"Good shot, Max," Martha said.

"I was merely illustrating the dangers of leg theory."

After a few minutes, Hart was able to stand, most of the blood now having been soaked up by handkerchiefs. "I'm going to make someone suffer for that, Mr Dalton. But not you."

"All right," Max said. "I'll tell you what I know if you let the others go now."

Hart smiled. "You don't understand, Mr Dalton. You will all soon have your throats cut. The choice you have is whether you're all tortured first."

"That's not a fair choice," Martha said, apparently more annoyed by the lack of sportsmanship than by their impending murders.

Flora, straining at her ties, glared at Hart. "I know a few people in the East End who'd like to meet you lot," she said. "And some of 'em is Jewish."

Hart watched her coolly for a few seconds. Then he turned back to Max and said, "We'll start with the maid, I think."

At this, Flora's face went white. She tried to speak, but the terror inside was too large. She instinctively looked at Eric, who was struggling with all his energy to free his wrists from their binding. The effort only made the rope tighter.

"Ten fingers, and ten toes," Hart was saying. "One at a time."

"I'll cut your bleedin' head off," Eric shouted. "One at a time."

"Well said, Eric," Martha said.

"Listen," Max said, "There's nothing I can tell you. Honestly. I met Burton, but I was drunk. I can't remember what he told me, and he didn't give me anything."

"Well then…"

Hart glanced at Wilhelm, and said, "*Das Dienstmädchen.*"

Wilhelm reached into his pocket and pulled out a handkerchief, which had been knotted in the centre. Flora fought hard, but couldn't stop the gag being stuffed into her mouth and tied around the back of her head. Then Wilhelm removed his flick knife. Without any passing expression on his face, he pressed the button and the blade shot out, gleaming beautifully in the light. He turned Flora's chair around so that everyone could see her tied hands. Then Wilhelm caught her small right finger in his wiry hand and put the blade to it.

"No," Eric cried.

Then the blade sliced slowly into Flora's finger, and bright crimson liquid, which seemed too red to be blood, seeped out over her white skin as she writhed in agony, her screams sounding throaty, crackled by the gag.

Then the blade stopped its progress, and Wilhelm froze, and everyone looked to the door where an unseen hand knocked on its wood and a voice said, "Hello?"

Martha opened her eyes wide and thought, *Thank God. It's Lindsey.*

Max rolled his eyes and thought, *Oh, no. It's Lindsey.*

Everyone waited, silently, except poor Flora, who was sobbing.

Then Hart made a sign to his two men, and they dragged the tied prisoners away from the line of sight of someone at the door. To the fat one, he said, "Anyone makes a noise, shoot them in the knee, and I'll take care of this person."

Hart then put his hand in his jacket pocket, held his gun there, and went to open the door.

"It is," Lindsey's voice said. "I thought so. I was down the road in that little pub. Can't recall the name. Anyway, I look up and see you and think, 'Hello, that's old Hart. Must be popping in to see Max.' He is here, isn't he? I say, what happened to your nose?"

Max heard Hart say, "Are you alone, Mr Lindsey?"

"All alone, old boy. Mind if I come in? Is Martha here?"

Max sighed and waited for Lindsey to join them. Martha desperately wanted to shout a warning, but that would've certainly condemned Lindsey to death.

Lindsey walked in and stopped short when he saw the scene.

Then he did something odd. He walked up to the fat man, reached into his jacket pocket, removed a small pistol and shot the fat man through the eye.

The crack of the gun made everyone jump, and thereafter they were so stunned by this surreal action that they simply stared. All, that is, except the fat man, who dropped down dead.

Lindsey then turned and aimed at Hart, who fumbled with his gun. Lindsey fired and missed and fired again, but by this time Wilhelm had made a dash for the door, and Hart decided to follow him. Lindsey sent a few rounds in that direction, but they'd escaped.

Lindsey strode to the window and looked down. After a moment, they all heard shouts from the street, and police whistles, and what sounded to Martha like the crackling of a log fire. Max, though, knew what the sound was.

Lindsey slipped his pistol into a shoulder holster, turned to the stupefied people in the flat and smiled. "Right, then. Let's get Flora's wound sorted out, then I'll make us all a cup of tea. After that, we'd better have a chat. You two have been pretty busy, I understand."

Chapter Forty-Two

"Of course," Max was saying, "I suspected there was something off about him, even at the dinner party."

"You did?" Martha said. "You seemed quite pleased when he asked you about your books."

"That was a ploy," Max said.

"A ploy? A ploy to get him here, tie us up and threaten us with torture and death?"

"Uh…"

"Very clever."

All five of them were now in the sitting room drinking things considerably stronger than tea. Two Special Branch policemen were outside, and a few more were by the building's front and back entrances, all of them armed.

Wilhelm was dead, but Hart had escaped in a waiting car.

"Damned annoying," Lindsey said.

Flora's finger was dressed, and would survive intact, albeit with a deep scar. Eric sat close by, on the sofa, determined never again to allow anyone to try to take her. Max had explained to him the real purpose of Hart's intrusion but Eric was convinced they'd been after Flora.

"Still, it's funny," Martha said. "Mr Hart seemed such a nice old thing."

"Front," Lindsey said.

"Yes," Max said. "I think that was what I found most strange at the dinner party, that he could seem so harmless and yet have these poisonous ideas about ancestry and race. That's the thing with these fanatics – *all* fanatics, they can try to pretend to be something other than they are, but they can't quite pull it off, they can't hide their beliefs because that's what makes them function. It's their Achilles heel."

"No sense of humour," Lindsey said. "Can't take a joke. Easy way to spot 'em."

"Germans?" Martha said.

"Nazis. Germans are fun. Nazis aren't. Make a joke about their Führer, won't crack a smile. Same with all zealots, what have you. Too important, see? Too serious to laugh at."

"Who were those other two hooligans?" Martha said.

"One with the knife was Wilhelm Klopfer, Gestapo thug. Fat one was Arthur Boyd, nasty piece of work. From Newcastle, one of Mosley's Blackshirts."

Max, meanwhile, had thought of something. He said, "How did you happen to be here, Lindsey?"

"We've been watching you for a while, old thing. Unofficial, you understand. Not our bag, Blighty."

"What on earth are you talking about, Tony?" Martha said.

"He means he's MI6," Max said. "Right?"

"Right."

"I don't understand," Martha said. "Max?"

"MI5 are responsible for internal security. Tony here is with MI6, who aren't allowed to operate in this country. They're foreign intelligence."

"Spies?"

"Officers, please," Lindsey said.

"And Burton?" Max said. "Rice?"

"Nothing to do with us. Pity. Got themselves killed."

"Wait a minute," Martha said. "Tony, you knew? I mean, you *knew* Max was innocent and you still let that awful Inspector Longhorn arrest him?"

"Yes. Sorry. Had to, you see, otherwise we'd have tipped off Hart. And we needed to find out what he was up to. Blown that now, of course, but…"

"But the four of us are alive," Martha said.

"Yes. Compensation, I suppose."

"You suppose?"

"We wouldn't have let anything happen to you, old girl. We've been watching you ever since old Burton got it. After that, one of our sources told us Hart had been talking to Frost at his club and managed to get an invite to your dinner party. Naturally, it was clear that we had to get someone there ourselves and, since you're an old friend, it was decided it should be me, which is how I'm involved. It was a joint intelligence thing. So, you see, you weren't in danger. Except for that stunt on the train when you escaped. That was quite a thing, by the way. I hear it was like *The Thirty-Nine Steps* or such."

Martha said, "There was a man on the train. Old Mr Tomlinson. He has heart problems."

"How in hell did you know that?"

"Is he okay?"

"Physically, yes. But mad as a hatter. Kept babbling about murder conspiracies and arms being chopped off."

Something had occurred to Max regarding the dinner party. "And all our drink, Lindsey," he said. "Was it part of your cover to consume two bottles of Sémillon and half a bottle of Médoc?"

"Sorry, old boy. Had to let everyone think I was a sop. Just an act."

Here Lindsey turned to Flora and said, "Very much apologise for my behaviour towards you, Flora. All part of the act, you see?"

"Yes, sir," Flora said, more concerned that Eric would question her about it than the incident itself. But Eric was dazed by information at this point and was trying to work out whether Max was in the Gestapo.

"So, maybe you can tell us, who the hell was Crawford?" Max said to Lindsey.

"Crawford was Branch."

"A branch?" Martha said. "I do wish you two would speak in English."

"Special Branch. They investigate agitators, political movements. That kind of thing."

"If he was a policeman, why didn't Inspector Longford know about him?"

"The Branch keep their business hush-hush, especially from the rest of the Met."

"So what happened to Crawford?" Max said.

"We don't know. He was supposed to meet your Major Rice and Sergeant Burton. He was going to interview them, at length, I understand."

"You were right, Max," Martha said. "That explains why Rice and Burton booked into the Peterborough hotel, and why they planned to stay a night."

"Yes," Max said. "And when Crawford didn't show, Burton and Rice had to improvise."

Flora and Eric were sitting listening to all this, trying to follow it. At one point, it occurred to Flora that Eric had possibly saved Max and Martha's lives by going to Huntingdon and smuggling them back to London. She gave Eric's hand a squeeze and said, "We should go to Southend one day."

Eric's face went the colour of a pig's heart.

"But why would Crawford want to interview them?" Max asked Lindsey. "What for?"

"Well, that's where things get tricky. We don't know. According to his Chief Super, Crawford was investigating usual Branch stuff – Blackshirts, in this case. He ran a number of informants inside that lot, and had a call from one of them on Wednesday."

"Do you know what the call was about?" Martha said.

"Only that it was about a job the fellow had done a month earlier. In Swindon, I believe."

"Swindon?" Max said.

"You all right, old boy?"

"My God," Martha said. "Swindon."

Max explained to Lindsey that they'd asked Mr Bacon to find men from Max's old company.

"What he found was that in the last two years, three of my platoon have died, and Burton made that four, and three of those deaths were in the last few months. One of those deaths was a man called William Halford, a private. He died of a supposed heart attack in Swindon last month. And Crawford was meeting a Blackshirt who wanted to talk about a job he did in Swindon, a month ago. That's too much coincidence."

Lindsey thought about that for a moment, then nodded and said, "I'll put a call through to the locals, get the details of the death. I have to say, though, I think you might be right. It might've been murder; a heart attack is easy. Digitalis, for example. I'll let Swindon police know."

"But we still don't know what happened to Crawford," Max said.

"The Branch have been trying to locate his informant, but they can't find him. Crawford telephoned his office after meeting him and told them that he had to follow it up."

"When did Crawford call?"

"Some time Wednesday afternoon. Shortly after four o'clock."

"He must've called Rice at the same time. Rice acted urgently, and was at Burton's by Wednesday evening."

"I'll check with Lincolnshire police," Lindsey said. "They interviewed Rice's wife."

"Do you know where he telephoned from?" Martha said.

"A phone box in Cheshunt."

"That's in Hertfordshire, isn't it?"

"Yes. Just north of London. His phone call came from a box outside the railway station. The police are checking the coins for fingerprints."

"I know where Crawford is," Max said suddenly.

"Impossible," Lindsey said. "Even his own office don't know where he is."

But Martha was looking at the expression on Max's face. His eyes darted here and there across the floor, reflecting the firing of thoughts and ideas. "Max?" she said.

He looked up at Martha, and said, "It was your circle."

"Circle?" Lindsey said.

"What about it?"

"What on earth are you two on about?" Lindsey said.

"Martha had a brilliant theory. She reasoned that if Rice and Burton had both travelled to Peterborough, then there must've been a reason. And if Crawford was booked into the hotel at the same time, they must've chosen Peterborough because it was a central location for them all, thus most convenient. So, she drew a circle with the centre in Peterborough and the radius reaching Lincoln, which is where Rice lived."

Lindsey thought about this for a moment. He said, "Maybe Crawford lived in Peterborough."

"Oh," Martha said. "I hadn't thought of that. Did he live in Peterborough?"

"No," Lindsey admitted.

"So the theory is still valid," Max said.

"Well, I suppose so," Lindsey said. "Tell me, then. Where did this circle of yours get you?"

"It skirted Nottingham, Leicester, Coventry, a lot of empty space in East Anglia, and just north of London."

"Still doesn't help us."

"Not by itself. But when Burton met me he had the late edition of the *Evening Standard*. I knew there had to be a reason for that, so I got hold of a copy. There was a short piece about an unidentified body found in Enfield Lock on Friday. A body will bloat with gas after death. Now, a man killed on Wednesday and weighted down in the water might float to the surface two days later. I think Detective Crawford is currently in a mortuary near Enfield."

"So that's why he didn't show up," Martha was saying excitedly to Lindsey. "Crawford, you see? So then things really got interesting."

"We think," Max said, "that Rice and Burton must've assumed something bad had happened to Crawford, and they came to London."

"To see Max."

"They arrived at King's Cross, bought the paper and read of the death in Enfield. They must've realised it was Crawford, which is why Burton brought the paper along when he met me at the pub."

Then it was Martha's turn to have an epiphany. She said, "And I know why Burton had Crawford's driving licence."

Lindsey shook his head. "You've both been watching too many films."

Even Max was surprised by Martha's declaration. "You do?" he said, a little too doubtfully.

"You're not the only logical genius here," Martha said. "Actually, it's rather obvious. Look, what did Rice have on him?"

"Nothing," Max said. "So?"

"So, they killed him and took all his papers. Tony, why would a killer take all the documents from a dead body?"

"To confuse the authorities. Give one more time to do what one has to do."

"Exactly. Now, if we assume the same people who killed Rice also killed Burton, they would've searched him too. In which case, why would they leave a driving licence?"

"They wouldn't."

"You see? They didn't fail to take the driving licence, they left it themselves. And that's why his face was beaten badly – to make identification difficult, which is what happened."

"But Burton had a train ticket too," Max said, "and they didn't take that."

"Because it was in his hatband, which was lying a few feet away in a gutter. They killed him and took all documents except the ticket – which they'd missed."

"I think the old girl's got something," Lindsey said.

Martha smiled brightly and poked Max. "So, what does that tell us about the fact that Crawford's driving licence was found on Burton?"

"Um…"

"Lindsey?"

"Uh…"

Martha sighed elaborately and said, "It tells us two things: first, the people who killed Burton likely killed Crawford, and took from him his identity papers. And it also tells us that they probably panicked with regards to Burton. They must've seen him talking to Max in The Lion and they got worried, so they killed Burton and then planted Crawford's driving licence on him…"

"To confuse the police. I understand. Yes, I think you're right."

Lindsey whistled and said, "Think you'd both better come with me. Right now. We'll talk in the car."

"Where are you taking us?" Max said.

"To see the German Ambassador."

"You can't," Martha said sharply.

"Why not?"

"Look at my hair, and my dress. I'd need an hour, at least."

Chapter Forty-Three

About five minutes later, Max and Martha were holding on for dear life as they raced down the Bayswater Road in Lindsey's Alvis Speed 20, slaloming between cabs, trucks, carts, cyclists, motorbikes, buses, cars and the odd pedestrian, and all while Lindsey was speaking with a cigarette in the corner of his mouth.

"Hart was born in England, certainly," he was saying. "In 1886. His father was a doctor. Very respectable. When old Dr Hart joined the choir, Edward was seven and his mother took him back to live with her family in Munich. He has just enough Britishness in him to speak without an accent, but not enough to conceal his difference. Not one of us, see?"

Lindsey slammed on the brakes as a cyclist cut across the road. He punched down a gear and roared off, the engine buzzing with power. "At the start of the war, he was studying for a doctorate at Cambridge. Philosophy. Or History. Something like that. Anyway, he volunteered for the army in '14. Because of his background, the army put him in Intelligence, which was bloody stupid of them. We think he was a double, you see? He was supposedly working for British Intelligence, trying to recruit German agents. In fact, we believe he was passing information to the Germans that he was pretending to recruit."

"Why is he still around, then?" Martha called from the back seat.

"Two reasons. First, we can't prove anything. In fact, nobody even suspected him until after the war, when some eager bod in the Corps decided to review and file all the wartime intelligence reports. All the received intelligence was graded, according to its importance, and this chap noticed a pattern with the information Hart had come up with: it was good to begin with, and then became useless very quickly."

"In other words, he baited the line and we kept biting," Max said.

"Exactly. In fact, most of it was likely false information. Who knows what damage he did."

"But even if you can't convict him," Martha said, "surely you can throw him out of the country?"

"Ah, well, old thing, that's the second reason he's free – we wanted him in place. We knew what he was, you see? But he didn't know that we knew. So, we could watch him, find out what he was up to. Meanwhile, we could allow him to see whatever we wanted, so we could get the Germans to think what we wanted them to think. That's blown now, of course."

Martha, who'd known Lindsey for fifteen-odd years, was stunned into silence by these cumulative revelations. The fact that Lindsey was a spy or secret agent or officer, or whatever, was incredible enough. The fact that he had, indeed, had a job for years was even more amazing. The thing that flabbergasted her most, however, was simply that he had never spoken as many words in her presence as he was now speaking. It was as if someone had put a penny in him and off he went.

"We think he met Hitler sometime in the early thirties," Lindsey was saying, "and became a member of the National Socialists. He's quite senior, an Obersturmbannführer in the Schutzstaffel."

Lindsey braked sharply and rolled the car to a stop outside a rather dull newly built semi-detached house in Shepherd's Bush.

A man in a dark grey suit opened the door. He was about six and a half feet tall and almost as wide. He nodded to Lindsey, who brushed past him and led Max and Martha into a drawing room at the back of the property where a slim, elegant man in his mid-fifties sat in a large Victorian chair, reading a red-bound book.

"Max, Martha, may I present His Excellency Leopold von Hoesch, German Ambassador to the Court of St James," Lindsey said.

Von Hoesch stood sharply and, very erect, bowed slightly. Max thought he was going to click his heels. Instead, he took Martha's hand and touched it to his lips, then straightened up and shook Max firmly by the hand, smiling warmly. "It's a great pleasure," he said. "My friend Lindsey has been telling me about your, uh, adventures. He telephoned me earlier today, in fact, and told me that he thought you might be in some trouble. I'm sorry we could not be of help."

"Yes," Lindsey said, answering Max and Martha's glances. "Would've blown things."

"And I am truly sorry you have suffered at the hands of my fellow countrymen," Von Hoesch continued.

"It's not your fault," Martha said.

"Perhaps so, but… I feel… uh… responsible. I am the German Ambassador, after all, and they are German subjects. Unfortunately, they answer to a different authority."

"The Nazis," Max said.

"Yes," Von Hoesch said, "the Nazis."

He paused for a moment. "Shall we sit?" he said.

Everyone having made themselves comfortable, Von Hoesch continued. "I felt, and Mr Lindsey agreed, that you should know something of the truth of the matter. It might be of help."

The ambassador here glanced at Lindsey, who gave a small nod. "For some time now," Von Hoesch said, "the policies of my government have led me to question my role, and, indeed, my loyalty."

He let that sentence go into the air, then he sighed deeply and said, "They don't like me. And I confess that I don't like them, and they know it. I was appointed to the position of Ambassador a year before Hitler came to power, and I've raised objections over some of the German foreign policy. I particularly opposed the recent remilitarisation of the Rhineland, for instance. Hitler is one who doesn't abide opposition. So, I feel I don't have much time. I've known this for a few years, of course."

"What do you mean, sir?" Max said. "That you don't have much time?"

"I expect to be recalled shortly, and I would expect Von Ribbentrop to take my place. Hitler is worried about Britain. He knows that he isn't in a strong enough position – presently, at least – to do what he wants if he antagonises the British. France, he doesn't care about. It's the Royal Navy he fears. We saw the effects of a blockade during the war. That's why the naval agreement was of such importance. Your government failed to see the consequences of that agreement. I was sidelined, so I wasn't able to warn your government. You see, Hitler doesn't care about agreements, unless they're in his favour. He sees this as the start of a naval programme."

He frowned and shook his head, as if he'd failed to explain something simple to a class of children. Indeed, it occurred to Max that Von Hoesch had something professorial about him, explaining clearly and concisely what must have been obvious to him and yet was so obscure to the students, or, as in this case, the British government.

"So," Von Hoesch said, "he wants people in place who will… facilitate? Yes, facilitate a convivial relationship with Britain. Von Ribbentrop will be appointed with that mandate. But, he has, what is it you say? A card in his sleeve."

"An ace up his sleeve," Max said.

"Yes. He has some sort of information, secret information. I learned this about four months ago. In the embassy we have… intelligence personnel. I think that would be a good description?" Here he looked at Lindsey, who nodded once.

"Gestapo?" Max said.

"I believe so," Von Hoesch said. "They're Nazis, of course, rabid and ruthless. Probably Gestapo, or something like them. They took over a department in my embassy and have direct access to their superiors in Berlin. I don't know who those superiors are, but I know they have access to Hitler, via Himmler. I'm afraid I know very little of their operation. I was…"

"Frozen out, old boy," Lindsey said.

"Yes. An odd term. I never quite understand some of your phrases. Anyway, never mind. I doubt I shall get the chance now to understand. It won't be long before they realise that someone inside the embassy has been helping British intelligence. After that…" He held his hands wide, and let them drop to his side.

"You can get asylum, though," Martha said. "Can't he, Tony? Max?"

"Of course," Max said.

Lindsey said nothing. But it wasn't necessary, because Von Hoesch said, "No, young lady. It won't happen. If I'm given asylum, it will be an admission of treason. For myself, I do not care. But for my family…"

"You mean—" Martha said.

"Yes. They won't want to make it plain, of course. It won't look like murder. It would be…" Again, he let the sentence slide off into space, probably not wanting to contemplate what it might be.

Lindsey said, "So, His Excellency passed a message to MI5, and they asked our mob to look into a few things abroad."

"Linz," Max said suddenly. "Lindsey, you were in Linz last week. Skiing, you said."

Lindsey watched Max evenly and without a flicker of emotion, much as a man in a poker game might watch the player opposite, especially if that player were deciding whether to call a bluff.

"I don't understand," Martha said.

"Hitler," Max said.

"What does Hitler have to do with skiing?"

"Linz is a town in Austria," Max explained. "Oh, they have skiing there, and lots of tourists from Britain and other places, but it also happens to be the place where Hitler grew up."

"Was it?" Lindsey said casually.

"Tony?" Martha said.

Lindsey ran his tongue over his lips. "Can't confirm or deny, of course. But if one were to attempt to uncover Hitler's past, his nature, his beliefs, one might try in his home town, one might speak to those who knew him, casually, of course, and on purely friendly terms."

"I can tell you his beliefs," Max said. "Total domination, the suppression of resistance to his will, ruthless dogmatic faith in his own and the Aryan people's right to control others."

There was a brief silence following this statement. It was true, of course, which, perhaps, was why it was treated with silence.

"There's more," Lindsey said after a moment. "Recent events have tied in with something His Excellency has discovered. Herr von Hoesch was able to intercept part of a message. Sir?"

"Mr Lindsey is correct. It was a message sent in three parts, each with a separate courier who carried the message among… uh… valid diplomatic documents. The messages were coded, but would have been one complete message to the chief security officer at the embassy, a man who calls himself Gerhard Sommer, which I believe is false. Most likely, the message would have been an order, or series of orders. In this case, I was unable to learn of the content of the first two parts of the message. But the third part, when decoded, contained only two words – 'töte ihn': 'Kill him.'"

"My God," Martha said.

"Kill who?" Max said, immediately realising the stupidity of that question.

"We don't know," Lindsey said. "Seems to be an assassination order. That's why it's imperative that we find out. It was why we left Hart in place. Why we couldn't step in to help you two."

"Is that why the papers have been quiet? The *Chronicle*, for instance," Max said.

Lindsey nodded. "We put a D-notice on the whole thing. Had to. We *have* to know what Crawford was on to. Who is the target?"

Von Hoesch looked at Max and Martha. He said, "I'm unable to help. There are always eyes on me at the embassy."

"Max?" Lindsey said. "Martha? Can you help us?"

Max and Martha looked at each other. "We can only try to work out what's going on," Max said. "Much as we have done so far."

"Like Nick and Nora Charles," Martha added.

"If you can give us anything, anything at all, it might help."

Max and Martha were quiet for a while, both trying to dredge up some useful information. In the end, Max shrugged and said, "We've been trying to work it all out ourselves. There are details missing. Don't you have any information on what Crawford was up to?"

"No. As I said, he was Branch, meeting one of his informants. It was routine until he disappeared."

Martha turned to Lindsey, her brow scrunched up. "You said Crawford telephoned from Cheshunt."

"Yes."

"So why was his body disposed of in Enfield Lock?"

Lindsey didn't have an answer for that. Martha said, "Klopfer was German, wasn't he? And the English man, the fat one—"

"Arthur Boyd," Lindsey said.

"Yes, Boyd. He was from Newcastle. They wouldn't know the local area, so why would they know that they could dispose of Crawford in Enfield Lock?"

"Assuming they did," Max said. "We don't know that for sure."

"But it's logical, based on evidence," Martha said.

Meanwhile, Lindsey had been listening and wondering. He suddenly looked at Martha and Max and said, "My God. The Small Arms Factory. Enfield. It's right there, by the lock."

"Sabotage," Max said.

"Yes, and more. Assassination."

"How so?"

"Easy. They rig the place with explosives, then wait for a royal visit or some such."

"Goodness," Martha said.

"And somewhere like the Small Arms Factory, well, there are lots of important visitors – government, military, royalty. Then there are the engineers, the clever bods designing weapons."

Lindsey stood and strode from the room. The others could hear his voice, and that of the tall man, conferring urgently. Then Lindsey came back into the room and said, "I have to meet some people, arrange protection, so on. Not going to be able to help you, I'm afraid. Can't spare the men. Understand?"

"I have a gun," Max said.

"Good."

"Is it really that serious, Tony?" Martha said.

"Yes, old girl. Now, I'll take you two back home. Herr von Hoesch, Murray will take you to Euston Station, where you can catch a cab."

"Of course," Von Hoesch said. "And good luck, Mr Lindsey. Good luck to all of you."

When they were back in the car, Lindsey became quiet and thoughtful. Max and Martha, sensing his distance, didn't speak.

They were taking a different route back. It was a slower and more circuitous journey, as if the car's engine were a mirror of Lindsey's mind: urgent on the way out, pensive on the way back.

The car skimmed past the back of a double-decker as it weaved through the bustling traffic of the Hammersmith Road. Then they turned off and headed south towards the

Thames, cruising past tall red-brick Edwardian mansion flats, and then through the rows of Georgian townhouses, plane trees lining the pavement. Further and further south they went, and into the more crowded streets of Fulham, heading towards Sands End, where the terraced houses were a single unbroken line and the brickwork had been blackened by soot.

The sky was a milky grey colour and had seeped low so that the greyness veiled the chimneys of the power station in the distance and made them spectral.

Martha watched the people moving around in their daily routines, unaffected by the politics of foreign powers. She watched two girls playing five stones on the pavement, utterly absorbed in the game, unaware of her or anything. She saw a couple of elderly women standing outside the corner shop, one with a full basket cradled before her, the other with an empty basket. The women exchanged gossip and kept an eye on the rent man, who was moving gradually up the road.

The car turned on to Townmead Road, where the large brick blocks of factories and the heavy industry of the dock area made Martha feel oppressed, stifled. As the car slowed for a moment, she saw a small boy with huge eyes and a grime-smeared face. The boy was sitting on the kerb, his feet in the road. He was playing with something in his hands, ignoring everything else around him. He looked up and saw Martha and stared at her, open-mouthed, until the car moved on and away for ever.

The silence was broken when Lindsey said, "Listen, you two. Shouldn't be telling you this, but I trust you. Besides, after what you've been through, I think it's only fair. Old

Von Hoesch has been gathering information regarding the German rearmament, Nazi dispositions, that sort of thing. And he's been passing it to a fellow at the FO, chap called Ralph Wigram. He's been giving it to Churchill."

"Why?" Max said. "I mean, why isn't the information going to MI6?"

"Oh, it is. Eventually. Trouble is, we're subordinate to the Foreign Office and they're not keen on stirring up trouble. They tend to ignore it, or keep it quiet, at least."

"Whereas Churchill is free to shout as loud as he wants," Martha said.

"Precisely. Now, you might want to have a word with this Wigram chap. He might have some ideas. I don't know. It might be worth it. I can't do it, of course. And Von Hoesch has to be careful at the moment. If we can find out who precisely is the target…"

Lindsey had become quiet again.

Chapter Forty-Four

A slim young woman opened the door and looked up at Max and Martha. She had a pleasant face, smiling eyes and a serene, almost modest, manner, but Martha sensed that the fragility she saw wasn't characteristic per se, but, rather, the result of some stress or pain, much as if a delicate flower were being bent to breaking point by a bitter and pitiless wind.

"Mrs Wigram?" Max said. "I telephoned earlier. I believe your husband is expecting us."

"Oh, yes." She opened the door wide to admit Max and Martha. Then she pointed down the hall and said, "He's in his study."

Max and Martha waited for her to lead them through the hallway, but she turned away from them and started up the stairs, stopping on the fourth step. "It's my son," she said. "He's not very well at the moment. Would you mind showing yourselves in?"

Then she continued up the stairs. Max shrugged to Martha and led them down the hall. He knocked on a closed door and heard a voice call out, "Yes?"

They entered the study and found themselves standing before an old walnut desk in front of the window. Almost all of the walls were filled with bookshelves, many of which were neatly lined with leather-bound volumes, tooled beautifully and gilded.

The man behind the desk had risen and walked around it, holding out his hand. Like his wife, Ralph Wigram was slight, not tall and not with any weight to him. His eyes were intense and dark, and seemed more so because of his very white skin. What Martha had detected with Mrs Wigram, both now saw in her husband.

"Mr Dalton," Wigram said, shaking Max's hand. "Would you believe I have one of your volumes?"

"I'm honoured," Max said. "I rarely meet anyone who's read one of my books, and never anyone so… uh…"

"So established?" Wigram said.

"So important."

"Ah. Anyway, it's I who should feel honoured. I found it exceptionally well written, although I'm not sure I entirely agree with your conclusions. As I recall, you were rather critical of Ney and Murat. Still, we should probably leave that conversation for another time."

Max introduced Martha, who said, "What a lovely room."

Wigram, shaking her hand, said, "Thank you. Yes, it's my sanctum."

They took seats, and Wigram tidied away some papers, putting them into a green binder.

"Now then," he said, "would either of you care for some tea?"

"Well—" Max said.

"That would be lovely," Martha said. "Now, I noticed that your wife was rather busy, so would you allow me to go and make it? I'd love to see your kitchen."

This statement baffled Max, who secretly believed that Martha had a phobia of working areas. Martha didn't wait for a reply, hurrying from the room before either man had a chance to stand. She closed the door behind her.

"I spoke briefly with Tony Lindsey. He seems to think there's a possibility that the Germans are going to assassinate someone," said Wigram.

"Yes," Max said. "But he doesn't know who."

"I don't know how I can help."

"You've seen a lot of information from the embassy; it might tie up with something I've learned."

"In that case, you'd better tell me what you've learned."

Max related to Wigram the events of the last few days, beginning with the Friday evening he met Burton. As Max was talking, Wigram stood and went to a cabinet from which he removed a tantalus. He poured a glass of brandy from one of the decanters, offering it to Max, who shook his head.

Wigram returned with the glass to his desk.

Max finished by explaining what had happened with Hart hours earlier.

"My God," Wigram said.

There was a long silence.

"I wasn't there," Wigram said finally. "I mean the Western Front. Or any front."

"I'm glad," Max said.

"I should've been."

Max didn't know what to say to that. He wasn't even sure whether Wigram was speaking to him.

Wigram was silent for a long time, and Max, allowing him the space to think, remained still and quiet. Then Wigram spoke, in a faraway voice. "We're heading for war," he said.

"We're not just heading for war," Max said. "We're running towards it with our arms outstretched."

"It wasn't supposed to happen again. Never again. It wasn't supposed to be like that. Don't you see?"

"Yes," Max said.

Wigram had a sip of his brandy, took his time about it.

Max waited, seeing the pain in the man, wanting to help him, feeling that he knew him intimately, even though they were so very different.

"It's not what was supposed to happen," Wigram said, gazing into space, apparently unaware of Max's presence. "You're born into a good family. Your father is a functionary, helping the empire tick along. He puts you through school – one of the good schools, one of those that makes men who believe in it all, but nothing gauche like Marlborough or Charterhouse, nothing that needs to shout 'look at me', just something… proper. Then you go up to Oxford and study History or the Classics. And then you leave and get a job in the City or in the diplomatic corps or something, and you join a club in London, but not the Athenaeum…"

He paused for a moment and had another sip of brandy, gently cradling the glass in his hand as if it were a treasured possession. He smiled at some private joke and Max, who had become mesmerised by Wigram's tone and demeanour, felt as though he were watching an old man passing judgement on his failures, as if his words were a valediction.

Wigram looked up and smiled again, but briefly and with more sadness than joy.

"And you join a club," he said again. "Nice and proper and English. And you marry a nice smart woman and she bears you a son whom you raise to be like you, squeezing him through the system so that he can become something in the City or the diplomatic corps or whatever. And after you've done your forty years you retire with your knighthood for services and wait out your time pruning roses in Hampshire and visiting the MCC to watch England lose again to Australia. That's how it's supposed to be. It was always like that. It was always supposed to be like that. It was written in stone, the words carved into a tablet and handed to Moses: thou shalt be British. Thou shalt be decent. Thou shalt do thy duty. Thou shalt not kick up a fuss."

He was quiet again, watching the smoke from his cigarette coil and drift and diminish. "But it wasn't, was it? It wasn't like that. You see, I can't blame the system. I can't blame anyone or anything, except myself."

He turned to Max. "You do understand, don't you? I mean, you know what it is, what it feels like."

And for the first time, Max found that someone had voiced the vague feeling he'd had for so many years. He said, "I don't know much about my parents. But I know they were poor and ordinary and ignorant. I didn't know it then, but I came to understand it when I was adopted by richer people, and I became ashamed of them, my parents. So I denied them, like Judas denying Christ. I wanted to be more than them, to be beyond them, all of them. Now... now I want to be just like they were. But it's too late."

He looked at Wigram, the glass of brandy cradled in his hand and his eyes delicate and intense. "The fact is," Max said, "I don't belong in a good club and I never went to a good school."

"But you understand," Wigram said. "All that other stuff is baubles – your family, your school, your college tie. It's just the silk lining. It's the body beneath that counts. It's this country, this impossible belief."

Max found himself nodding, not really knowing why. And then, barely aware of his own words, he said, "I understand. It was the war. History records that empires crumbled and monarchs fell, but Britain survived. Well, we didn't. We just pretended we did. The *system* pretended we did. And that's the great lie. That's what we know."

"Yes," Wigram said. "Yes."

"And that's what's wrong; because we know it's a lie, and we believe in it anyway."

"Yes," Wigram said, but this time quietly, with a finality. "It's funny, everything we're told to believe in, all the honour and truth, the safeguarding of weaker peoples – you act in that belief and they condemn you for it."

Both men were quiet for a long time. Max felt that he'd discovered a truth of great potency. It was a kind of epiphany, and one that would take a long time to comprehend.

He blinked when he heard Wigram speak. "I'm afraid I can't help," Wigram said. "I don't know who might be on the Germans' assassination list. Frankly, they seem to be benefitting quite well with all our senior figures right where they are."

"Well, it was just an idea."

"You know, this is the sort of story that needs to be told. It needs to be in a newspaper."

"There's a D-notice on it."

"Ah. Still, there are ways."

"Ways?"

"Yes. As I said, I'm not able to help. But I know someone who might be."

*

Once outside, Max said, "Since when are you interested in kitchens?"

"I'm not. But I thought he might talk more openly without a woman present."

"Hmm. You were right."

"What now?"

"Now," Max said, "We're going to meet Winston Churchill."

"Goodness. My parents will be livid."

Chapter Forty-Five

The elderly and rigid Mr Willoughby pointed to a thick oak door across the wide lobby. Max thanked him and then he and Martha walked across the tiled floor, their feet clicking and echoing in the vast chamber, which was more like a church.

"Only Mr Dalton, I'm afraid," Mr Willoughby said.

That brought Max and Martha to a sudden stop.

"What?" Martha said, turning and giving Willoughby her fiercest glare.

"No women," he said.

Martha appealed to Max, her eyebrows raised. But Max, knowing he would suffer for it later, could only shrug. "Don't you dare," Martha said to him. "I've done as much as anyone in this case."

"Martha, please," Max said weakly.

She turned back to the – now nervous – Willoughby and said, "This is an outrage. I demand to see Mr Churchill. Bring him outside if necessary."

Max, fearless on many occasions, decided to make a run for it, and slipped quickly through the door, pulling it closed behind him. He heard Martha call his name, and add an expletive.

The room was large, with shelves made of dark oak along parts of the walls, oak panelling and large, foreboding oils of foreboding statesmen staring down in apparent disapproval and disdain.

"MAX!" Martha screamed.

There were a half a dozen men in the room, spread out, each alone and ensconced in deep chairs or studded leather club seats. Several of the men woke up and glared at the door, which, though very solid and firmly closed, wasn't up to the job of preventing the commotion without from being heard.

Max saw Churchill sitting at a small table in the corner of the room. Before him were documents, which, pen in hand, Churchill was appraising and amending.

When Max introduced himself, Churchill, who remained bent over his work, looked up and appeared about ready to charge him. His mouth was tight in a frown, and his forehead creased in thought. His face was quite unlined, though, and his soft, puffy cheeks gave him a baby-like appearance.

A considerably diluted glass of Scotch sat within reach of Churchill's left hand, and to his right a half-burned cigar rested in a silver ashtray. The cigar was lit and the rich, heavy tobacco smell filled the air.

Churchill reached over to the ashtray, lifted the burning cigar, and stuffed it into his mouth where it smouldered, along with his face and demeanour. He said, "Hmm."

After a moment, with Max waiting patiently, he removed the cigar, blew out a stream of blue smoke and signalled to the chair opposite, in which Max seated himself.

"I received a curious telephone call recently," Churchill said in a gruff, lispy voice, "from Ralph Wigram. He advised that you wished to speak with me, young man, and that I might be remiss if I didn't allow an audience. So, do you wish to speak to me?"

"Yes, sir," Max said. "And so does my wife."

"Your, uh, your wife?"

"Yes," Max said, glancing towards the door, behind which could still be heard the stream of sharp words and Willoughby's occasional plea for calm and reason. "She's a woman of ability and opinion."

"And that noise would be she, would it?"

"It would."

"She strikes me as a woman of great purpose," Churchill said, laying down his pen. "I myself am such a person. I admire all those of great purpose, provided such purpose is not, uh, detrimental to the welfare of our kingdom. Do you think it would be wise for me to speak to her also?"

"I'd say so."

Churchill nodded, as if Max had confirmed to him that the empire was in safe hands and had a good future. He stood and walked to the great door and opened it. Max followed nervously.

Martha had the unfortunate Willoughby by the shirt and was explaining why she was more qualified than most men to enter the club, when Churchill's portly figure presented itself.

"Madam," he said severely, "I hope by this action that you don't mean to harm my friend. He is already accomplished in years and I fear, through your agency, might rapidly be shuffled off this mortal coil."

Martha let go of Mr Willoughby and, breathing hard, turned to Max and Churchill. She glared at them both, defying them to prohibit her from something, anything.

"Now, it is a fine day," Churchill said, "and I am in the habit of breathing fresh air and partaking in nature. Would you both accompany me to the park?"

The park in question was Green Park, at which place they shortly arrived. The few people scattered around didn't seem concerned by Churchill's presence, although one man in a bowler hat, sitting on a park bench, glared at him.

Max and Martha, now sufficiently calm, walked either side of Churchill who, for the most part, had strolled there with his hands behind his back and his head down, cigar clenched at the left side of his mouth. He listened to Max recount what had been happening recently. This took Max, with Martha's occasional help, a long time to fully explain and they were, by now, well into the park.

After Max had finished relating events, Churchill said, "Humph."

Then he was silent, his head bent, as if the solution to everything must be on the ground somewhere. He continued to puff on his cigar. Max and Martha waited and became more anxious the longer the silence continued.

At that point, amid the limes and planes and poplars of Green Park, Churchill stopped and stood and thought. He looked around and, spying a bench, walked over to it and sat. Max and Martha followed suit. Instead of referencing the case in hand, Churchill glanced at Max and said, "Have you ever seen war, Mr Dalton?"

"Yes, sir. I was on the Western Front."

"As was I. A terrible thing. You may not believe me when I say I do not like wars. I have seen my fair share of them, over, uh, many years and many continents. There are those who believe me to be a warmonger. On the contrary: *Si vis pacem, para bellum.* If you wish for peace, prepare for war. That is my belief, and the only way to deal with a man like Hitler."

"He's a madman," Martha said. "They all are."

"Hitler is most certainly mad, young lady, but he's a madman with an army, and that makes him most certainly very dangerous. He believes in the Aryan race as an ideal. Soon millions of others will believe it. By then, Nazism will be a religion, and those in it will be worshipping an idealised race. It won't take them long to decide that the other races are subordinate to them, and when that happens it's a short distance to determining that they should and can control those other races. In their minds, we, here, in this land, are like them. Does that mean we should stand aside and watch as they destroy other lands, other peoples?

"You see, that's the thing with a fervent belief – with, if you'll forgive the word, 'faith'. Faith must, by definition, discard that which does not adhere, and the more strongly one has this faith, the more determined one is to expunge that which contradicts it. But therein lies the Nazis' flaw, their Achilles heel – they believe themselves superior, as such they treat everyone else as inferior, and they underestimate us. We've already seen it in the way they treat their own citizens. And that's how we'll win. We British are not perfect creatures, to be sure, but we try to be and we keep on trying."

"You're talking as if we're already at war," Martha said.

"Oh, we are at war, certainly. Mark these words, young lady; the second Great War has already begun."

"Is there any way you can help us, sir?" Max said. "Ralph Wigram thought you might be able to."

"He might be correct, but until we know what the story truly is, I cannot help. You understand that I have very little power. I feel sometimes like a shepherd ignored by his sheep while a wolf lurks, hungry and slavering."

After these words, Churchill became pensive. His cigar was extinguished, but remained clenched in his mouth. Finally, he looked at Max and Martha. "You said that nothing was found on the body of your friend, Burton, and nothing was found in the room where he and Major Rice were booked?"

"Yes," Max said.

"And two men attempted to, uh, infiltrate your home after these murders."

"Yes, sir."

"Humph. Young man, madam, I don't believe I can do anything to help you, not without some form of evidence. However, these scoundrels who tried to gain entry to your flat must have been looking for something, and that thing must be of considerable importance, given that they were prepared to expose themselves to such a risk of discovery. I suggest you go home and look for whatever this thing is."

Chapter Forty-Six

Back at the flat, Max and Martha were trying to work out what Klopfer and Boyd could've been looking for.

"They must've thought Burton gave you something," Martha was saying.

"But he didn't," Max said.

"If he'd slipped something to you, you wouldn't have known."

"Yes, but whatever it was would have to be in the suit I wore."

"And you've checked that?"

"And I've checked that. Lots of times."

Something else was bothering Max, however. It was that book in Rice's house; the history of the Grenadier Guards in the Great War. But rather than the actual words in the book, it was the image of the dog-eared page, the notation – Lies – that kept coming back to Max. Rice was fastidious, and yet he'd scrawled, in ink, over his book and had turned back the corner of a page and cracked the spine, all so that something on that page would remain prominent. Max went into his study and grabbed the book and opened it to the same page. There, as in Rice's volume, was an account of how Max had brought Palgrave back to the British lines.

He took the book back into the sitting room and sat and started to read from the top of the page.

Martha was watching him while he read the book. She often watched Max reading, often surreptitiously. She loved to watch the calmness and concentration on his face while he was absorbed in a book and unaware of being observed.

In this instance, though, Martha didn't see calmness in Max's concentration. She saw distress, pain, confusion.

Then a key turned in the front door and Flora entered with a basketful of shopping, followed by Eric, who seemed now determined to shadow her until all threats were smothered.

"Flora," Martha said.

"Yes, ma'am?" Flora said, kicking the door closed behind her.

"Have you seen anything new?"

"Er…"

"I mean, have you come across anything that doesn't belong? Anything in the clothes Max was wearing on Friday?"

"No, ma'am," Flora said, putting the basket down by her feet. "Except that ticket, of course."

Max dropped the book. "Ticket?"

"Yes, sir. The one that was in your jacket pocket."

"What are you talking about? What ticket? Which jacket?"

"Your dark grey jacket, sir. You couldn't find a suitable jacket for the dinner party on Saturday, sir, so Mrs Dalton told me to iron the one you'd worn on Friday night."

"My God," Martha said. "That's right. And you found a ticket?"

"I had to take it out when I ironed the jacket. I put it on the window sill, in the kitchen."

Max dashed out of the room. Martha, Flora and Eric waited, listening to Max's footsteps on the kitchen tiles, and then hearing him slamming a drawer closed. When he came back in, he was holding a ticket in one hand and a Webley service issue revolver in the other. "King's Cross. Left luggage. Martha, stay here."

For once, Martha decided not to argue. There was a febrile intensity in Max, his eyes fierce and darting around, sweat on his forehead. And there was the pistol he held, which frightened her.

Max pocketed the ticket and then broke the Webley open. From his pocket he took a handful of cartridges and loaded the gun, snapping it shut and handing it to Eric. "I need you to stay here with the ladies. Don't let anyone take them."

"Count on me, sir."

Then Max was gone, with Martha's faint words following him.

"Be careful, Max. Please be careful."

Chapter Forty-Seven

Thirty minutes later, Max emerged into the crowd outside King's Cross Station with a brown leather briefcase clutched under his arm. The case was of fine quality, with a sturdy brass lock. Above this were three gold embossed letters: FJR. Frederick James Rice.

There was no key, so Max decided to find a butcher's or fishmonger's or similar, and ask them to cut the leather strap. He was too impatient to wait until he got back to the flat. Besides which, this was too important to delay. He had to know what the case contained, although he had an idea.

He decided to head down the Gray's Inn Road. There'd be someone down there with a knife or scissors. There were bookbinders, that sort of thing.

He turned left towards Pentonville Road and stopped abruptly as a man walked up to him. Max was about to step aside and let the man pass when he was surprised to see the hatted head tilt up. He was even more surprised to see that the face belonged to Edward Hart.

The gun in Hart's hand, however, didn't surprise him at all.

Chapter Forty-Eight

For some minutes after Max had left, Martha, Flora and Eric had remained in situ, all quietly considering what had happened. Despite the dangers they'd experienced, it was Max's behaviour that most affected them. They could all see it, and they all felt frightened.

Finally, Martha suggested that Flora put the shopping away and further suggested that Eric might help her, which he was pleased to do.

In truth, Martha wanted some moments alone. She stood and went to where Max had been sitting. He'd left the book open, and Martha sat and started to read.

'It was during this assault that a company from the 3rd Battalion were caught by artillery fire while several hundred yards from either the enemy or their own lines. One shell landed among the men, killing several instantly and fatally wounding their Commanding Officer, Captain Richard Palgrave, DSO. Despite himself having received a severe head injury and disregarding intense enemy fire, Lieutenant David Maxwell Dalton carried Captain Palgrave back to British lines. For this action, Lieutenant Dalton received the Military Cross.'

Martha closed the book and tried very hard not to weep.

Chapter Forty-Nine

Hart stood a foot from Max, a short Bayard .32 automatic pistol in his hand, pointed directly at Max's stomach. Hart had guided Max to one side of the exit, but still in plain sight of dozens of people, all of whom passed by. "Hand me the case, Mr Dalton."

"I don't believe I'll do that."

"It was not a request."

"And supposing I don't?"

"I would shoot you. I don't want to, but I shall. I would burn the contents of that case. Then I would simply hand myself in to the police. I have diplomatic immunity, you see."

"Ah," Max said, not having considered that he might actually get shot.

Hart smiled a nasty smile. He said, "That's the problem with your country, Mr Dalton. There are those, like you, like your wife, who still believe in the fairy tale of honour among peoples, among the nations. How can you still fall for that idiocy, after all you've seen? After what you experienced on the Western Front? It's a fool's paradise, and you're a fool to believe it."

"I'd rather be a free fool than a dog that serves a rabid master."

The smile had gone from Hart's face, and Max knew he was heading into dangerous waters. Still, something in him didn't want to back down, not in front of a snivelling maniac.

And all this while, streams of people had passed within a few feet of them, going to the station, leaving the station. Porters with barrows of luggage and trolleys of sacked mail, cab drivers collecting fares, depositing fares, fathers and mothers and children and businessmen and workmen and young lovers going on holiday. All of them passed by and knew nothing of the fearful and desperate situation that was uncoiling. A situation that would have consequences for decades to come.

"Germany doesn't want to be an enemy of England's," Hart said. "We respect the English. I'm half-English myself."

"But only the respectable half."

Hart tried again to smile. He was attempting to use reason and cordiality to win Max over, but that last comment had hit home, as Max saw in the twitching of Hart's eye. And Max knew, now, that therein lay the anger and hatred, and the need to dominate for people like Hart. It was the mental sickness of the envious and spiteful. They were the characteristics evident in Iago and Richard III and the Lucifer of *Paradise Lost*, but without their wit and charm and intelligence. Hart was nothing more than an empty shell of malice.

"Mr Dalton," Hart said darkly, "give me that case and we can continue to be friends, our countries will continue to be friends. Our ambition is not to take anything from you. Your empire is yours, we allow that. Allow us to create our own empire, a Greater Reich."

"And enslave foreign peoples?"

"They're not people," Hart said, his face now contorted with fury, with hatred, "they're *Untermenschen*. The Soviets, the Poles, you would choose them over *us*?"

"I'd choose obsolescence over you. I'd rather we lost our empire and became an insignificant, powerless group of islands just so long as we did it fighting you and all those like you."

Hart pushed the gun into Max's gut, and pushed so that it hurt to breathe. Still Max didn't retreat. Instead, he met Hart's furious gaze with his own cold fury, his eyes locking with Hart's, watching as the venom in Hart's blood moved and pushed. Max was compelling his own murder, he knew that.

"You British will never understand. Our Germany will never be defeated," Hart said as he crumpled, unaccountably, to the floor.

Max blinked and stood still, unable to comprehend what had just happened. One second he was expecting to be shot through the stomach, and the next he was standing over Hart's body.

Then he realised he'd heard a small pop, and he became aware of the motionless people, the gasps and horrified looks. He heard a car door open and he glanced over to see two men emerge from a black sedan.

Sergeant Pierce holstered his pistol and buttoned his jacket. Inspector Longford was behind him, crossing the street.

"What are you doing here?" Max said when the detectives had arrived on the scene, moving people away from the body of Hart.

"Well, sir," Longford said, "you can thank Mr Churchill for that. He felt you might be in danger and contacted our Commissioner, who sent us, seeing as we were already acquainted with the case."

"Look, there's not enough time to explain things," Max said. "I need you to do three things for me, and I need them done very urgently."

"Just tell us what to do, sir," Longford said.

"First, I need you to take me to The Lion pub. I believe you know it."

Chapter Fifty

As soon as Max got home, Martha, without saying a word, walked to him and wrapped him in her arms. She rested her cheek on his chest and said, "You're safe. Thank God you're safe."

Max kissed the top of his wife's head. "Why wouldn't I be?"

"I was scared, Max. I... I read what you did for Palgrave."

Max looked over at the book he'd left open. It was now closed. "Everything's fine," he said.

"I was scared," Martha was saying. "I was scared you were going to do something."

After a moment, Max realised that she was weeping, very quietly. "It's all right," he said.

Flora and Eric, who had been in the kitchen making tea, came into the room and, observing the scene, decided it was time for them to leave. Eric made a presentation of the Webley revolver to Max, who said, "I knew I could count on you."

Eric left beaming, as did Flora.

Martha, who had now composed herself sufficiently and was seated, said, "What happened?"

"Hold on, darling," Max said.

He then went into the bedroom and unearthed an old shoebox, which he brought into the sitting room.

"What's that?" Martha said, dabbing her eyes with a small handkerchief.

"Mementoes, photos, that sort of thing."

After a few minutes of riffling, he held up a small photograph and said, "Got it."

"What?"

"The answers, Martha. These are the answers."

Next, he went into his study and came back with a pencil and a piece of paper. He scribbled on the paper.

"What are you doing, darling?"

"Making a list. I have a compulsion to summon everyone to the library and explain the plot."

"We don't have a library," Martha said.

"Well, I'll send Flora to get one."

Chapter Fifty-One

The Lion was closed, and a simple handwritten sign on the door read 'Private Function'. That was an understatement, but adequate. Since the pub was a small place and only had one room, all the tables had been moved to the cellar, and the chairs arranged in a large semicircle facing the bar, against which Max was leaning back, a smouldering cigarette between his fingers and both elbows on the counter. Now and then he took a sip from a glass of water, which was on the counter to his left.

He was wearing a single-breasted grey pin-striped suit from Savile Row. It was his best one, because this was the most important speech he would ever have to make. Beneath his jacket he wore a shirt so white it dazzled and, to top it all off, he was wearing his Guards tie and tie pin.

Martha was sitting on the chair closest to Max, to his right. She was wearing a pale grey Schiaparelli two-piece, the jacket and skirt so slim that it made her seem more ethereal than usual. She sat, as she sometimes did, with her ankles back and her knees together but angled to one side. It was elegant in extremis and Max wondered how it was that she didn't sprain something.

It was a bright spring morning. Sunlight shot through the dirty windows, lit patches of the sawdust-covered floor and lacerated the clouds of cigarette smoke.

The first to arrive was Alwyn Frost, who greeted Martha and Max coolly before hanging his chesterfield on the Victorian coat stand. He unpeeled his leather gloves, slipped them in the pocket of the coat, then removed his bowler and placed that on one of the eight hooks at the top of the stand.

Only after Frost had done all that did he nod to Jack Connor, who was standing behind the bar, over to the left side. Max, who'd watched Frost's act with growing annoyance, wanted to walk over and tip the whole coat stand over.

"Why are we meeting in a public house?" Frost said.

"Because we don't have a library," Martha said.

Frost then went and sat as far away from everyone as possible, which was in the centre of the semicircle.

Next came Mr Bacon, who chose to sit beside Martha, placing his briefcase on the floor between his feet.

Flora and Eric turned up together, followed shortly by Inspector Longford and Sergeant Pierce. Both couples sat in the chairs next to Mr Bacon. Flora moved her chair closer to Eric, and further from Longford. Pierce was now seated next to Frost, and introduced himself to that man, receiving a curt nod in return.

Longford was still sporting a bandaged head, but had somehow managed to squeeze it inside his hat, which he removed and placed on his lap. Martha smiled sheepishly at him and received a raised eyebrow in reply.

Tony Lindsey himself had collected Lilly Burton and Mrs Rice from the station, and now brought them in and walked them to their seats, which were in a corner, away from the door, directly opposite Martha. Lindsey then seated himself next to Mrs Rice, took out his cigarette case, lit a cigarette and relaxed into his seat, his ankles crossed, as if he were at the pictures.

Lilly Burton was very pale and nervous. She licked her lips and clutched her hands in her lap. Jack Connor noticed this and brought her out a glass of brandy.

"Get this down your neck," he said. "I'm sorry to hear about your loss. Yours too, Mrs Rice."

Mrs Burton thanked him and sipped the drink. Mrs Rice failed to even acknowledge Connor.

Churchill arrived next, a cigar clenched in his mouth and a homburg crammed on his round head. He viewed those present, then made for the bar in the manner of a bull charging the matador. Jack, who, as far as Max was aware, had never been nervous in his life, stood upright and said, "What would I... I mean, what can I get you, sir?"

"I'll have a glass of your brandy, if I may."

"It's not the best quality."

"That's fine. The best drink in bad company is far worse."

Jack reached below the counter for the brandy, took a large wine glass from the shelf behind him, dusted it and poured the drink. He handed it to Churchill, saying, "On the house, sir."

Churchill nodded his thanks, lifted the glass, gazed for a moment at the picture of the black boxer behind the bar and said, "Hmm."

He took his drink and his cigar and sat heavily next to Frost, who ignored him.

The last person to arrive was General Monroe, who strode in and glared at everyone, especially Max and Churchill.

"Winston," he said, "what are you doing here?"

"Same as you, I expect – defending the realm."

The general then took the final seat, which placed him with Lindsey on his right and Churchill on his left.

Once all but he and Connor were seated, Max introduced each person individually, ending with Martha, "The most glorious wife, and a damned good detective."

Alwyn Frost, always ready to pour cold water on warm feelings, said, "Is it necessary to have Mr Connor here? We *are* talking about issues of national security."

"Good point, Alwyn," Max said. "First, Jack's a material witness. Second, he, at least, didn't bring a Gestapo agent to our flat for dinner."

Here, Frost drew in a long breath, stared sternly at Max and went very slightly white.

"Third," Max was saying, "this is his pub. And, finally, Jack is as good a Briton as I've ever known and I see no reason why he shouldn't be here."

"Quite right, young man," Churchill said. "And may I add to Mr Connor that I have heard of him, and his… uh… illustrious forebear, the great Tom Molineaux."

Max glanced at Connor and was amazed to see that the huge man's eyes were glistening.

"On the issue of security," Lindsey said casually, "I must remind everyone that they're party to information covered by the Official Secrets Act. No chat about this, please."

Then Lindsey nodded to Max, who killed his cigarette, pushed himself away from the bar and said, "Now I'll begin."

"Begin what?" General Monroe said.

"A story, sir. The most important story you'll ever hear."

Chapter Fifty-Two

"I'll begin by explaining why Sergeant Dan Burton and Major Frederick Rice became involved, and how they met their deaths."

Here, everyone in the room glanced at Lilly Burton and Mrs Rice. Lilly Burton was silent, a small lace handkerchief to one eye. Mrs Rice stared white-faced at a point on the carpet while her hands trembled in her lap.

There was silence for a few seconds, in honour of their suffering.

"There was a man called John Crawford," Max said quietly. "He was a Special Branch detective who had the routine job of keeping an eye on potentially dangerous political elements. Part of his work was to speak to informants and receive from them any intelligence, which could then be reported back to his superiors for further investigation, if necessary."

Here, Max glanced at Inspector Longford and Sergeant Pierce.

"Inspector, I understand you've spoken to your colleagues at the Branch?"

"That's correct, Mr Dalton," Longford said as he took a notebook from his pocket and opened it. "And I've learned the following: On Wednesday March 18th, Detective Crawford was scheduled to meet one of his informants, a man named Ralph Hall; a cab driver by trade and a known member of Mosley's Blackshirt group. No trace of Ralph Hall has been found and he is considered a missing person, most likely deceased."

This was too much for Mrs Rice, who sobbed loudly. "I don't understand all this," she said. "I don't understand what Mosley and all that has to do with my husband."

It was Sergeant Pierce who went to her aid. He rose, walked over to her and knelt down. "We are very sorry, madam. Would you prefer to wait in our car?"

After a moment, Mrs Rice sniffled and wiped her tears away with the lace handkerchief that Lilly Burton had handed her. "I'm all right, now. Really, I'm all right. Please, I want to know what happened."

Jack, having brought over a brandy, handed it to Pierce, who gave it to Mrs Rice. She sipped the drink, nodding to Pierce. He returned to his seat. Again, a hush descended on the room.

Then the inspector cleared his throat. "Referring to Detective Crawford, he telephoned his office Wednesday afternoon to say he had vital information that he had to follow up, and that he was going to see Mr Rice and Mr Burton."

"Mrs Rice," Max said, "did your husband receive a telephone call late on Wednesday afternoon?"

"Yes. About four in the afternoon."

"That telephone call was from Detective Crawford," Max said. "What I believe happened was this: Crawford met his informant, Ralph Hall, who, as Inspector Longford mentioned, was a member of the Blackshirts. Hall told Crawford about a job he'd done a month or so earlier – the murder of a man in Swindon. I suspect the killers used Hall as a driver. He owned his own cab, which would allow them to conceal their movements. Then Ralph Hall had been told to do another job and had been given two more names and addresses – those of Major Frederick Rice and Sergeant Daniel Burton."

Max paused again, allowing the information to filter through his audience, most especially Lilly Burton and Mrs Rice. When it was clear that those two ladies were fine, he continued. "Hall knew it would be a similar job, ie murder. Losing his nerve, he'd called Detective Crawford and arranged to meet him near Enfield. It was about then that Crawford disappeared. But I'll come back to that. Shortly after that call from Crawford, Rice went to Wisbech to see Dan Burton. Lilly, Lindsey showed you a photograph of Major Rice earlier, is that correct?"

"Yes, sir. He's the one who came to our house on Wednesday night."

"Thank you. And first thing the next day – Thursday – Dan Burton left his home and arrived at a hotel in Peterborough where Rice was waiting for him. Crawford was also registered in that hotel."

Here, Max slowly took his cigarette case from his right jacket pocket, put a cigarette between his lips and took his lighter from his left pocket. He held it up to the cigarette, but paused. It was a silver, engine-turned Dunhill number given to him by Martha the previous Christmas. On one side was a small clock. On the other was a cartouche with an inscription, which read: All my love, M.

It was odd. He'd never really thought about the lighter that much. It was nice, certainly, and he'd liked it and had thanked Martha, of course. But now, holding it in his hand, he thought it one of the most beautiful things he'd ever seen. It was elegant and practical. It was slim with beautiful lines. He looked up at Martha and saw her looking at him as if she knew exactly what was going through his mind. Perhaps she did. She smiled slightly, almost shyly.

Finally, aware that everyone was waiting for him, Max lit his cigarette, sucked down a lungful of smoke and said, "You know, I don't think I realised until just now how important Martha has been to working out what happened. A few days ago, when we knew nothing of Crawford, Martha and I wondered why he'd want to meet Burton and Rice, and why they'd felt it necessary to book a hotel room. And then Martha mentioned something about Burton's clothes. Lilly, can you remember what Dan wore?"

"They were his best clothes, sir. His Sunday suit. And he wore his Guards cufflinks."

"Would he often have worn those things?"

"No, sir. Never, except for special occasions. Weddings and such. And church, I suppose, although he didn't go to church often."

"Right," Max said. "It was Martha who suggested that Burton's dress was akin to a woman wearing her best frock and diamond brooch, which reminded me of the last time I'd worn my Guards tie and tie pin – these very ones, in fact. I'd worn them to a job interview because I wanted to be smart and to impress my interviewer. When Lindsey told me Crawford had been a Special Branch detective, it all made sense. He was going to interview Rice and Burton, question them about something, but something unspecific, which is why Rice booked the rooms – because, as Martha mentioned to me, they didn't know what they were looking for. That is partially correct. They didn't know *specifically* what it was, because they didn't know what I now do. But they knew approximately what it was. I know this because I saw a book at Rice's that had been opened at a certain page and on which he'd made annotations. But I'll come back to that. So, Rice and Burton were in the hotel in Peterborough, prepared to give their testimonies to Crawford."

Max took a drag of his cigarette. It was an intentional pause, designed to make his next statement more dramatic. He exhaled the smoke and said, "But Crawford didn't turn up because he was dead. I think we can assume that Ralph Hall was discovered to be an informant and put under watch. He was killed. Then Crawford was murdered and disposed of in Enfield Lock. I suggested yesterday to the inspector that the police dredge the lock."

"We're doing that, sir. We expect to find Hall's body soon."

"After these murders, the killers were in possession of Crawford's notes, and the details of the meeting in Peterborough with Burton and Rice. Then it was simply a matter of despatching men to keep those two under surveillance.

"Meanwhile, Burton and Rice were very anxious about Crawford's failure to appear. They realised how urgent the situation had now become, so the next day, Friday, they travelled to London. On reaching King's Cross Station, they bought a late edition of the *Standard* – which was found in Burton's coat pocket – and read about the discovery of a body at Enfield Lock, close to where Crawford was last known to be. A body submerged by weights would bloat with gas, and might resurface a couple of days later. This was the case with Crawford. I would imagine that it was at this point Burton and Rice decided to write down as much as they could regarding the general subject of Crawford's investigation."

Max flicked the ash from his cigarette into the ashtray on the bar counter. "From now on, Burton and Rice knew they were in danger, and that their testimony was, perhaps, the last piece of evidence. So they did two things: first, they placed their signed testimonies in a safe place – the left luggage at King's Cross. Then Burton, possibly on his own initiative, came to find me. He might've done so to warn me – which would've been ironic since he actually put me in danger. He might've come to ask me to file a story with the newspaper, just in case something happened to them. I have no doubt that Rice was intending to go to Scotland Yard to speak to someone in Special Branch, but he was killed in his hotel room before he had that chance.

"Now we get to the evening of Friday last. I'm ashamed to say that on that night, in this very room, I was drunk. The whole Rhineland thing had hit me hard, and I could only see that we were heading again for war. Many in this room know what that means, and it seemed to me on Friday that the indescribable horrors we'd all hoped had been banished for ever were crawling towards us again."

"Quite right," Churchill said.

"That's when I saw Dan Burton for the first time since the war. He'd tried to find me, no doubt, at home and then at the *Chronicle*. He eventually found me here in the pub.

"So there's Dan Burton trying to tell me something and I'm too drunk to take in what he was saying and too stupid to realise how important it is. Martha and I came here a couple of days ago and spoke to Jack. And I asked him what he could remember of that evening. He recalled one thing. Jack?"

"I told you that he was trying to get you to remember something. He said, 'Do you remember, Max?'"

"Right," Max said. "Then Burton left hurriedly, not even paying what he owed Jack here. But that only shows how urgent his actions were, right, Lilly?"

"Yes, sir," Lilly said. "It must've been very urgent if he didn't pay Mr Connor. He was always very honest."

"Yes, I know he was. And the urgency was due to the fact that he saw two men enter the pub. These men weren't interested in drinking or chatting. They were here to kill Burton, and to take something from him. And when Burton saw them, he knew he was in danger, and that whatever he was carrying on him had to be disposed of quickly. He left the pub and was murdered by these two men."

"Who were they, sir?" Lilly Burton said. "The men what killed Dan. Who were they?"

"They were very dangerous men, Lilly. Martha and I met them, as did Eric and Flora."

"They tried to take Flora," Eric said.

"Yes," Max said doubtfully. "Eric discovered them trying to break in to our flat and fought them off, bravely. Lindsey, would you tell Lilly who these men were?"

"Glad to. The two men in question worked for a man called Edward Hart, who was the chief Nazi agent in Britain. The first man was a German, Wilhelm Klopfer of the Geheime Staatspolizei. Gestapo, for short."

There was a gasp from Lilly Burton, and General Monroe half rose from his chair. "Gestapo?" he said. "In England? My God."

"Yes, sir. Gestapo, to be sure."

"Did you know this, Frost?"

"I'm afraid we at the FO are the last to hear from the intelligence services."

Ignoring this, Lindsey continued. "The other man was English, fellow called Arthur Boyd, a thief, suspected murderer, a member of the Blackshirts and a man who has a record of… uh… assaulting women. Eric certainly did save young Flora."

Upon saying this, Lindsey gave Eric a little salute and Churchill said, "Excellently done, sir."

Even Monroe and Connor were nodding their agreement.

Eric almost burst into tears, such was the welling of emotion. Flora moved ever closer.

"Those," Max said, "are, essentially, the facts behind Rice and Burton coming down to London to see me, and what happened to them."

"But what does that tell us?" Sergeant Pierce said. "I mean, we don't know *why* they wanted to see you. What would they have wanted to tell you?"

"Ah," Max said dramatically. "That's the real heart of this story. To explain it, I have to go back a little. Mrs Rice, do you remember a book on your sideboard?"

"Yes," Mrs Rice said, shortly, as if she were not yet convinced that Max was innocent of her husband's death.

"Could you tell us which book it is?"

"It's an edition of the Official History of the Grenadier Guards during the war. It was a birthday present from me, as a matter of fact."

"And did you bring it with you, as Mr Lindsey asked?"

Mrs Rice answered by reaching down to her handbag and pulling out the book. She handed it to Lindsey, who flicked through it, stopping at the dog-eared page.

"There's a note here," Lindsey said. "Margin of page three hundred and nineteen. Is this your husband's writing, Mrs Rice?"

Mrs Rice glanced at the note and nodded. Lindsey then handed the book to Max and resumed his seat.

"This history was commissioned in 1922 and completed two years later. An official history like this is composed of regimental and divisional reports, front line despatches, eyewitness interviews, that sort of thing. I saw this book in Major Rice's house. The thing that caught my attention was that the book was open, the spine cracked, a page dog-eared and a note written in the margin. Major Rice was a long-time army officer. I knew him to be fastidious, and his house confirmed that; all his books were in perfect order. Except this one. So, I wandered over and looked at the page he'd dog-eared. There was an account on that page of my attempt to rescue Captain Palgrave…" Max said.

"You didn't rescue him," the general said. "Because you wanted him dead. And you got away with it. With murder."

"I said, 'my attempt to rescue'. But, as you say, I didn't rescue him. And I did want him dead, for a moment. And I'll suffer the guilt of that for the rest of my life. Next to this account in Rice's book he had written one word. That word is 'Lies'."

"Exactly," the general said. "I knew Rice, and I'd known Palgrave too. And Rice felt, as I did, that your citation was a mockery."

Martha sprang to her feet and faced Monroe directly, sticking an accusing finger out at him. "Don't you dare say that. Max is the bravest, most honourable man I've ever known. I know you're some important soldier, but I don't care if you're the King himself, you will not talk about my husband in that way."

When she'd finished, there was a long period of silence.

Then Flora said, "Too bloody right."

Martha turned and saw Max looking at her, a very small smile on his lips and something bright in his eyes.

"Well," Martha said, suddenly very self-conscious, "I just wanted to make that point."

She sat down again.

Max cleared his throat. "I want to tell you all something that I've only ever told to one person – that being my wife, and, even then, only a few days ago. When I was in that shell hole with Palgrave, I was badly concussed, and Palgrave had a serious wound. I don't know how long I sat there, staring at him. He tried to speak a few times, but the words didn't reach me. When, finally, I understood what he was saying, it was as if I'd been wounded as badly as he, as if I too were dying. I can still see his face, ghostlike, and I can still hear that one word: 'Traitor'."

He looked directly at the general, as if challenging him. But the general, his face fierce, to be sure, said nothing.

"When I read the word 'Lies', I felt certain that, as the general just said, Major Rice blamed me for his friend's death, and that all of this must have had something to do with that event, in a shell hole in a muddy swamp in 1917. Passchendaele. But that wouldn't account for Hart and his men. So I dug out my own copy of the Guards' *History*. I found the same page, and read from the start of the chapter. It detailed preparations along the line ahead of the push on the next day, which was when Palgrave was killed."

Max opened the book to page three hundred and nineteen. "I'm going to read from the same page, but from the first paragraph: 'Along the line, in the early hours of the 19th of October, preparations were made for a consolidating push, by which it was hoped to straighten out the somewhat ragged line, and frustrate German attempts to find a weakness. Consequently, many patrols were sent to raid the enemy trenches, and to mark, as well as possible, the positions of wire, machine guns, pillboxes and other strongpoints. In this particular instance, the trench raids up and down the line achieved no success and merely served to alert the Germans of the impending attack.'"

Max closed the book.

"For those of you unfamiliar with battle tactics, I'm going to explain it in lay terms. On the 19th of October, several divisions, including the Guards Division, were intended to push forward according to a detailed plan. The idea was to straighten the line, which had become disorganised in the previous fighting. In other words, to consolidate the gains made. A ragged line can result in salient points, which are bulges, if you like. They can be useful, but in this case they were weak points, allowing the enemy to attack on three sides. This was a large, coordinated push, and, as often happens in these instances, on the previous night patrols were sent to raid the enemy trenches in the hope of obtaining some kind of intelligence that would aid the attack. Palgrave often selected Burton's section for patrol duty. He did so this night. I was, as often happened, also on that patrol.

"After I read the entry highlighted in Major Rice's book," Max explained, now addressing the room, "I realised something. And I came back yesterday and asked Jack a question. Jack?"

"You asked me if Mr Burton might have been saying 'Don't you remember, Max?', and when you put it like that, I agreed. That's what he was saying, that's what he kept saying, over and over until he was almost shouting it. 'Don't you remember?'"

"And can you recall what I was saying, more or less?"

"Yes, Mr Dalton. You were saying 'No, it wasn't me'."

"Thanks, Jack," Max said.

He was quiet for a while, and the whole room was silent with him, as if in some sad remembrance of things past.

Then Sergeant Pierce cleared his throat and said, "I'm sorry, sir. I don't understand the difference."

Max nodded. "It's a subtle difference, I'll agree. But there is a difference. 'Do you remember?' could mean something indefinite, unidentified. For example, I could ask Martha, 'Do you remember what we had for dinner last Sunday?' and she might remember, or she might not. However, if I were to ask her, 'Don't you remember what we had for dinner last Sunday?', it would imply that I expected her to recall it. Do you see? The difference is in the assumption of the enquirer. Burton was *expecting* me to remember something, and he was becoming frustrated when I couldn't."

"I still don't follow, sir," Pierce said.

"The reason I kept telling Burton that it wasn't me was simply because it wasn't. I hadn't been there. As a result of the explosion that threw me into Palgrave's shell hole, I was concussed. When I got back to our position, I was sent behind the lines for a couple of days to recover."

Here, Max hesitated and became thoughtful. He had to explain the next part clearly, especially to those who were unfamiliar with military terminology, such as Lilly Burton. "In normal circumstances, any intelligence gleaned by our patrol would be reviewed by Palgrave as my CO, and anything of note would be sent immediately to Battalion where it might be sent on to Division or, if it was clearly important, straight to GHQ. Now, when Palgrave died, I became the de facto company commander and it would've fallen on me, as the most senior surviving officer in his company, to collect his papers, assemble his affairs, pass on reports etc. But I hadn't been there. I'd been evacuated because of my head injury."

Max looked around the room, trying to see whether anyone was confused. But the silence and stillness told him that every word he said was being absorbed, even if the effects of those words differed between the people in that pub. "Yesterday," he continued, "as I was beginning to understand what was going on, I asked Mr Bacon here to see what he could discover of the fate of other members of my old company. After all, if Burton and Rice were linked to me, so were others."

Max glanced at Harold Bacon and said, "Would you tell us about William Halford?"

"Certainly, Mr Dalton. William Halford died of a heart attack in Swindon, approximately one month ago."

"My God," said Frost.

"Yes, indeed," Max said. "Klopfer and Boyd – a Gestapo agent and a known Blackshirt – are taken to Swindon by Ralph Hall – Crawford's informant – approximately one month ago. At the same time and in the same place, one of my platoon dies. Inspector, Sergeant, if you learned this, what would you think?"

"Can't be coincidence," Sergeant Pierce said.

"I'd investigate thoroughly," Longford said.

"My former company seem to be mostly alive," Max said, "in work and in good health. There were one or two deaths along the way, but nothing of particular note. However…" Here he paused again, for effect, Martha knew, even though she was rapt by his words, as were all the others. Even General Monroe had nothing to say.

"However, when I ignored the company as a whole and looked solely at the men in my platoon, the death rate rose sharply. And when I looked solely at Burton's section, something terrifying became apparent."

He reached into his inside jacket pocket and took out a small photograph. "I took this picture in August 1917 when my battalion was in the rear. It's Burton's section."

He handed it to Martha, who looked at it then passed it to Mr Bacon. It passed down the line. When it got to Lilly Burton, she began to weep. Mrs Rice put her hand on Lilly's.

The photograph was handed back to Max, who looked at it for a while. From a tiny moment, almost twenty years previously, nine men sat in the sun, smiling, smoking, glad to have just a moment's respite. "Of the nine in that photograph, six survived the war. Of those six, I discovered that four have died in the last few months, including Dan Burton. Yesterday, I asked Inspector Longford to urgently find the remaining two men and to take them into the protection of police custody. Inspector?"

"Yes, sir. I despatched men as soon as we located the man. He's in our protection, sir."

"Just one?" Max said.

"Yes, sir. Walter Kiffin. The other man, Andrew Poole, was killed by a motor car in January of this year."

Martha gasped. "Oh, no," she said.

Flora was sniffling, with Eric patting her on the back, trying his best still to protect her.

Lindsey shook his head sadly, while Churchill mopped his forehead with a handkerchief and General Monroe glared at the floor.

The news hit Max hard and he cursed himself for being drunk that night. "You see," he said eventually, "after Crawford spoke to Hall, he had to interview Rice and Burton immediately, and put them into protection. They were rapidly becoming the only witnesses left who would be able to provide a testimony."

"A testimony of what?" Inspector Longford said.

"The trench raid," Max said.

"What?" Frost said.

"What are you talking about, man?" General Monroe said.

"I'll explain shortly, sir."

"What about you, Mr Dalton?" Churchill said. "You were also present on this raid."

"Yes, sir. Martha made that same point to me the other day. She asked me why nobody had tried to kill me, given that the others were being systematically murdered. How did you put it, darling?"

"I said that perhaps it wasn't an accident that you hadn't been targeted. I said that perhaps you weren't on the list."

"That's right. And I asked you which list you meant. And you said, 'the death list'."

"Yes."

"In answer to your question, sir," Max said to Churchill, "it was common for a trench raid to be commanded by a sergeant or corporal, but very rare for an officer. It was Palgrave's practice, for personal reasons, to send me out with Burton. The next day, after Palgrave had been killed, his notes would've been sent up the line to Battalion HQ by whichever officer was present to do so. As I mentioned earlier, this would normally have been me, but I was wounded.

"Now, since Palgrave and Major Rice were old friends, it was natural for Rice to tidy Palgrave's affairs after the battle. In short, it must've been the case that Palgrave hadn't yet despatched his report of the raid to Battalion HQ. So, when Rice was sorting through, he made a report of the raid, but had no idea that I would've been ordered to accompany it. The despatch that he sent to Battalion Headquarters contained the names of those in Burton's section, but not my own."

"I don't understand," Frost said. "What has this to do with a death list?"

"That report *was* the death list. Every one of the men on that trench raid is now dead with the exception of Private Walter Kiffin who, as we've just heard, is now safe in police custody. And Major Rice was on the death list because it was he who sent the report. Wilhelm Klopfer and Arthur Boyd didn't realise that, as Martha pointed out, I wasn't on the death list, because my name hadn't been included in the despatch regarding the raid. When they saw Burton talking to me, they had to find out who I was and what I knew. They reported it to their boss, Obersturmbannführer Hart of the Schutzstaffel and Gestapo. That's when Hart approached Alwyn at his club and claimed to be interested in the Napoleonic war. Frost led Hart straight to me."

"But why?" Frost said, ignoring the scold. "What was so important about a damned trench raid?"

Max was quiet for a moment. He glanced at Lindsey, whose face remained as passive and relaxed as if he were watching a game of cricket, even though, as Max knew, he was far from that state.

"That," Max said, addressing Frost, "is the most important question of all. The reason is that, as Rice realised a few days ago, the official account of that raid is a lie. Remember that the official History recorded there were *no significant results from the trench raids.* But, on that night, we *did* have a success. We managed to hit a command post and take them by surprise. We gathered what intelligence we could and returned to our lines. I gave it to Palgrave myself, but I didn't review it. The official history doesn't record any intelligence, but there was some, and it was significant. So, why wasn't that recorded? You see, it was the *gathering* of that intelligence that Burton was trying to get me to recall."

"But how is that significant?" Longford said. "If the intelligence wasn't sent before the attack, what use was it afterwards?"

"Because that attack was only one part of a push, a series of attacks over three days. As I said, we were trying to secure our gains from previous attacks, straighten the line. The first day was only part of it."

Max dropped his cigarette and trod it out. Connor made a noise at the back of his throat. Max reached down for the butt and dropped it into the ashtray on the bar counter. He reached for the glass of water, his hand trembling as he put the glass to his lips.

Everyone was quiet for a moment. Only Lindsey seemed indifferent to the account Max was giving, which, as the tension in the pub attested, clearly hadn't finished.

It was Mr Bacon who broke the silence, and asked the question that they were all holding in their minds. He said, "I don't understand, Mr Dalton. What does it mean?"

Max lit another cigarette. "It means that Palgrave didn't forward the intelligence to Battalion."

"That doesn't make any sense," General Monroe said. "Why would Palgrave not forward his report to me if it contained intelligence a few hours before a major offensive?"

"I'm glad you asked me that, sir. When Palgrave saw the intelligence, he concealed it because he knew what it meant. I found out why in that shell hole, twenty years ago, but I didn't know until yesterday. The reason is in that word: traitor."

"What does that mean?" Frost said coldly.

"It means that when Palgrave saw the intelligence, he knew it would identify a traitor in the British army."

"A traitor?" Churchill said. "I can't believe it."

"There was a traitor, sir, and there still is. And he's sitting on your right."

The stunned silence that followed this announcement was such that it seemed to Max as if the whole world had suddenly stopped – sound disappeared, life halted, the air itself froze.

All eyes turned to General Monroe, who, in a dark voice, said, "What did you say?"

"I said you were a traitor. And Palgrave knew it, because of the intelligence he saw. And you were his friend, and he didn't know what to do, so he concealed the intelligence. And then, dying in a filth-filled hole in the middle of a wreckage of bodies and blood and wire and mud, he sat opposite me, the man he hated more than any other in the world, and he knew he was dying, and he knew he had to tell the truth. And he told it to me."

All the while Max had been talking, Monroe had been grinding his teeth; his face was blood red, his eyes wet with ferocity.

Martha watched the general coolly. Connor, his arms folded, stared at him as if he would be happy to commit murder. Frost didn't know what to do, along with Pierce, Bacon and Longford. Lindsey surveyed his thumb nail. Mrs Rice was white with shock. Lilly Burton stared at Monroe, her mouth open, her hands clenched tightly into fists.

Churchill glowered at the floor in front of him, chewing his cigar. Even he was unable to utter a word.

Slowly, and with manifest difficulty, General Monroe composed himself. "That's ridiculous," he said.

"It's the only thing that makes sense."

"What proof do you have?"

"Well, there's the *Official History*. The intelligence was sent to you at Battalion. Rice sent it, and I'm a witness to the fact that there was something to send. So, you were the only one in a position to destroy it, which you did. That's why the

Official History doesn't record it, and why Major Rice knew it was a lie."

"There are a hundred reasons why that intelligence didn't reach me. You know how difficult communications were. It was chaos, man."

Max pulled an envelope from his inside pocket. "These are the signed testimonies of Major Frederick Rice and Sergeant Daniel Burton, both formerly of the Grenadier Guards."

"Forgeries."

In answer to that, Max showed the handwritten and signed testimonies of Burton and Rice to their respective wives.

"That's Dan's writing, sir," Lilly Burton said. "And his signature."

Mrs Rice didn't say anything, but nodded.

"According to the testimony of Major Rice, he personally handed the intelligence to you at Battalion. He remembers it distinctly, because it was the first opportunity he'd had to inform you of Palgrave's death," said Max.

"Maybe he did give it to me. I can't remember. You can't expect me to recall something like that after so long."

"Hart was in the Intelligence Corps. I asked Lindsey yesterday to check up on Hart's movements at the time of that October attack during the third Ypres offensive – otherwise called Passchendaele. Lindsey?"

"Hart was attached to GHQ in that sector. One of the intelligence officers."

"He could easily have gone to Battalion HQ," Max said. "That's where you handed him the details of the next day's attacks, and he handed it to his so-called agents, who were still working for the Germans."

"That's it? That's all you have? Speculation?"

"It's good enough for me," Churchill growled around his cigar.

"Of course it is," Monroe snapped. "You're paranoid, Churchill. You seem to think everyone is a Nazi or a Nazi sympathiser."

"Not everyone," Churchill said. "Only those who are."

"What was it?" Max said to Monroe. "What was in those papers? What did Palgrave find? Were they plans you'd leaked to the enemy? Did you tell them we were coming? Were they in your handwriting?"

Monroe didn't utter a word. He merely stared at Max, his face fierce with cold burning fire. Everyone in the pub then knew it was true.

Max continued speaking, all the time his gaze lancing Monroe, sticking him with words and relentless logic. "Hart was a German spy during the war. Once Hitler came to power, Hart offered his services, eventually becoming a Gestapo officer and Obersturmbannführer in the SS. I have no doubt that Hart secured that position because he knew the value of having the Chief of the Imperial General Staff as an agent. So they reactivated you and were determined to erase any possible threats, hence the death list."

Monroe stood abruptly, slamming the chair backwards. His hand reached for the holstered pistol on his belt.

"Uh-uh," Lindsey said, his pistol already in his hand and pointing at the general.

Monroe spluttered for a moment. "You'd never get a court verdict on that evidence," he said.

Mr Bacon coughed politely. "I'm afraid he's right, sir. It wouldn't stand in court."

"Would never go to court anyway," Lindsey said.

"It's absurd. You have nothing. Nothing."

"Well, not unless we can one day get into the Gestapo records or break the German codes," said Max.

Monroe glared at all present, and marched out. They heard his feet hammering the paving stones, then a car door slam shut. Then the sound of the car's engine as it pulled away.

"Is that it?" Lilly Burton said. "Is that all that's going to happen to him? Are you letting him go?"

"He killed my husband," Mrs Rice said. "What are you going to do about it? What are you going to do about that… *traitor*?"

Max couldn't offer an answer. Neither could Frost or Lindsey or Bacon or Longford or Pierce. Not because they refused to, but because they couldn't. Monroe was Chief of the Imperial General Staff. Few had authority over such a figure.

Churchill stood slowly, and said, "Mrs Burton, Mrs Rice, you have my solemn word that one day, that man will pay for his treachery. He will pay for what he's done to you."

Chapter Fifty-Three

Slowly, as if following a funeral, the people began to leave. Lindsey took Mrs Burton and Mrs Rice to a hotel, and stayed with them for some time. Mr Bacon quietly took his leave, enjoying the small but pleasant thought of buying a pork pie for supper.

Inspector Longford shook Max by the hand and apologised for the doubt he'd had. He then shook Martha by the hand and told her that his head would be fine, and there'd be no charges against her.

Max looked at Churchill, and said, "I haven't thanked you for sending the police to protect me."

"After you visited me, I thought it prudent that you should have some form of protection. I, uh, may not be in a position of power, but I have friends, and they are in positions of great power indeed."

"Well, thank you, sir," Max said. "You saved my life."

"On the contrary, young man, thank you."

Martha walked over to Churchill and planted a kiss on his round head, which ripened instantly and resembled a shining cherry. "That's for what you promised to Mrs Rice and Lilly," Martha said, "and for saving Max yesterday."

"Charming woman," Churchill was heard to mention to Frost as they wandered along the road.

Eric said he'd better get Flora home just in case anyone was hanging around. "They might wanna take her."

Flora left with her arm in Eric's.

Connor poured Max a pint of best and offered Martha a gin and tonic. He poured himself a pint and raised it up and said, "I never woulda thought. The First Lord of the Admiralty hisself, in my pub. Cheers."

He swallowed the beer in about three seconds.

Then, allowing Max and Martha some time alone, Connor went out back.

"Do you remember why all this started, Max?" said Martha.

"Of course. The war."

"I mean, with Burton. On Friday."

"Ah. You mean because I was drunk."

"No, that's not what I mean. It's the reason you were drunk. You were so sad, so angry. You felt like the world was going to hell and you should've been able to do something."

"Yes."

"Well, you did."

"We did," Max said.

"Yes. But the anger, Max, the sadness and bitterness, those things you felt… they… they were wrong. Hope is the future. It has to be. We must have hope, not doubt or despair, otherwise we're all finished, and I just can't believe that. I won't believe it. There are too many good people to ever let that happen."

Max smiled softly, and kissed his wife on the top of her head.

EPILOGUE

Leopold von Hoesch, German Ambassador to the Court of St James's, died suddenly on 10 April, 1936, a little over two weeks after the events herein depicted. It was reported that Von Hoesch's death was due to a heart attack. Tony Lindsey believed that the assassination order Von Hoesch uncovered at the Embassy was, in fact, his own.

Von Hoesch's replacement as Ambassador to the Court of St James's was Joachim von Ribbentrop.

Ralph Wigram died suddenly on 31 December 1936, approximately nine months after he first met Max Dalton. He continued to meet Max and Martha until his death. Many people, including Churchill, believed that Wigram committed suicide.

On 31 July, 1942, while fishing on his estate in Perthshire, General Sir Clifford Monroe apparently fell as he attempted to ascend the river bank, and was knocked unconscious. He drowned in the mud.

It was twenty-five years exactly since the start of the third Battle of Ypres, which would become known as Passchendaele.